Women of the West

For Angie Grantman —

Thanks for the inaugural tickets. I had a wonderful time!

My best,

Judy Comeau

Women of the West

An Anthology
of Short Stories
by Contemporary
Western Women Writers

Edited by Kathryn Ptacek

A DOUBLE D WESTERN
DOUBLEDAY
New York London Toronto Sydney Auckland

A DOUBLE D WESTERN
PUBLISHED BY DOUBLEDAY
a division of Bantam Doubleday Dell Publishing Group, Inc.
666 Fifth Avenue, New York, New York 10103

DOUBLE D WESTERN, DOUBLEDAY and the portrayal of the letters DD are
trademarks of Doubleday, a division of Bantam Doubleday Dell Publishing Group,
Inc.

Acknowledgments

Introduction, copyright © 1990 Kathryn Ptacek.
"All Bets Are Off," copyright © 1990 by Nancy R. Herndon. By permission of
the author.
"A Passion for Trees," copyright © 1990 by He Sapa. By permission of the
author.
"Moonseed," copyright © 1990 by Kristl Franklin. By permission of the au-
thor.
"Size of a Silver Dollar," copyright © 1990 by A. R. Morlan. By permission of
the author.
"Dust," copyright © 1990 by Anke Kriske. By permission of the author.
"Planting Time," copyright © 1990 by Lucy Taylor. By permission of the au-
thor.
"Just As I Am," copyright © 1990 by Joyce Gibson Roach. By permission of
the author.
"Sunday Morning, Wednesday Night," copyright © 1990 by Johnnye Montgomery. By permission of the author.
"Rain Shadow," copyright © 1990 by Melanie Tem. By permission of the author.
"History of the Branded Heart," copyright © 1990 by Jo-Ann Mapson. By
permission of the author.
"The White Woman," copyright © 1990 by Ashley McConnell. By permission
of the author.
"Taking Miss Charlotte Back," copyright © 1990 by J. L. Comeau. By permission of the author.
"Buried Alive, or: Lunar Mischief," copyright © 1990 by Nancy Holder. By
permission of the author.

Library of Congress Cataloging-in-Publication Data applied for
ISBN 0-385-24647-1

Contents

Introduction

I grew up in the West, specifically New Mexico, and have always had a deep abiding love for it. When I moved East, I began to appreciate the West even more—certainly I seemed to long for it, my interest in western matters grew keener, and every time I went back home I saw things I hadn't noticed before.

And when I moved East I had a typically western attitude: I didn't think anyone would want to know about where I'd come from. I couldn't have been more wrong. Those outside the West are interested in that region, extremely so. Nearly everywhere I've traveled, people have always wanted to know more about New Mexico, more about the West.

What is so incredibly unique about the West that it holds a fascination for us all? Why does it seem to reach almost mythic proportions in our history, fiction, and lives?

Perhaps, the fascination with the West—its legendary nature—lies in the fact that it was the last frontier of this country, the very last untamed, unspoiled wilderness (unless you count Alaska, which is still sparsely populated, but no longer unspoiled).

There was simply the matter, too, of the region's size. The West was huge—the sky seemed to go on forever; the plains stretched until the eye could no longer distinguish them; the forests seemed endless; a storm could be watched as it formed hundreds of miles away, then swept toward a settlement; the mountains were higher than anything the pioneers had yet encountered. There were new animals to see, new trees and shrubs and flowers, new minerals. And this was a fresh land: there were plenty of fish in the lakes and rivers and streams, abundant bison and moose, beaver and deer, elk and mountain goats. All these resources were seemingly without end, the first settlers thought. Also, there was hardly anyone living there—only Indians scattered here and there throughout the thousands of miles—hardly the bustling, populous centers of the East. And there were the tornadoes that dropped unpredictably out of ugly clouds in a matter of seconds; there were great prongs of lightning that seemed to delve the very earth when they struck; there was an *energy* that the South and the East didn't seem to possess.

The West.

Many images are conjured by that term. Bigger than life. Tall tales. The last frontier. New hopes and new dreams. A new life.

And freedom. The settlers believed, above all, that the West would bring them freedom—of religious choice, from slavery, from persecution because of class or country of origin. Freedom from all the intolerance that had grown since the country began.

Of course, we know that wasn't always the way it happened. The settlers, alas, brought their prejudices with them. But for many the West meant their freedom.

You always hear a lot about the men who made the West—they make up the majority of characters in television programs and films and novels set there—these are the cowboys and railroaders and pioneers and marshals and outlaws. You hear less about the women. Yet the women were there, dying in the same numbers; working just as hard, just as long hours; trying to make their own dreams come true.

Dee Brown, in his 1958 nonfiction study of women of the Old Wild West, *The Gentle Tamers*, concentrated on pioneer women, army wives, the "soiled doves," the actresses, the Carry Nations and Calamity Janes and Belle Starrs. I thought that was a good starting point; but I really wanted to do more.

A few years ago when I decided that I wanted to do an anthology about women *in* the West by women writers I wanted to open the field up. I wanted more than the typical western story and the typical western woman. I wanted the writers to reach for something different. I didn't want Annie Oakley or Belle Starr or anyone equally famous, and I made that quite clear in my guidelines.

And I didn't want any stereotypes, like the spinster schoolmarm. Yes, there were such teachers, but I was looking for something more unusual.

I wanted outlaws, ranchers, reporters, pioneers, madams, prostitutes, Indians, sharpshooters, Asian immigrants, writers, artists, merchants, miners, army wives, camp followers, scholars, suffrag-

ists, missionaries, soldiers, religious leaders, scamps, Spanish settlers, educators, reformers, actresses—in short, the entire gamut
of what women really were in the West.

Writers sent tales about a Chinese immigrant along the California coast, a dryad in Arizona, a woman preacher in a wagon train,
Indians—Cherokee, Apache, Shoshoni, Sioux, Navajo, and a host
of others—an artist, a launderer, a salt vendor, a miner's wife,
singers and musicians, mail-order brides, ranchers, farmers, medi-
ums, prostitutes and madams, a photographer, Cattle Annie, outlaws and Pinkerton detectives, Mormons, dance-hall girls,
Basques, saloon owners, freed slaves, hunters, lawyers, quilters
and other needlewomen, doctors and midwives, horsewomen, a
bathhouse owner, massacre survivors, Baby Doe, settlers and pioneers (more of these than I ever wanted to see), Paiute leader
Sarah Winnemucca, bounty hunters, murderers, and even one
woman who ran a mining company scam.

I received stories about old women and middle-aged women,
and about girls and women just starting their lives or careers—they
were daughters and wives and mothers and grandmothers and
sisters, but most of all they were women, characters in their own
right.

I wanted more than just stories about a typical day in the life of a
woman pioneer or rancher. I wanted humor and horror, romance
and mystery, adventure and nostalgia, even stories that couldn't be
placed in a typical genre. I got those, and many more.

In my guidelines I had defined the West as everything north and
west of Texas, including it as well. And stories along the plains of
Nebraska and Kansas and the Dakotas would be considered as
well. Alaska and Canada (Saskatchewan and westward) were also
included as part of the West.

There was some mild confusion at the beginning. Some writers
thought you had to *live* in the West to contribute a story. Not
precisely. I soon quashed that idea. Stories I read (close to two
hundred) came from all over—Canada and the Midwest, the
South, the Northwest and Northeast, and of course the West. As it
turns out, most of the stories selected were from writers who live in
the West. Only a coincidence, though. These writers live in Montana, Virginia, Texas, California, Florida, Wisconsin, Colorado,
New Mexico, and Connecticut.

The response from women writers was overwhelmingly enthusiastic—"It's about time," most of them declared in their cover letters. I agreed. For far too long women have been relegated to a minor role in the history of the West.

I hope that long out-of-step notion will change with this volume.

So, whether from the Old West or the New West, these characters are definitely Women of the West. Thirteen stories, by newcomers and old hands, the very best of today's women western writers.

KATHRYN PTACEK
Newton, New Jersey
May 1989

Women of the West

All Bets Are Off

Nancy R. Herndon

Nancy R. Herndon was born and brought up in the St. Louis area. She has a B.A. in English and a B.J. in advertising from the University of Missouri, where she was Phi Beta Kappa, a sorority president, secretary of the student government association, and writer for the campus humor magazine when it wasn't suppressed for offending the Dean of Students. She now holds an M.A. in English from Rice University. She's lived in Florida, Missouri, Mississippi, Massachusetts, Connecticut, and Maryland; written or proofread advertising copy in Houston, St. Louis, New York, and Bridgeport, Connecticut; and taught English literature and/or composition at Rice, New York University, Ole Miss, Florida Atlantic, and the University of Texas at El Paso. This is the second story she sold. A gourmet cook and compulsive reader, she lives in El Paso with her husband, a chemistry professor, and has two sons.

Nancy sent me three wonderful stories about spirited Caroline Harley in the Wyoming of the early 1900s. I liked them all, but had promised myself no more than one story from each contributor. Then I had to make the difficult decision about which one to take. I'm looking forward to when Nancy will gather her other Miss Caroline stories into a single volume.

The great horseracing scandal of 1905 drew the largest mob of spectators ever assembled for a trial in Douglas, Wyoming—in fact, every adult, male or female, who could squeeze into the old courthouse. The men of the community called it a shocking thing for a girl, especially a pretty one, to disguise herself in men's clothes, ride in the most important race of the year, and win. Naturally the racing judges declared her ineligible; they said they did it because no one told them the owner was switching jockeys, but everyone knew the real reason: she was a girl. Then Miss Caroline, who wasn't one to hide her light under a bushel, filed suit against the judges, which was the last straw as far as the men were concerned, because after that none of the bets could be paid off till the case went to trial.

The women of Douglas were mostly of another mind, being uncommonly independent—the result, folks said, of having had the vote ever since territorial days. They didn't see why a girl shouldn't ride in a race if she had a mind to, although most disapproved of women wearing men's clothing, and all disapproved of gambling. Still, the women had other fish to fry and hadn't gone out of their way to support young Caroline Harley, who was a spirited girl but doubtless would have appreciated a few well-wishers.

Clayton Merriweather, who was said to be sweet on her, felt a tad sorry for Miss Caroline when he saw her sitting alone at the plaintiff's table in the old courtroom with its water-stained, bullet-holed ceiling and walls and its splintered judge's bench and jury stall. There she was, lawyerless and outnumbered by the three defendants and their three lawyers—all six experienced men and substantial members of a community to which she was a stranger. Clayton suggested to her uncle, Oliver Chatman, that they sit right behind her, but Oliver refused and took a seat to the rear, where he slumped down and tried to look like he wasn't there at all.

The selection of the jury proceeded through the first three members without much comment from Miss Caroline, and folks thought maybe she'd lost heart. She didn't even react to all the joking between the defendants' lawyers and the prospective jurors. But when the fourth male juror made his appearance, Miss Caroline jumped up and cried, "Your honor, where are the women?"

"Which women would that be, Miss Harley?" asked the judge.

"Why, the women jurors," Miss Caroline replied. "I understand that jurors are chosen from among the voting population. Since women vote in Wyoming, why are there no women jurors?"

Judge Henry Lateen looked real surprised and had to consider that question a minute or two. "I couldn't say, Miss Harley," he finally answered. "We've never had women jurors. I suppose no one ever suggested it."

"Then I suggest it," she cried. "In fact, I—"

"Women don't want to be jurors," announced Mr. Barclay, attorney for the head racing judge, "and men don't want women to be jurors. I object to this outrageous suggestion."

"You interrupted me, sir," said Miss Caroline, planting her hands on her hips and displaying such a trim waist and fine bosom that half the young men in the courtroom would have jumped to her defense if it hadn't been for all that money bet on the race. "Your honor, I think in a case of this sort, when the matter obviously involves prejudice against a woman—"

"She's arguing the case before we even have a jury," objected another of the lawyers.

"You interrupted me again," said Miss Caroline, the blue and yellow flowers on her navy blue straw hat bouncing with indignation.

The judge, who had an eye for a pretty girl, sighed. "You'll find that's a common courtroom occurrence, Miss Harley. Are you sure you don't want a lawyer of your own?"

"There's not a lawyer in Converse County brave enough to take up my standard, your honor," said Miss Caroline. "I believe I've asked them all, so I must defend myself." With that she unpinned her hat and put it down on the table, and all the young men sighed at the sight of her black curls escaping out of the ladylike bun on top of her head. It was that shiny black hair that got her in trouble in the first place.

"Well, I'm sorry to hear that, young lady, but there are no women jurors around to choose from," said the judge, all kindly like.

"I'll volunteer," shouted Mrs. Liz Ryan, and several other ladies then offered their services.

"You see, your honor, there are plenty to choose from," said Miss Caroline sweetly, "and I am a reasonable woman; I shall only ask that half the jury be female."

"I won't accept female jurors!" shouted Mr. Barclay, not much affected by black curls and blue eyes.

"Why not?" Miss Caroline shot back. "Don't you think the women of Wyoming are responsible citizens?"

A chorus of female voices belabored poor Mr. Barclay, and his own wife, from her seat in the first row of spectators, gave him a warning poke with her Sunday umbrella. Nonetheless, he turned to the judge and said, "Your honor, this is a serious matter. There's a powerful lot of money bet on this race, and—"

"What's that? Betting?" Miss Caroline whirled, blue skirts flying, to face the judge. "Your honor, gambling is illegal in Wyoming; therefore, betting on a horse race is illegal. I demand an investigation of these illegal activities. And I think that gentleman should be disbarred."

She pointed right at Mr. Barclay with one little hand, while she spread the other dramatically over all the tucks and lace on her shirtwaist. Fifteen more young men were smitten on the spot and forgot all about the horse race, but likely they didn't have any money bet.

"How are we to have civilization on the frontier when officers of the court use in their arguments the protection of illegal activities?" cried Miss Caroline, who had really begun to hit her stride. "For shame, Mr. Barclay! It becomes clear to us all that you do not wish to have women on the jury because women would not be swayed by your emotional appeals for the protection of your secret vices."

Right then everyone heard Mrs. Barclay asking her husband if he'd been betting on the horses again. He wouldn't say, so she turned to the judge and announced, "Henry, if betting is what this trial's about, I want to be on that jury."

"Sorry, Maude, but we can't have the wife of a defendant's lawyer on the jury," said the judge.

"I am willing to accept Mrs. Barclay," Miss Caroline offered with a generous smile as she straightened her cameo broach, which was nestled in the lace of her high collar right under a chin that, when you looked at it, had a real stubborn tilt. "I don't doubt that Mrs. Barclay will render a fair and impartial verdict."

"Well, I doubt it," muttered Mr. Barclay.

"You willing to accept women jurors, Barclay?" asked the judge.

"He is," said Mrs. Barclay. "If I can't be on the jury, then Liz Ryan can. She's not related to any lawyers."

"I object, your honor. Mrs. Ryan is a friend of the plaintiff. In fact, the plaintiff spent the night at her house, and Mrs. Ryan accompanied her to file this suit."

"Those three fellows up there are all friends of yours, Jess Barclay," said his wife. "You better get rid of them, Henry—I mean, your honor." Mrs. Barclay sat down, looking smug.

Judge Henry Lateen sighed. "We'll never get a jury, Jess, if we start worrying about friends and enemies—not in Converse County. Step up, Mrs. Ryan."

Mrs. Ryan was accepted by both sides, but the attorneys for the defense managed to hold a quick powwow before the next woman came forward, and Mr. Barclay got up to question her. "Mrs. Halloran, whose horse did Ben bet on in the race in question?"

"I object," cried Miss Caroline. "Mrs. Halloran, are you the legally wedded wife of Mr. Halloran?"

"Of course I am," said Mrs. Halloran, who, being the mother of seven, took that question amiss.

"Then I advise you to take the Fifth Amendment."

"Where is it?" asked Mrs. H., a mite confused.

The judge explained the Fifth Amendment and then turned to Miss Caroline. "I don't know why we're getting into this, Miss Harley. Would you care to explain your objection?"

"Certainly, your honor. In the eyes of God, Mr. and Mrs. Halloran are one. Therefore, if she admits that her husband bet on that race—betting being illegal in the state of Wyoming—she would be incriminating herself."

"I'd hate to rule on that," muttered the judge.

"Besides, a wife does not have to testify against her husband," Miss Caroline added triumphantly.

"That's true," said the judge with relief. "You don't have to answer that question, Mrs. Halloran, and you might as well stop asking it, Jess."

"Well, I don't mind answering it," declared Mrs. Halloran. "If I find out that Ben was betting on that race, I'll have his hide, and that's all I got to say on the subject. Now let me ask you, Jess Barclay, do you know something I don't know about what Ben's been up to?"

"You better take that up with Ben later, Mrs. Halloran," the judge interposed. "Now, are there any more questions for this juror?"

"I am certainly willing to accept Mrs. Halloran," said Caroline Harley, "and may I say that she strikes me as a model citizen of whom Wyoming can be proud."

"I object to the plaintiff buttering up the jurors," said Mr. Barclay.

"Yes, yes," muttered the judge, "but do you object to Mrs. Halloran?"

Mr. Barclay accepted Mrs. Halloran, and after a deal of wrangling, three men and four women more got chosen for the jury. Clayton Merriweather said to Oliver Chatman that Miss Caroline was "doing pretty good." Oliver grimaced and slid down farther on his seat.

For her first three witnesses Caroline Harley threw the opposing lawyers into confusion by calling their clients. She got the racing judges to admit that the rules of the race—which no one had a copy of—had nothing to say one way or another about female jockeys. All three claimed they didn't know whether any other last-minute, unapproved changes of jockeys had been made, but they all said that should any such a change be proved, they'd disqualify the horse just like they had Oliver Chatman's. Miss Caroline took that claim amiss since the posted jockey and the substitute jockey that she knew about, although she didn't know their names, had evidently left town before they could be hauled into court to testify.

The three attorneys then cross-examined their own clients to the effect that no rules had ever been made against female jockeys because it was understood among folks in Wyoming that horse racing was too dangerous for ladies.

Miss Caroline snorted and called as her fourth witness Mrs. Ryan, but Judge Henry Lateen claimed she could not call a member of the jury. Finally she called herself and testified that she had heard with her own ears one young fellow saying to another that he couldn't ride in the race, after all, because he had a boil on his posterior, to which his friend replied that he'd do the riding, which he had. "And Judge," said Miss Caroline, "I haven't seen them since. Now, where did they go? Everybody sees everybody sooner or later in Converse County. What I think is that those lawyers"— at which point she shook her finger right under Mr. Barclay's nose —"those lawyers and the racing judges made them leave town. That's what I think."

The judge sighed. "You can't testify to what you *think*, Miss Harley. You can only testify to what you *know*. Now, do you have anything else to say, anything else that's admissible?"

Miss Caroline scowled at him but went on to explain that she had ridden because Mr. Harry Benson, her uncle's jockey—who had also left town—had been deathly ill at race time. "He had the—ah

—trots," she explained delicately, "which is much worse than a boil on the posterior." Then she testified that she had heard her uncle say he had his heart set on running his horse at the Douglas State Fair, and being a loving and dutiful niece, she could not bear to see his heart broken. That's why she'd taken Harry Benson's place.

Oliver Chatman practically slid out of sight right then, but it didn't help. Mr. Barclay called him to the stand, when it came the defendants' turn, and made him say that he hadn't asked nor wanted Miss Caroline to ride his horse.

Miss Caroline was so angry that she didn't cross-examine her uncle at all. Instead she gave him the lecture of his life about his ingratitude in the face of all her sacrifices for his sake: her long hours making fruit preserves, her days in the saddle training his horse after his clumsy jockey had fallen out of a fruit tree, and, last but not least, her first-place finish—which she told him Harry Benson could never have managed had he been in the best of health. And all the time she was scolding Oliver, Mr. Barclay was objecting to harassment of his witness and the judge was trying to tell her that she was supposed to question the witness, not dress him down. Miss Caroline finished up by smiling as sweet as pie at the judge, fluffing out the lacy gathers of her sleeves, and saying, "I beg the court's pardon." Then, sweeping the judge a fine curtsy, she glared at Oliver and marched back to her seat.

"I gather the plaintiff has no questions for you, Mr. Chatman," said the judge. "You are excused. I will now hear the final arguments."

The lawyers for the defendants split up their presentations, and each one had his say on a different subject. John Bates covered Miss Caroline's claim that she had not been the only unannounced substitute jockey. "I ask you, ladies and gentlemen," he said, "where is the mystery owner who made this substitution? Where is the unknown jockey who failed to ride? And where is the rider who did ride? If they exist, why do they not come forward that they may be disqualified?"

"Now, there's a stupid question," said Mrs. Barclay right out loud for everyone in the courtroom to hear.

"Why is it that no one knows of this secret substitution but the plaintiff, my friends? Why can she not tell us their names?" continued the lawyer, trying to ignore Mr. Barclay's attempts to hush up

Mrs. Barclay and all the snickering in the audience. "Does it not seem strange that the plaintiff bases her case on information that only she can confirm?"

"Your honor," cried Miss Caroline, who had been sitting at her table pinning up stray curls, "I want to sue that man for impugning my honor. He is calling me a liar."

"You'll get your turn, Miss Harley. It's his turn now."

"I want the sheriff to find out who ran those people out of town," Miss Caroline continued, jumping out of her chair, just as mad as she could be. "There is something fishy going on here."

"Miss Harley, please."

"Your honor," said John Bates, "I know the young lady is not familiar with courtroom procedure, but—"

"I am too," snapped Miss Caroline, whose brother in Texas was a lawyer.

"Do you have anything else to say, Bates?" asked the judge.

"I believe I've made my point," said Mr. Bates with a sulky frown.

"I wish you were under oath," said Miss Caroline loudly.

"Miss Harley!" The judge tugged real hard on his beard, which is what he does when he's extra put out with a lawyer or a criminal or his wife, who's more outspoken than Mrs. Barclay or even Miss Caroline. "Miss Harley, Mr. McLaren will speak next, and I do not want you to interrupt him. Save your complaints until you summarize. Then you can say whatever you want."

"And I will too. You just wait." Miss Caroline scowled at the three lawyers and resumed her seat.

Mr. McLaren got up to address the question of Harry Benson's mysterious illness and disappearance, but he kept looking nervously in Miss Caroline's direction as he stammered and stuttered his way through his ideas on the matter, one of which was that Miss Caroline herself had probably poisoned young Harry with her fruit preserves. Miss Caroline just turned her back on him and muttered to herself about how lawyers and liars had more in common than the letter *L*, which caused folks to laugh all the harder and embarrassed Mr. McLaren half to death.

Lastly Mr. Barclay took the stage and bowed to Miss Caroline. He was the most famous of the lawyers, being as he planned to run for governor and owned his own motor car, the first in Converse County. Also he had the touchiest point to make, which was com-

ing out against women jockeys in such a way as to win over the
ladies in the audience and on the jury without infuriating all the
men who claimed racing was a man's prerogative.

"Ladies and gentlemen of the jury, consider what lies at the
heart of this conflict in which we participate today." Mr. Barclay is
Converse County's finest orator—most long-winded, too. "Is it a
clash between men and women? I submit to you that it is not. Is it
an attempt to take unfair advantage of this pretty young lady because she is a member of the fair sex? I submit to you that it is not."
Mr. Barclay tucked his thumbs into his waistcoat and nodded solemnly. "Rather, it is a misunderstanding—a clash of cultures, if
you will. Miss Caroline Harley, my honorable and, if I may say so,
beautiful opponent"—again Mr. Barclay bowed gallantly to Miss
Caroline—"is a visitor to our fair state, a stranger in our midst—
and a welcome stranger, I may add, for Wyoming has always been
known for its hospitality. Therefore I say, 'Welcome, Miss Harley.
Welcome to our fair state.' "

Miss Caroline and the judge yawned at the same time, and Mrs.
Barclay told her husband to "get on with it."

Mr. Barclay cleared his throat and took a sip of water. "We
citizens of Wyoming honor our sister state of Texas, Miss Harley's
home. Ah, yes, how many, many of our own fine citizens have come
to us from fair Texas—countless fine men and women, I assure you
—but I say to you, ladies and gentlemen of the jury, that Texas is
not Wyoming. No, and Wyoming is not Texas. And why do I say
this? I say this because our customs are different. Nothing could be
clearer to us after the words heard today in this courtroom. Our
customs are different. Miss Harley feels that she is being discrimi-
nated against by Wyoming customs, but I say to you, ladies and
gentlemen of the jury, that she is not. No, no. Rather she is being
honored—honored by Wyoming custom—as it is our custom in the
fair state of Wyoming to honor our ladies, and not only *our* ladies,
but all ladies—including Texas ladies."

Mr. Barclay bowed again to Miss Caroline and took another sip
of water.

"Yes, we of Wyoming honor our ladies, and we love our ladies,
and we protect our ladies. We put our ladies upon a pedestal, as it
were. If we did not honor our ladies, why then from the beginning
of government in our fair state did we wish to have them vote at

our side in public elections? I say to you that we gave our ladies the vote because we honor them.

"And we love our ladies. If we did not love our ladies, why then did we strive over the years in the searing heat of summer and the bone-chilling cold of winter, through blizzard and drought, through peace and war, to make Wyoming a safe and pleasant place for our ladies to live? Why, if we did not love our ladies, did we work ourselves into early graves to assure their happiness?

"And I say to you, ladies and gentlemen of the jury, that we protect our ladies. Never would we see a lady come to harm. And that, my friends, is why we of Wyoming shudder to think of ladies riding in horse races. That is why we of Converse County say a prayer of thanksgiving that our fair visitor rode unscathed through the tumult. And you may ask, How did it happen that our fair visitor rode unscathed through the tumult? I say to you, ladies and gentlemen of the jury, that her life was preserved because we of Wyoming protect our ladies. Is it then fair that this young lady should ask to be declared winner when other riders made way for her? I leave that to your consciences and your sense of fair play, ladies and gentlemen of the jury.

"And to you, Miss Harley, I say again, Welcome to Wyoming. Live among us in peace; enjoy our beautiful mountains and our bountiful plains; and foremost I say to you, Miss Harley, honor our customs. They are meant to honor you, as we do honor you, and all ladies. They are the mainstay of your happiness and your safety." Looking real happy with himself, Mr. Barclay bowed one last time to everyone in the courtroom. Then he said, "I thank you, ladies and gentlemen of the jury."

Miss Caroline jumped up, knocking her blue straw hat off onto the floor, and cried, "I say to you, Mr. Barclay, bosh!" She glared at him and bent to pick up her hat. "Yes, Mr. Barclay, I say, bosh! That was the most hypocritical, nonsensical speech I ever heard in my life." She slapped the hat down on the table, causing all the yellow and blue flowers to flutter wildly. "No one made way for me. I rode 'unscathed through the tumult,' as you put it, because I am a good rider and I was riding a good horse. No one even knew it wasn't Harry Benson on that horse until my hair fell down, and by then I was four lengths ahead, and no one had to make way for me if they'd had a mind to—which I doubt. Or are you trying to say that everyone in that race was honoring, loving, and protecting Harry Benson?

"And as for Harry Benson's mysterious disappearance, there is nothing mysterious about that. He went off to the university in Laramie, as everyone well knows. The mysterious disappearance is the disappearance of that other bunch, and I think you and your colleagues had something to do with that.

"So let's get to the real issue. You just don't want women winning your horse races. That's the real issue, not all this loving, honoring, and protecting ladies. I am sure your wives and mothers and grandmothers would be very surprised to hear that they were sitting around on pedestals while you were doing all the working and suffering. And don't talk to me about voting either. It's perfectly obvious that the women of Wyoming have a lot more right to vote than the men because the women are better citizens. The women, at least, aren't running around breaking the law, betting on horse races and such." With that, Miss Caroline turned her back on Mr. Barclay as if he were beneath her notice and looked at the jurors with a real stern eye.

"So I ask you, ladies and gentlemen of the jury, if women are good, law-abiding citizens and vote in Wyoming, why can't they be good riders and ride in Wyoming? I submit to you that women *are* good riders, just as they are good citizens. I submit to you that I am a good rider. I won, didn't I? I even trained the horse. So I should not be disqualified, and shame on you for even trying it." She then stalked over to the defendants' table and shook her finger at the embarrassed racing judges before she sat down.

Judge Henry Lateen harumphed and instructed the jury to retire to consider its verdict. During the fifteen minutes or so the jury was out, Miss Caroline didn't say one more word; she just sat at her table with her arms folded while the defendants and their lawyers buzzed among themselves about what the verdict would be. In the jury room a very loud and fractious argument was taking place, which no one heard in the courtroom because dozens of loud, bad-tempered arguments were taking place there too—mostly between husbands and wives. Then the jury filed back in, still arguing, and the foreman announced that they could not reach a verdict.

"Well, you've only been out a quarter of an hour," snapped the judge. "Go back and reach one."

"Your honor, we're split six and six. I reckon you can figure how that might be, and everyone's mad at everyone else. I, for one, ain't goin' back in there. I never been so insulted so much in such a short time in my whole entire life." The foreman sat back down like he never intended to move again.

The judge looked over the angry men and women on the jury and said, "I declare a mistrial. Case dismissed."

"You can't do that!" cried Miss Caroline. "I demand another trial! I demand justice!"

"Your honor," shouted Mr. Barclay over the uproar, "we have to have a verdict. What about all the bets?"

The judge glared at him. "Do you expect me to rule on an illegal activity, Jess?"

"Someone's got to, or we'll have anarchy in the county."

"Very well," said the judge. "All bets are off. How do you like that?" Then he got up and left.

As soon as the mistrial was declared, Oliver Chatman said, "That does it. I need a drink." And he scooted out, leaving Clayton Merriweather to rescue Miss Caroline from the free-for-all that broke out when the judge declared all bets off.

Miss Caroline was still demanding another trial when Clayton got to her and began to haul her toward a side exit. "Miss Caroline, you did real fine," he shouted in her ear. "Had I been on that jury, I'd sure have voted for you."

"Then why weren't you? Let go of my arm! This is a miscarriage of justice, and I insist that I be granted another trial."

"If we don't get out of here, you may need to be granted another life. Does that look like a friendly crowd to you?"

"The women are friendly."

"Not to the men, they're not. I expect you've just caused one whopping big drought in the Wyoming baby crop come next summer."

"Mr. Merriweather, that is a lewd thing to say. And please unhand me. I do not wish to leave. I insist on complete victory in this matter. And besides that, we've left my hat behind. That's my favorite, second-best hat."

Clayton picked her up and carried her, squirming and complaining, through the door to an alley, where he had a wagon waiting. "Hang on, Miss Caroline," he shouted as he dropped her on the seat and whipped the horses into a dead run. "We're making a hasty exit."

"I will not be kidnapped, Mr. Merriweather," Miss Caroline shouted back.

"No, ma'am, but you will be rescued, and since your no-good uncle ran off, it looks like I'm the one stuck with doing it." And he didn't let the horses slow to a trot until the wagon was two miles out in the countryside. "Reckon we're safe for the moment," he decided.

"How can you tell? I may push you off the seat and head back to Douglas."

"Now just simmer down, Miss Caroline. You won a victory today. Maybe you didn't win the case, but neither did they, and that's a moral victory if ever I saw one."

"Do you really think so, Mr. Merriweather?" Miss Caroline looked real pleased.

"No question, Miss Caroline, no question. You ever heard of women on a jury before—even in Wyoming? No, ma'am, you haven't ever heard of that, but you sure brought it about today. You ever heard of one pretty little female outlander making absolute jackasses of six prominent Wyoming citizens on their own stamping ground? No, ma'am, but you did it."

"I did do that, didn't I?" Miss Caroline gave Clayton a big smile. Then she added, "That Mr. Barclay was ridiculous, don't you think? He sounded as if he were running for office."

"Yes, ma'am, but that's partly because he *is* running for office. Still an' all, you've got him talked to a standstill when it comes to public speaking."

"Really? Maybe *I* should run for office."

"Well, now—"

"After all, how are we women to make our mark in public life, if we don't run for public office?"

"Well, I don't—"

"Take the matter of gambling. Those gambling laws should be enforced."

"I don't think that would be real popular."

"I could run for sheriff."

"Sheriff!" Clayton looked horrified. "Miss Caroline, ladies don't run for—"

"Why, I could run for governor!"

"Oh, lord."

A Passion for Trees

He Sapa

He Sapa is the professional name of Marnia Wormus. Native to the high plains of the Rocky Mountains, she lives in Bozeman in southwestern Montana. She is currently working on a second novel. This is her first professional sale.

Michael Seidman, then editor at Tor, had recommended that Marnia contact me. We talked over the phone, and she sent me several stories, which I rejected after some consideration. Then we talked again, and she mentioned that she had others—with a bit weirder topics—that she wanted to send to me; I told her to go ahead. One of them really intrigued me—a story about a present-day dryad. I trust you won't soon forget it.

She was unusual, but her unusualness was not the fact that she was a dryad, kachina of trees, living in an abandoned hogan in the northern Arizona desert on scant income from her weaving (learned one lazy summer from a breeze-blown arachnid and stupendous even by Two Grey Hills standards), presently suffering from the growing distraction of the lack of a druid, a heavy singer for the trees, invariably agitated each spring when her sap began to flow. No.

She was unusual because, finding herself in a blessedly temporary but appallingly destructive culture overstuffed with unmet needs, unarticulated wants, ubiquitous worries, and rampant fears, she had only one problem: she urgently desired the company of trees.

Well, you may snort, if she wanted trees why did she live in the desert?

A fair question. Cold, but fair.

When first she'd inhabited the hogan there had been a grove nearby, a lovely grove of piñon pines. She, being a dry-land dryad, a spirit loving the marginal hillsides of the world, had delighted in the little pines, their nuts a sweet treasure collected joyfully by the children of a people old in the land. In her association the trees flourished, increasing the happiness of everyone—children, trees, herself—with every passing season. Perhaps the love of the children for the trees replaced the worship of a druid; in any event she had no problems at all until the Army Corps of Engineers in complicity with the Bureau of Land Management at the behest of the Bureau of Indian Affairs razed the grove in order to graze cattle there.

Without the pines to cast a loving shade and hold precious water near the surface of the earth, the grass withered. Cattle were removed, goats and sheep brought in. The sheep ate the grass down to the ground, the goats ate the roots, and the shepherds took the herd away and left the place to prickly pear, small barrel cacti, and tumbleweeds.

She was responsible in no measure for this unfortunate sequence, it being a simple biological imperative.

When, she thought, digging her toe into the cracked earth, causing it to pop up into sun-made mud pies, oh, when are the greedy bastards going to realize it never pays to desecrate a grove?

After all, piñon nuts had been bringing $16 a pound in gourmet shops when the children felt like selling any, which they rarely did, preferring to eat them in squash-blossom soup and chocolate chip cookies.

She considered moving to Wyoming. Rumor had it there were still a few groves of wild native locust, their pods fodder for other children, four-legged ones whose parents also deplored the use of bulldozers as gardening tools. There being no hogans in Wyoming, abandoned or otherwise, she would have to inhabit a tree, no problem for her but considerable hassle with the loom. She was unwilling to give up the pleasures of weaving. Besides, living in a tree would bind her life to the life of the tree, and she was acutely aware of the possibilities of death by clear-cut.

She wanted a grove; a grove required protection. Why was there never a druid handy when you could use him? She would have to cultivate one herself. Together they would replant the grove, she would bless it, and he would preserve it. This plan was sound, basically, except it required a lifetime commitment on the part of the prospective druid draftee, and she was aware that lifetime commitments were virtually extinct in the present bulldozer-dominated culture.

Short-term, a dryad could always use sex as bait, but this project demanded a lure initially irresistible and subsequently substantial. It was going to take love.

Love is a complicated affair for anybody, often dangerous, but for a dryad it can be lethal, conferring, as it does in any but its most superficial states, mortality. Thus, foremost in her profile of the as-yet-unmet candidate was irascibility, a quality she found annoying enough to keep her safely distanced. She was looking also for a person of remarkable sensitivity and stubbornness. (It is, of course, a given that all druids are first poets.) She refined her requirements carefully: this project needed an irritating poet of environmental extremities, reasonably young, healthy, disillusioned romantically, discouraged financially—possibly even abjured.

Upon advertising obliquely in the *High Country News*, she had numerous respondees forthwith. After culling the letters written in aggrieved tones, there was left a possibility of three. She read their brief letters into memorization and discerned in one—from a failed actor turned failed economist—so insidious an undertow of desperation its strength she knew would prove invincible. Two remained: a sculptor and a writer of science fiction short stories. She interviewed them on consecutive weekends.

The science fiction writer was a man of mixed ethnicity embodying the concept "medium": medium height, medium weight, medium coloring, medium despair. His distinguishing characteristics were his ears, sticking straight out from his head like handles on a jug, and his eyes, wearing a hazel veil behind which the dryad suspected depths both lonely and kind. A member of the Nature Conservancy and the Audubon Society, evidently his passions also tended to medium.

The sculptor, an Earth Firster, was a dark green-eyed giant well over two meters, exhibiting great physical strength, a deep melodious voice, and a masculine beauty so profound as to be, practically speaking, perfect. He looked deeply into her eyes, and she felt the slow syrup in her veins liquify and zing.

That night on her heap of fluffy sheepskins she felt his hands upon her, graceful and strong, and the coarse muslin sheet over her became his kisses. Worse, she could feel her own hands tender on his massive shoulders, turning to silver streams in the dark and flowing down his arms, across his back, over his belly. When she found herself returning the sheet's kisses she knew beyond question who she must hire.

Earnest Yabey, the writer. What he lacked in irascibility he also lacked in excitement. She had no intention of compromising her immortality, however pleasant the process might prove.

She hired him on a two-year contract: room, board, a small stipend, and regular time off. Room was his own pile of sheepskins in the one-room hogan, board was the sharing of simple meals jointly prepared, and after six months the only time he took away was for brief trips to a trading post to sell her weaving. It was not her he was loath to leave, but the seedlings.

The two had traveled by rickety truck to groves hidden deep in the reservation for infant trees, together planted them, but their care was his alone. The channel of arboreal tenderness she had by dryad magic opened in him the young trees themselves perpetuated.

The desert sun burned his skin brown and his hair white while he fashioned miniature *ramadas* to protect the little grove. The veil over his eyes began to lift. In his eighteenth month, completely enamored, he wrote the trees his first poem. By the time his contract had run out he was composing regularly. The dryad encouraged him to keep the poems in a journal, rather than submit them for publication. The last thing she needed was for him to become a famous poet.

She also let him negotiate her into a five-year contract renewal.

It was shortly after this that she became aware of his eyes upon her. She would look up from her weaving to see him standing quietly, studying her. He seemed suddenly to inhabit doorways, shadows, and, most disturbing, her stray thoughts.

The trees were now old enough; by moonlight she sought relief in the grove. It was a beautiful night, full of stars and the alert silence of desert animals. She danced. She held out her arms to each young tree and sang a blessing. She turned to shimmering and slipped into one slender trunk.

Perhaps it was coincidence, perhaps not, but Earnest, too, sought the solace of the midnight grove. He sat on the ground, evidently not knowing any dances, leaned back on his elbows so he could admire the little branches against the stars, and began softly to cry. He walked about on his knees, caressing the limbs of each sapling in turn, murmuring to them. When he crawled at last to the treelet containing the dryad, she heard his words.

"You are so beautiful," he said. "So beautiful. I love you." The sincerity of his emotion passed through his fingertips deeply into the flesh of the little pine, and the dryad shuddered. He kissed the tip of a limb gently, and she melted out of the tree into his arms. He didn't seem surprised.

They loved each other by moonlight on the grass in the grove, sanctifying it. She found he was not a man of medium passion after all.

Under such influence, the piñon pines grew mightily, attracting the attention of prominent persons on the reservation, two of whom came to see what precisely was going on.

Earnest was prepared for their visit, conducting them on a tour and answering questions. Finally the younger man mentioned how surprising it was, a man and woman living on the reservation, without permission, in what amounted to tribal housing. Earnest instantly invited them into the hogan. The older man, thus far silent, looked into the nut-brown dryad's smiling black eyes as she offered him refreshment, said to her, "Haven't seen you in a long time," and to Earnest, "What do you think?"

Earnest thought the tribe should immediately register the site as a Tribal Treasure, for such was the only way to protect the grove from future depredatious whims on the part of the BIA or private enterprise. The tribe would also select the grove's caretakers and bequeath to the children, in perpetuity, the nuts.

The old man's eyes crinkled. "An organic trust fund," he said. "Sounds good." Then, "She stays. You too." He sipped from his cup, nodded once thoughtfully. "Maybe you would like to visit other trees on the reservation?"

They made the circuit through the orchards, cherry and peach, and to secret piñon stands, while the legal work went off without a hitch. Earnest tore up his contract.

The dryad began to droop.

"What's wrong?" he asked, kissing her thin shoulders, dappled by moonlight through leaves. Her fingers wandered in his hair; his lips traveled softly over her, loving the small depressions in her especially. She trembled against him, and when she spoke her voice was thick with fullness and with loss.

"Earnest Yabey," said the dryad, "I love you."

He kissed her temples, her eyes, caressed her arms, held her near him.

"Not to fear," he whispered in her ear. "Do you love the trees, yes? Love me as you love them, as they taught me to love them, and there can be no danger. They don't make us choose between isolation and self-annihilating surrender; that wouldn't be love." He kissed her tears; she offered him her lips, touched him deeply with her star-silver hands. "Tell me how you love the trees," he whispered.

"It feels like music," she whispered back. "A harmony, accommodating each individual, in celebration."

"Like this?" he breathed, gliding as sweetly into her as she into the flesh of trees.

"Ah! Yes. . . ."

Later, she cradled his head in her lap, smoothed his eyebrows with her fingers. "You weren't this wise when I hired you," she said. "What happened?" The leaves rustled in a tender breeze. His eyes laughed; he touched her face.

"You made me a druid," he said. "Wisdom goes with the territory."

"It never did before. Not really."

"Maybe because you let me alone, and I learned to love the trees, not worship them. So I could love you too, simply, without need or fear."

"A harmony . . ."

". . . in celebration. Yes."

She smiled, bent, kissing him in the tent of her thick hair. "I'm not scared anymore," she said.

As beautifully as the cherry trees they blessed, the dryad began to bloom.

Every year since, the dyad plants a scion dryad, unless they plant twins. Even so they can't keep up, for in the reservation orchards the limbs have to be propped up with two-by-fours to keep from breaking under the weight of peaches, and with the money from surplus piñon nut exports the tribe annually plants new groves.

Moonseed

Kristl Franklin

Kristl Franklin emigrated from Germany as a child. With the help of TV shows such as "The Mickey Mouse Club," "Sky King," and "Broken Arrow," English quickly became her second language. Although she has lived in New York, Louisiana, Texas, and Oklahoma and now lives in Denver, Colorado, she still considers the South her home. A few years ago she began writing again after a lapse of twenty years. Her work has appeared in *My Weekly, Piecework, Byline, Lives of Real People, Woman's World,* and *Women of Darkness II.* She is married and has three children. A member of Horror Writers of America, Kristl is currently working on a psychological suspense novel titled *Hush, Little Baby.*

Kristl had sent this story of the Cherokee in Oklahoma to me when I was editing the first *Women of Darkness.* I had to reject the story because it came when I had just closed the anthology. I never forgot the story, though, and when I started working on *Women of the West* I hoped Kristl would send it back to me. Luckily she did.

TSA-LA-GI', OKLAHOMA—1967

It has begun, Beloved. Our bones bleach together with the buffalo, with the white wolf.

The words were in her consciousness without volition. Like a flash of lightning burning an image on the back of her eye. Then the thought was gone before she even missed a beat in her presentation to the tour group gathered in front of her.

"The Cherokee brave," she heard herself reciting, "hundreds of years ago, provided for his family with ingenuity. Using only natu-

ral materials, he fished by methods other than the conventional
hook, line, and sinker."

The group leaned forward expectantly.

"One way was to bait a trap like this one made of willow." She
pointed to a small basketlike structure on the ground. "The fish
swam in through the narrow neck and then were trapped by these
spikelike pieces"—she bent over, her arm sweeping over the con-
traption—"that point inward."

Before straightening, she picked up two shallow buckbrush baskets and held them for the visitors to see.

"To catch a large quantity of fish," she continued, "the Cherokee used ground red-berry moonseed. The berries, which ripen in
the fall, were dried, pulverized, and then sprinkled on the water.
When ingested, the acid poison of the moonseed plant caused a
mild paralysis of the breathing organs, and the fish would, in fact,
drown. The catch was then harvested by net. Pounded buckeye
root and green walnut hulls were also effective in stupefying fish."

Several of the visitors peered more closely at the woven bowls,
one of which was filled with dried whole berries, the other with a
coarse powder the color of old blood.

"Sounds kinda cruel to me—unsportin' like," one visitor remarked.

The young guide hooded her eyes so all she could see were the
visitor's laced canvas shoes with rubber soles—sneakers, the new-
est fad. The *u-ne:-ga* wore them everywhere. She tried to keep her
voice low and controlled as she answered. "The Cherokee in those
days didn't fish for sport, sir."

She didn't look directly at him. She never looked directly at any
of them, these *u-ne:-ga*, lest she meet their eyes, lest they read what
lay hidden in the depths of her own.

"If enough food couldn't be caught or killed to feed the tribe,
the only alternative was starvation. And it was usually the very old
and the very young who died first."

She allowed herself to look up as far as the visitor's knees. Below
madras shorts, his legs were bare and stark white, sprinkled with
freckles and covered with a fuzz of reddish hair on the backs of the
calves. Dark blue veins bulged prominently. The sight made her
feel slightly ill.

She could feel him staring.

She'd never gotten used to it: to the visitors who came to stare—

not at her but at what she was—like this one, who took in every detail, raking down the animal-hide shift that molded against her body. Her figure had turned in the last few years from the straight line of a young girl into the generous fullness of a woman. Too generous, she'd complained once to Tomie. He'd chuckled deep in his throat and had nuzzled closer to her breast. Just right, he'd countered.

The thought of Tomie gave her courage. Taking a deep breath, she continued her lecture. "An interesting note is that the ancient Chinese used a similar technique to stun fish for food gathering."

Just at that moment the rain that had been misting all morning turned to a definite drizzle. Her small group of visitors lit out like a nest of yellow jackets hit by a stick. Watching as they raced for the exit and the safety of the main pavilion outside the gate, she called out softly, "The next tour starts in fifteen minutes at the south gate . . . if it stops raining."

She smiled and lifted her face to the sky, her eyes closed, welcoming the rain. Her hair was already soaked, and cool water seeped through the thick strands to the scalp. Now fingers of raindrops started trickling down her braids.

Beloved, wipe the tears off the eyes of the weeping nation, clear their ears and throats, take away all sorrow from their hearts.

She listened for more, but all she heard was the rain as it pelted her dress with tiny plops. When she looked down, she saw water pool on the doeskin surface and then run off. She would have to hurry. The skin had been rain tanned but not waterproofed. Tomie would be furious if the costume took enough water to ruin it.

Turning toward the center of the camp, she hurried along the concrete path that led around the dwellings and displays. The fine coat of red dust that always settled over everything had turned to slippery liquid mud on the hard surface. She paused to take off her moccasins, securing them under the tie at her waist, and then continued on the grass sod alongside the pathway. Already the ground was soaked, and brown-red water oozed between her toes.

Ahead of her the rain shrouded the mud-wattle summer huts with a gray mist. Interspersed among the huts were *o-si*, or winter houses, that sprouted like giant mushroom caps in front of her as she wove her way to the other side of the camp. This replica of a primitive encampment with its ten-foot stockade fence had been billed a living museum: Come see the real live Indian work and play in his natural habitat. How ironic, she thought, that this "new" Indian town had the ancient name Tsa-la-gi', the Cherokee. It was built for the sole purpose of herding the visitors through at fifty cents a head. She still found the whole idea incredible.

She made a graceful leap over a drenched fire placement. The strong odor of partially burnt oak hung in the air, stinging her nostrils. She went on until she passed by Alma's display. She raised her hand in greeting, but the older woman didn't look up.

Alma, protected from the rain by a shelter of branches and leaves, sat crouched over a soft piece of doeskin that she worked with pony and crow beads. The details were right even down to the children, also dressed in buckskin, who played at the older woman's feet. There's no magic here, the young girl thought. Why would anyone pay to see it?

If only she could be practical and content like Alma, she thought, as she maneuvered her way across logs and partially built dugouts. If only she could be like Tomie, who took life slowly, tapping the goodness out of it as if he were collecting sap from a maple tree. Tomie, in his easy sliding way, dismissed the humility of being on display with an "it's part of the job" shrug. Alma, oldest and perhaps wisest of the three, simply withdrew into her own world, her leathery-brown hands grinding hickory nuts into a paste for *kenuche*. The older woman seemed oblivious to the fact that every fifteen minutes the visitors came to her display, huddled around the earthen wickiup, and stared—at her animal-hide dress, at her broad Indian features, at her black hair falling straight as a waterfall down her back.

"Can't complain," Alma often told the younger girl. "It pays good money."

It was good money, money the young girl needed. So she swallowed her reluctance like swallowing the juice of bitterroot, refusing to let the feeling turn into shame. Now that summer neared its end, she had almost convinced herself that working as a tourist guide really wasn't so bad. Once she'd learned her lines, the fishing display was easy enough. She enjoyed grinding hickory nuts in the hollowed-out stump when she replaced Alma in the nut-paste demonstration. And she had Tomie.

She continued with easy strides past the seven-sided tribal council building that stood at the center of the village until she reached a grove of scrubby blackjack oak.

There on the other side of the grove, several yards away, was Tomie with his group of visitors. The rain had abated somewhat so she stopped to watch. Bare to the waist and dressed in fringed deerskin pants, *chaleco* vest, and red loincloth, the young man shook the rain from black hair that just skimmed his shoulders. He held a long cane blowgun at arm's length, raised it to his lips, puffed his cheeks, and in a quick motion blew a dart to its target. Bull's-eye.

Tomie turned and gave her a big wink. She was barely aware of the patter of hands clapping around them, for the wink was his way of saying he'd claimed another victim for her.

"Every time I land a bull's-eye, think of it being one of your dreaded *u-ne:-ga*," he'd told her. It had made her laugh. Tomie had a way of doing that. With a subtle gesture or a twist to his words, he could reduce her fear, her shyness, to the substance of a Ghost Dancer's shadow. The visitors who'd been observing the blowgun demonstration left quickly, dipping their umbrellas, sidestepping puddles, and headed for the next camp display. She wondered what the reaction of these *u-ne:-ga* would be if they knew about Tomie's little game that they were being eliminated one by one. The young man, blowgun in hand, loped over to her with graceful strides.

"Hey, better get out of the rain," he said, coming to a stop in front of her. She tried to assess his mood.

He looked in good spirits, his smile lighting up the world for her, the perfect white teeth against the bronzed skin irresistible. Even his eyes laughed.

Despite that, or maybe because of it, a hard knot formed in the pit of her stomach. She should have known from the beginning how it would end, she thought. How difficult it would be.

"I thought you couldn't shoot if the dart's fletch got wet," she commented, saying the first thing that came to mind. She hated having to dissemble with him like this. If only they could go back to their old relationship. For a moment the wistful thought softened her resolve. She would do anything for Tomie . . . anything, that is, except what he wanted most.

The tension between them was almost a visible cord tightening around them, strangling them both.

"Got a secret weapon," Tomie answered. He reached into the parfleche hanging from the waistband of his leggings and produced a long thin dart feathered with white thistle. The steady drizzle of the rain as it started again pelted the delicate thistledown limp while they watched.

"Guess that was my last show," Tomie said. He looked down in her face, searching, until his eyes finally met hers. The plea laid hidden in the darkness of his eyes, waiting for her.

She couldn't . . . wouldn't answer it.

Tomie dropped the wet dart and took another from the pouch, cupping it in his hand to keep it dry.

"You're going, aren't you." He made it a statement.

She nodded and looked away. "The notice came today. I've been accepted." She should have known he wasn't going to make this easy for her.

"Have it all planned, don't you?" He mumbled the words and came closer to her. His mood shifted like the wind that gusted around them. "Just gonna leave these dirty injuns behind."

Her head jerked up in response to his words and her body stiffened. She tried to meet his eyes again, but he wouldn't look at her.

"Why, you could even have a name-changing. . . . Let me see." He feigned a thoughtful look, stroking his chin. "Little Miss Apple. There now. That about says it all." The edge to his voice was sharp, much sharper than the words themselves. She'd heard the tone before, but this time he definitely wanted to cut, to hurt her.

"Don't call me that," she said through clenched teeth.

He turned away from her and palmed the dart he held into the long reed cylinder in his other hand.

"Why? That's what you want to be, isn't it? Red on the outside, white on the inside." He looked at her over his shoulder, his wet hair slung to the side. "Apple." He spit the word at her and raised the blowgun to his lips.

She reached out and grasped the end of the cane and held it, forcing him to look at her once more. His face was a mask, completely blank and void of emotion, except for his eyes, which held clouds of feeling. Rain bled from the ends of his jet black hair onto his shoulders.

"Tomie, you are my family—more than that, you're my friend. We're lovers. No one in this world knows me the way you do. You of all people know I have no choice in this. I'm called."

He jerked away. "It's not natural, I tell you. It's not natural. A rabbit doesn't become a mountain lion by wearing its skin."

"But Uncle said—"

"Your uncle was crazy, plain loco. He's filled your head with craziness too."

"Uncle taught us both, Tomie. He wanted us to know the ancient ways of the A-yv'-wi-ya'. But we don't live in an ancient world. Can't you see why I have to go to the white man's college? It's necessary to know the u-ne:-ga world as well. If we continue to live on the fringe of society, we'll soon cease to exist as a tribe, as a people. There'll be no place for us." She leaned in toward him, every nerve taut in the effort to make him understand. "Like the eagle, there'll be fewer and fewer of us until there are no more. There has to be someone who leads all the Real People, not just the Cherokee, to become united. It's the only way we can survive."

"Hey, I get it . . . girl Indian becomes savior for her race"— Tomie's face darkened, the features becoming hard—"and you're it. My God, girl, look at yourself!"

She pulled herself tall and straight, hands clenched at her sides. He's right, she thought. Who was she to count coup with the stars?

"As a woman," Tomie continued, "you're not even allowed to speak in the council meetings. How do you think you'll talk to nations? Silly little girl, do you seriously think you're the only visionary around?"

"It was Uncle who had the vision."

Tomie's hand shot out and grabbed her upper arm. The pain from his tightening fingers forced a small cry from her. He brought his face close, his eyes blazing and his mouth twisted with fury.

"You belong here." He spat the words at her. "You're mine, do you understand? Mine. No stoned son of a bitch with his crazy dreams is going to take you away from me." He shook her. "You hear me? You belong to me. The same as my car, my house, my boots. You are my woman."

He let go of her so suddenly she stumbled back a few steps to catch her balance. Once more Tomie placed the blowgun to his mouth. Sucking in his stomach, he blew full force into the reed. A *whoosh* of air sounded briefly, and the dart pierced the target across the clearing from them. The small missile landed and then barely clung to the outside border. He'd hit the target from a distance of sixty feet.

Tomie faced her again, calmer, but more frightening in his calmness. His eyes looked like two dark holes bored into his head. There was no laughter in them now.

"You're not leaving, and that's that," he stated flatly. "I'd hoped you'd come to your senses by now."

"And how, Tomie Grayhorse, do you intend to stop me?"

Even before she'd completed the question, an answer formed in the back of her mind. Silence filled the air. Then, with the deliberateness of a rattler before he strikes, Tomie's eyes looked at the target with the dart hanging from it and then back at her. A quiver of fear raised the hair on the back of her neck as understanding hit her in the pit of her stomach.

"You're a smart girl, you figure it out," he whispered. Without another word, he flung down the blowgun and stalked away. She watched his back, straight with anger, as the fog of rain swallowed him.

She stood in the rain for a long time, her eyes never leaving the spot where he'd disappeared, until the rain intensified and came down so hard each drop felt like a tiny slap. Finally the drops united, becoming sheets of water, and drenched her to the bone. Out of the corner of her eye she saw people scattering like quail for shelter.

She hitched up her dress, earthy smelling and heavy with moisture, as far as she could and sprinted through the mud toward the council building ahead. Her leg muscles ached with the effort. She tried to pull her thoughts together but they flew with panic, screeching and dodging like bats awakened out of an underground cave. Her mind sought the nightland, needing it much as the bats needed the dark. But there was no response.

Now the sky seemed to tear open and pour on the earth. Seeing was impossible through the solid rain. Only instinct guided her search for shelter.

Run the race, Beloved. The swiftness of the wind is in thy heart and the nimbleness of the deer in thy feet. Win the race.

She Who Races the Wind. She used to run often when she was younger, not as an athlete or part of a program, with regulation shoes and timing devices, but as a free young thing, darting through the trees and open meadow in the early dawn hours while everyone slept except for her and Tomie.

Windracer, She Who Races the Wind, Tomie had dubbed her

before this "apple" business started. He'd caught her in his arms after one long run and pulled her to the ground and then rubbed her neck and arms with dry sweetgrass as if she were a racehorse.

"You're always running, Little Bit," he said, using her childhood name. Even Tomie didn't know her secret-unspoken name, and she was still too young for her adult naming. "Always going somewhere in a hurry. Why, I bet you'd even try to race the wind," he whispered as he covered her body with his. Still out of breath from the run, chest heaving, she sought his eyes and for a moment thought she caught a glimpse of herself reflected in their darkness, as if she were on the verge of seeing who she was.

"Gotta have a real name," he teased her, "if you're gonna be one of the A-yv'-wi-ya', one of the Real People."

"I am real! I am," she protested. "Does this look fake to you?" She held up an olive-complexioned arm for his inspection, secretly pleased that he'd picked a name for her. When he solemnly kissed the soft place where the elbow bends, she tickled his nose with the end of one long dark braid. "Just because my mother is white doesn't mean I'm not A-yv'-wi-ya' like my father." But despite her words she hadn't been sure.

Ever since she'd been old enough to understand the word "half blood," she'd wondered. In which world did she truly belong, the *u-ne:-ga* or the A-yv'-wi-ya'?

That's what she had wanted to shout at Tomie when he'd left her standing in the rain, when she rubbed the bruise on her arm; she'd wanted to throw the words at his back like darts.

Who am I? Where do I belong? But the cries stuck in her throat. She had kept silent.

Without warning the hardened mud structure of the lodge bit into her shoulder, halting her in her tracks. She flung herself spread-eagled against the side for a moment as if to hug the warmth it still held. She let the rain beat at her back and legs before making a dash through the entrance passage that was purposely built only big enough for one man and his weapon to enter at a time.

The dark that had been almost complete in the entrance portal was softened by strategically placed spotlights around the large interior chamber. Small pools of light shone out from under the log-benched gallery that circled the room.

Stale and dusty air enveloped her as if the raging storm outside had cut off the only source of air to the room. For a moment she couldn't catch her breath. A streak of lightning stabbed the sky and flashed through the smoke outlet at the roof's center. In that second of illumination the room looked as if a picture had been taken using a giant flash.

The birch poles holding the roof showed white behind the ornaments of tomahawks and clubs that hung from them, the feathers not moving in air still as death. In the middle of the lodge, an artificial fire burned, the alternately revolving red and yellow lights simulating the flickering of flames. A soft monotonous tribal chant drifted from the partially hidden sound equipment.

Tomie will be mad, she thought. Someone should have turned off the speakers and lights after the last tour.

Tomie. What was she going to do about Tomie? She rubbed the upper part of her arm where his fingers had pressed into the flesh. Feeling vaguely faint, she leaned against a tall pole that stood sentinel at the front of the room. The rain continued to pound on the roof, demanding entrance.

The eyes of my soul come onto thy body.

The clarity of the thought made her alert. She strained to see through the shadows of the room. She relaxed once more. She was alone. For the first time completely alone.

She gathered her braids together and squeezed water out of the ends. The rain had soaked her, and the animal-hide dress felt like a coat of armor, plastered to her skin. She undid the tie at her waist and let it and her moccasins fall. After a moment's hesitation she unlaced the neckline down the front, slipped the shoulders down and let the garment drop into a sodden heap around her feet. In a brief motion she stepped out of the wet clothing and kicked it aside. She leaned against the birch pole again. The warm air wrapped around her chilled body like a blanket. When she hugged her arms around bare breasts and chafed her upper arms in appreciation, the blue marks on her arm caught her eye. The imprint of Tomie's fingers was clearly visible.

Tomie. What was she going to do about Tomie? It wasn't a question anymore. That he could stop her there wasn't a doubt. He claimed her; he had rights. In a society where the women ate together in the kitchen after serving the men in the dining room, where the wife walked several paces in back of her husband, Tomie had indisputable rights.

Her breath became uneven and ragged. Her chest heaved as she struggled to breathe. Loving Tomie was like being poisoned by moonseed, she thought. Who would think, looking at the heart-shaped leaves on the moonseed vine with its thick clusters of blood-red berries, that a small taste could paralyze? Just like loving Tomie paralyzed her.

Windracer put her arms back and tried to bring her hands around the ceremonial pole she leaned against. The slick nylon of her underwear made her slide a little at first, but then, muscles straining, she grasped her hands together as if they were tied.

Prisoners, stripped and beaten, faced their conquerors this way three hundred years ago, she mused.

Now she too must face her captor.

She released her hands and slowly unbraided her hair while staring with unseeing eyes into the center of the dark room. Against her back the wood felt rough from the scars and gouges Tomie's hatchet made, demonstrating the way the warriors voted on tribal issues. The women voted only when war was the issue. *It was the women, Beloved. . . .*

Once more she became alert. But only shadows darkened the rows of crude benches that semicircled the room. Leaving the pole, she sat on the nearest log bench, stretched out on it, and arranged her hair like a peacock fan across her body so it would dry. After making a pillow of sorts with her arms, she let her eyes drift half closed. The hypnotic chanting in the background seemed to grow louder. Somehow it seemed to be of itself, no longer a part of the audio system.

If she looked hard enough, she could almost see them—the women—dancing, the turtle-shell rattles attached to their legs making a soft rhythmic sound. Dozens of them moved in a circle, shoulder to shoulder around the fire. The figures were barely visible through the smoky haze. The odor of burning herbs drifted to her. The smell was familiar; where was it she'd . . . ? Oh, yes, at a second cousin's funeral. The smell of the ceremonial mixture of sage and tobacco had been strong.

"No one remembers for sure, Little Bit, why it's done," Uncle had told her. "The Tsa-la-gi' have always burned remade tobacco and sage when someone dies. Some say it purifies and drives away the Ones from the nightland."

Windracer closed her eyes completely. The chanting continued to drone in her ears.

It's the women, Beloved. . . . The women of the tribe decide who shall live and who shall die.

Her eyelids flew open. She half expected someone to be standing in front of her, but the room was empty, no shadowy figures, no smoke. It was just a replica of days gone by when the Tsa-la-gi' went to war.

A wisp of memory came to her, one that had been on the edge of her dreams many times but always eluded her. It was something Uncle once told her.

They'd been sitting on the wooden steps of the farmhouse. Uncle shared his figs, sour milk, and fry bread with her. In between chews and swallows, he told her about the trials of endurance, the adoption of captives, the manner in which some of them died.

"There was only one person in the whole world, Little Bit"— Uncle dropped a piece of fry bread into the milk to soak—"who, after the choices were made, had the power to reverse the women's decisions"—he paused for a moment to select a plump fig for her —"a special member of the tribe . . . a woman everyone called Beloved."

Something awakened her. Windracer opened her eyes and scanned the lodge, noting every detail. As far as she could tell, everything was the way it should be.

The hard edge of a knot in the wood poked into her side, waking her further. Shifting her weight, she turned on her back and scrubbed her face with her hands to help clear her thoughts.

How long had she been sleeping?

When she looked up for a glimpse of the sky, she saw the domed ceiling of the lodge was no longer in shadow. Instead, light flowed into the center of the room through the smoke outlet. Dust motes danced in the column of sun.

The rain. That's what had awakened her. The rain had stopped. She glanced at the opening to the passage leading outside. Although she was lying close to the entrance, she couldn't see past the darkness. If anyone came to the lodge, she wouldn't see them until they actually walked in the room.

She should get dressed.

She contemplated the wet heap of clothing on the floor and

wrinkled her nose in distaste. The last thing she wanted to do was put on that dress. Besides, it was warm in the lodge—perhaps a little too warm—almost steamy, and she found it hard to breathe deeply.

The air was completely still, without sound except for the tape of chanting in the background. She'd heard the tribal songs so much they'd become white noise to her, almost unnoticeable. No, it was another sound for which she listened. After a rain, usually a whole calliope of chirping and chattering broke forth from the animals in the encampment. But this time everything was strangely silent . . . except . . . she turned her head to look at the entrance.

Was someone coming?

The muted noise came again.

Her head jerked toward the column of light. The sound came from the back of the room, from the other side of the bright sun streaming on the floor. She'd heard the unmistakable soft scraping of moccasins against hard dirt. While she watched, a man came into view, as if he'd materialized right before her eyes.

For some reason it never occurred to her to be afraid, to scream, or even to question how a strange man came to be there. It was as if she'd lived this moment before, as if she'd dreamt it into existence.

Was she dreaming?

It didn't matter. The man approaching was her reality. He walked into the spotlight formed by the smoke hole. Now she saw him clearly. Every detail of his appearance was a tiny part of a whole she felt she should somehow know.

He was A-yv'-wi-ya', one of the Real People, round head with cheekbones so high they made small mounds below the far corners of his eyes. Of medium height and well built, he wore the markings of the Tsa-la-gi' on a quilled neck band around his throat. His hair, streaked with white, hung long around his bare shoulders, except for the crown, which was tufted and held a black and red feathered roach that disappeared down his back. Save for a breechclout dyed yellow with red symbols, he was naked, his skin shining darkly with oil, his ornaments, a small ax and a knife, both held to his side with a rawhide strap. In the back of her mind the fact registered that he was dressed for battle.

The warrior came to her with measured sliding steps, swaying in rhythm with the drums that played in the background. Her hands gripped the edge of the log bench on which she was lying while she held perfectly still, afraid to move. He knelt on one knee by her side. His black eyes glistened in the half-light. A dead calm permeated her.

The warrior placed his hand on the knife at his side and drew out the weapon.

He held it above her.

The blade, made from sharpened flint, was aged with use. Tiny feathers danced from sinews attached to the handle. He lowered the knife to her throat. At that moment terror rippled through her, urging her to react, but she couldn't move. His eyes drew her. His face filled her whole consciousness, blocking everything except him.

A gasp, more from surprise than pain, escaped her when the tip of the knife broke her skin just above and between her breasts. Raising her head, she saw a tiny bead of blood form around the point of the blade where it had entered. Then while she watched, he drew the knife down between her breasts, the razor edge barely breaking the skin. A crimson line bubbled in the wake of the knife as it continued down her body along her rib cage, stopping just short of her navel. Still she didn't move.

She felt strangely detached, not in her body at all but outside of it, hovering over the scene, watching as if out of curiosity. She saw her body lying supine on the planed log, relaxed, her abdomen rising and falling with each breath. At the same time she felt every sensation: the hard wood of the bench pressing against her back, the fresh burning of the cut.

What did he want of her?

As if in answer to her unspoken question, the warrior lifted her hand in his, palm up. After dipping the first two fingers of his free hand in the line of her oozing blood, he brushed the dark red liquid on her hand until the palm and the bottoms of the fingers were covered. When he finished, he raised her hand in a quick twisting motion, turning the palm toward him, and forced it against the upper part of his chest. Then, just as swiftly, he snatched her hand away as if it were a branding iron searing his flesh. Perhaps it had been, for there across his breast above the left nipple was the red imprint of her outstretched hand.

Windracer looked at her hand, incredulous. The strong odor of fresh blood filled her nostrils. For a moment the image of the warrior swayed sickeningly in front of her. She squeezed her eyelids tightly shut, trying to clear her vision, and reopened them in time to see him take a substance out of his parfleche and hold it in the hollow of his hand. After adding crumbled tobacco leaves, he spat in the mixture and stirred it. Very deliberately, while starting a low chant, he dabbed the concoction to her open wound. The aromatic odor of the tobacco filled her senses. She closed her eyes once more.

"The A-yv'-wi-ya' are dying, Little Bit," Uncle had said one evening long ago. Clouds of smoke ringed his face as he drew deeply on a pipe that hundreds of years before had served as a calumet. The odor was the same, tobacco mixed with dried sumac leaves. The same odor that soothed her now had on that day intoxicated her.

With the solemnity that befitted the last hereditary chief that he was, Uncle handed her the pipe. It almost dropped out of her small child hands.

Four feet long and wound with fine ribbon, the pipe was designed with white corals, porcupine quills, and green, yellow, and white feathers. The bowl was red marble, at least three inches deep and eight inches wide. Grasping the hard black wood of the stem, she struggled to hold it aloft in order to puff on it several times. Her eyes watered from the pungent smoke invading her mouth and throat and burning her lungs. She swallowed most of the smoke, choking down the urge to cough lest she disgrace herself. Her head seemed to be spinning, and she heard Uncle's words intermingled with drums and chanting from far away.

"Ay-ya-ee-ya." The chanting rose and fell, lifting her one moment, drowning her the next.

Was it her uncle she still heard now or was it the sound of the warrior who stood next to her and sang his own song?

His face and arms were raised to the heavens. His dialect, although very similar to her childhood Cherokee, was an ancient one. The intonation was different and many of the vowel sounds were absent. Still, she understood the words.

"The spirits of our ancestors," the warrior sang, "loudly call upon us, and it is our duty to obey them. By the ancient words, it has been said . . . it shall be a Woman. We will place her in the midst, and the other nations who seek to destroy us shall be man and live around the Woman. No one shall touch or hurt her but shall protect and honor her or he shall die. So it must be with all the A-yv'-wi-ya'."

She fought the remembered smoke-induced sickness that rose in her throat.

The warrior lowered his arms and turned his hands palms up over her. "Beloved, thou shalt be the Woman. Through thee the A-yv'-wi-ya' shall last as long as the sun and moon give light, rise, and set, as long as the stars shine in the firmament and the rivers flow with water." He brought one hand to his chest. "The sign of thy vision is on my breast." With that he drew his knife once more and raised it in the air. His other hand clasped the small ax from the rawhide thong at his waist.

Then with one leap and a chilling whoop, he began dancing, brandishing the weapons in the air.

The last thing she heard before she lost consciousness was the distinctive sound of the warrior's voice as he sang a dance of victory.

It was strange that she couldn't remember the exact time she had thought of it, . . . the precise moment. She should: the way people remember where they were when Kennedy was shot or every detail of the moment they were told they had cancer. But the knowledge that Tomie was to die had simply become a part of her like the secret darkness from the nightland that welled up in her dreams. She would push the thought away, pretend it wasn't there, but it always returned. He was to die or the dream would end. There was no choice.

Perhaps tonight . . . perhaps tonight would be the last time. Each moment they spent together weighed heavy and seemed like a small farewell.

The moonlight outside the open screened window streamed across fields that stretched as far as she could see in every direction. In a lazy motion Windracer raised her head and propped her chin in her hand, settling her bare stomach more comfortably against the rough sheets. The night's pale indigo light bathed the prairie lace that grew wild across the fields. The great masses of flowers resembled banks of blue snow, in among Indian blankets and false coreopsis, and grew right to the edge of the farmhouse. The long red tassels of the love-lies-bleeding that she'd planted in the spring had filled out bushlike to the windowsill and pushed against the screen.

The wind was still.

The thought occurred to her: when the moment came, would she be able to go through with it?

Beloved, thou art the living seed. The hope of a great nation. The beginning is with thee. Thou must endure to the end.

Understanding came to her, overpowered her, and left her breathless. She was to count coup.

She turned her head to look at the man lying asleep next to her. In the moon's reflected light a faint sheen of perspiration glistened on his back. His arm, the color of a piñon nut, almost touched hers. In that moment she wanted him. One last time.

"Tomie," she whispered.

The wind burst suddenly across their bed, sending the window's pulled-back cotton curtains flapping. A chill went through her. Tomie stirred and turned to his side. He was awake. She could feel him looking at her, his eyes laughing.

He reached for her, pressing gently against a breast already swollen from lovemaking, sending her an invitation. She held out her arms to him. She couldn't resist him. She never could. He filled her senses with his presence. The hard demanding body, the scent of passion, the completeness of him intoxicated her until she had no will left of her own. The moonlight painted his hair inky blue. The long silky strands fell against her cheek and neck and shut everything from her vision but him. The odor of sweet grass drifted to her. Then something else. It filled the room. A smell of sage and tobacco. And sumac. She pushed the curtain of Tomie's hair aside and looked around.

The moon held them captive on the bed in its light, but the rest of the room was so dark it looked almost as if it didn't exist. She saw a wisp of smoke curl lazily into their circle of light.

"Tomie," she said, a tone of panic sharp in her voice. She struggled to move under the weight of his body. At that moment she knew. His body was hard, tense with desire. But at that moment she could imagine rigidity in his muscles, the rigidity that comes with death.

She let out a short cry and rolled from beneath him.

"What the hell?" Tomie raised up, a startled expression on his face.

She huddled against the wall near the window, unable to stop shaking.

"I'm sorry, Tomie, I can't." She wrapped her arms around herself tightly. "I can't do it. . . ."

"Hey." Tomie raised his hands in a conciliatory gesture. "It's all right. Everything's cool. I was being a glutton anyway." He swung his legs off the bed and sat up. "Come here by me." He patted the mattress next to him.

A haze gathered and drifted in the spot of light made by the moon. The scent of sage was so strong it burned her nostrils. She went to him.

"Have you seen my smokes?" he asked.

"Over on the nightstand." She sat carefully on the bed next to him. Alert. Waiting.

Tomie stretched out, leaning on the bed, and grappled on the shadowed nightstand for his cigarettes.

"Hey, what's this?" He sat up and held out his palm to her. Even without seeing clearly in the dim light, she knew what he held.

"*Kenuche.* Alma ground some extra paste and gave it to me. So I made some this morning for you."

Tomie popped one in his mouth. "Thanks. I really love this stuff."

She rose from the bed like a sleepwalker and backed slowly into the shadows. Tomie ate two more nut-paste balls.

Time stood still. The young man on the bed coughed slightly when he swallowed the last of the sweet, as if the smoke that whirled in and around him made it hard for him to breathe. The second time he coughed it was more urgently, as if something had caught in his windpipe. A few seconds later he bolted upright, gasping for air, his eyes bulging. He clawed at his neck.

Out from the same spot where the girl had merged with the shadows, a warrior dressed for battle came forth. Clothed only in a yellow breechclout, his body shone with red paint. He started a low chant at the same time that he approached the young man writhing on the bed. The chanting grew louder and stronger, melodiously hypnotic. The warrior leaned over Tomie and placed his hand on the base of the choking man's neck. Immediately, the struggling ceased and the body was still. The eyes that had once laughed stared straight ahead, fixed by death. On the neck the bloody imprint of a hand counted coup.

Size of a Silver Dollar

A. R. Morlan

A. R. Morlan was born in 1958 in Chicago, moved to Los Angeles when she was three, then moved to Ladysmith, Wisconsin, when she was eleven. She graduated from Mount Senario College with a B.S. in English, and Minors in Theater Arts and History. She has worked as a motel maid and waitress. Her stories and nonfiction have appeared in *Twilight Zone, Night Cry, Weird Tales, The Horror Show, Grue, Dark Regions, 2 AM, Bone-Chilling Tales, New Blood, Grim Grafficks, The Scream Factory, Doppleganger, Supernova, Eldritch Tales, Scavenger's Newsletter, Writer's Nook News,* and the *Obsessions* anthology. She is a member of Science Fiction Writers of America. She has sold two novels, *The Amulet* and *Dark Summer,* to Bantam. She's single, and is owned by a houseful of cats, some of whom have made guest appearances in her stories and novels.

When I started reading A.R.'s story, I thought, "Oh no, *another* pioneer tale." For a while that's all I received and I was fast growing tired of soddies and such. But I kept on reading, and I'm glad I did. This is not your usual pioneer wife.

The town councilmen exploded the gunpowder on the anvils shortly after sunrise, but it wasn't until near on ten o'clock in the morning that enough folks had gathered in the town proper to make starting the celebrations worthwhile. And by that time, the sun was just high enough to shine painfully in Miz Myrtle Morgan's thin-lidded eyes as she sat on the high platform. The flimsy paper fan someone had gently pushed into her curled left hand was a poor shield against it. In fact, the red third of the fan made the filtered sunlight all the hotter, and after the Mayor gave her good morning greetings to the townsfolk assembled on Main Street, Miz

Myrtle Morgan let the fan slide from her fingers, where it dropped unceremoniously to the planks below her feet. No one came forward to pick it up and reposition it in her hand, for the time of the speeches had come, and all eyes were focused on the row of sixth-graders sitting on cane-bottom chairs behind the new microphone podium on the stage.

The little girl sitting nearest to Miz Myrtle (as the Widow Morgan was known to one and all present) wore her flax-colored hair in a long hangman's braid, which rested on her back, just touching the greyish stripe of sweat running down her spine. Miz Myrtle eyed the braid with a dull mixture of dread and fascination—dread because dread of death was a fixture of her one hundred years, fascination because . . . just *because.*

Before her, the Mayor (the town's second woman mayor; Kansas had been in the forefront of the woman's suffrage movement for close to fifty or sixty years) had launched into a short Fourth of July speech, clear thin voice loudly and uncertainly amplified across the heads of the people assembled below the platform, hastily erected close by the hardware store and across from the dress shop. Miz Myrtle could see the shimmering reflection of all those on the platform in the window of Hargrove's Dress Shop, a wavering blend of red, white, and blue, touched with washed-out pinks and the pale hemp yellow of the children's hair . . . with a blob of white-tipped black in the center of that pale mirror.

She, Miz Myrtle, was the shapeless black object: close on two hundred pounds, swathed in black like an obscene parody of the Holy Infant, and wearing a ridiculous parody of a pioneer woman's bonnet in thin white netting, like the little hats the Mennonite women wore. No help against the white glare of the sun, simply none at *all.*

Having reached the century mark, Miz Myrtle was not interested in looking down at the upturned, perspiring faces below her; she had seen those same faces from near infancy and had grown tired of them long ago. She had grown tired of the faces of the children too, because they all began to look the same to her—or, in certain cases, *worse* than the same. For she had never forgotten, despite the passing of sixty years, how the faces of her children had looked . . . before the Indians came.

Before the Indians came. . . . Those four words had become the line of demarcation in her life. First had come the forty years of

her life in which she was a wife, a mother, and a homesteader . . .
and then, after the Indians, everything was changed. For good and
beyond. Before the Indians came, she had been part of eleven;
eleven people in a soddy plowed from an acre of the Morgan claim,
eleven lives lived in a place of dirt sifting down from the earthen
walls, the cottonwood, willow, and sod roof. And muddy, soggy
floors when it rained. Horrible it had been, but she'd been a part of
it, mother to nine, wife to Mr. Morgan . . . all before the Indians
came.

Came to be that all she *could* think about anymore was that time
before the coming of the Indians out of the flatness of the land and
the hard blueness of the sky; curiously, what thoughts were old in
her remained the clearest, while new thoughts came and went like
pinpoints of hot twinkling light that fanned the ground in front of
an oncoming prairie fire. Miz Myrtle couldn't even remember exactly who it was who had half dragged, half hoisted her onto this
platform, who had led her to this stout chair and placed the ridiculous little paper fan in her hand. But she remembered *why* she was
here; the reason was unmistakably clear. She was here to be tortured—oh, not officially; on the face of it she was the guest of
honor, the woman of the day, as someone or other had told her
over breakfast. Another voice, another face out of many at the
home where she stayed, trapped for the most part by infirm limbs
and immense weight.

And ironically, if memory served her (as it did, oh, how faithfully
it did these days!) this just about *was* her day, as close as that to the
day of the Indians. The day nothing, even old age and a capricious
memory, would allow her to forget.

The Mayor's speech was coming to an emotional end, and as the
sluggish breeze tugged at the woman's flimsy voile dress (making
an almost imperceptible susurration that reminded Miz Myrtle of
dried grass whispering under an endless horizon), Her Honor
concluded. "Women gave up their best years, their very strength,
health, and material wealth, in order to tame and civilize the great
western lands. And the cost of their sacrifices is one that cannot be
totaled on any cash register or be figured in any ledger. That cost is
known only to the Almighty. And yet . . . some of the sacrifices
were not personal, but sacrifices which extended to the very *families*
of these brave women. And it is the fact that these women, women
such as our own Mrs. Morgan, not only survived such travails but

persevered and prospered *despite* the cruel blows of Fate. *It is that fact*, citizens of Walnut Center, that made these simple farm women the true royalty of the West. And no greater honor can be bestowed to any mortal woman." Amid the hearty clapping, hooting, and cheering that rose up from the heat-shimmering street full of people below them, the Mayor turned and applauded Miz Myrtle. Miz Myrtle pretended to nod off.

Having suitably honored the dozing Miz Myrtle, the Mayor returned to the huge microphone. "And now the sixth-grade students of the Walnut Center Elementary School will give their speeches. First up is"—the bob-haired woman consulted an index card—"Bessie Walters."

Miz Myrtle's strangely bonneted head jerked up reflexively at the mention of the curly-headed girl's surname. Walter—little Walter, the baby of the bunch—would have been sixty-one this year, come October. Only baby Walter hadn't made it to one year of age, let alone sixty-one.

With her good hand (her right arm was the only "good" limb left to her), Miz Myrtle groped for her drawstring handbag, sticking a fat finger into the puckered top and gently widening the opening until she could almost stick her whole hand into the bag. While worming her way into the bag, she let her eyes drift down to her lap, where she stared at the absurdity of her bloated hands. The fingers were vaguely articulated sausages, with nails resembling nothing less than blobs of richly yellowed fat stuck in the bottom of the casings. And on the backs of them, countless misshapen brown dots seemed to hover above the dead white of her skin, each speck of dark pigmentation seemed to float in the strong sunlight. Miz Myrtle was almost afraid the dots of color would peel off of her skin and drift away like ashes blown from an open fire. But most of all, she feared the shapes left behind on her hands after the departure of her age freckles, for how could she know what color the skin *underneath* them might be?

Little Bessie Walters was in place behind the microphone, standing on a footstool, wide-lined paper in hand. Her first few words were lost to the crowd, until a man came forward and adjusted the microphone head with an ear-stinging squeal. Only then did the child begin again.

"One—*one* hundred years ago a baby girl was born in Ohio, and her mother and father named her Myrtle. That year was eighteen

and twenty-nine, and twenty-two years later, little Myrtle was a
grown-up gir—*woman*, and she became a bride, and there was a big
celebration, and . . ."

Fingers firmly around what lay in her bag, Miz Myrtle bit a fleshy
lip and thought, No, little girl, it wasn't like that at all. Momma and
Poppa hated Joshua. Thought him an ingrate and a good-for-
nothing. And our union brought scant joy. . . .

The Myrtle Clarke of 1851 was a far cry from the Myrtle Clarke
Morgan of 1852; in less than twelve months she made the sudden
cocoonless metamorphosis from graceful, flighty young miss to
chastened, saggy-bellied, full-teated mother, and when she wrote
tearful letters to her dear mother, finally admitting her stupidity,
her blindness in wedding Josh, it was too late. The letters were
returned; her mother and father refused to pay the postage on
them. And baby Olive was always hungry, and the milk was slow in
coming out of Myrtle's body. Joshua only laughed, berating her for
her small breasts, laughing even as Olive squalled, red-faced and
too thin in her mother's arms. If only milk had flowed from Myrtle
like liquor flowed from the ever-present bottle in Joshua's hand!

Myrtle was careful in the next few years, not allowing Joshua's
seed to stay within herself long enough for a child to flower inside
her. Mostly he was too drunk to notice her swift departure from the
bed, to her douches and washings-away of his maleness. But before they left Ohio, when the government made cheap land in the
Kansas Territory available to white men, Myrtle was unable to
cleanse away all traces of Josh. Henry was born the year after they
came to the western plains, born in the filth and near-darkness of
the dugout Josh carved into the side of a low hillock that first year.
During all of 1856, the year of Henry's birth, Josh took bad with
the ague, alternately sweating and freezing. So it was dose Josh
with the quinine and sassafras tea, and nurse the baby, and tend to
toddler Olive, and tend to their patchy garden and sickly livestock
when she wasn't tending to her weak brood in the dank confines of
the dugout. Come the next year, when William was born, Josh was
well enough (and sober, although that was no blessing, since the
drink had at least kept him slightly jovial) to plow away blocks of
prairie marble from an acre of their land and stack them with
Myrtle's help into four walls a full two feet thick. Myrtle had helped
to shape wood into window and door frames; the fine soft hands of

her girlhood and youth were rough now, almost splintery to the touch. And the lifting and positioning of the sod made painful knots of muscle in her upper arms toughen, bulge slightly when she flexed her hands. She ended up cutting the roof of cottonwood and willow brush, for as the work neared completion, Josh's ague came back, most conveniently, Myrtle thought at the time. . . .

Her head of bright curls all but hidden from the crowd by the microphone, Bessie Walters finished her speech, which ended with the lilting words, "And that was how life was on the plains for Miz —Mrs. Morgan and her family. It was a hard life but a *pure* one," and with that Miss Walters stepped down from her stool and went back to her chair, where she did a little curtsy for the clapping crowd. Miz Myrtle hoped the little girl wouldn't win the prize for Best Speech (said prize displayed on an easel-back stand near the podium, a gold medal the size of a silver dollar attached to a bright blue ribbon); she had made everything seem just too nice, too simple. To quote Miss Walters, too *pure*.

Miz Myrtle's fingers slid over the leathery surface of the thing in the bag, caressing the well-worn roundness of it, but the vague movements of her fingers became jerky, tense, when the next child, a boy whose hair fluttered in the breeze like the silk of almost ripened corn, began his speech with the overemphasized phrase, "On the *plains*, life was hard and *many* settlers' children *died*, so the families had *lots* and lots of *young*sters." The boy paused dramatically, then went on, "And our Widow Morgan was no exception." The crowd below made a low murmur of disapproval. The subject of the speech was a touchy one, sure to displease.

But Miz Myrtle was too lost in thought to hear someone in the crowd grouse, "Don't the boy have any *consideration* for her?" In the depths of her brain, names came forth, and years, and small wrinkled faces: In 1857, William, cross-eyed but quick to smile. Pearl two years after, completely Josh's child. 1861 brought Carrie, she of the sad eyes and tiny mouth. Two summers later Josh was placated by Benjamin's arrival, and come 1865 Bernard brought the promise of more help on the farm, and perhaps a respite in later years for Myrtle. The next year was a setback, but Gertrude might be of use for housework, food gathering, and water hauling. Before 1868, Myrtle had her hands full with three very young blond children to run around after, but Walter's arrival all but broke her, and even his cheerful gurgle and inquisitive little fingers and darting eyes couldn't bring much cheer to his mother. For Josh was no help at child-rearing and little good as a farmer, not with his annual bouts of ague, his almost on-the-dot announcement each summer, "I dunno, Mother, feel mighty sickly, mighty peaked." Myrtle wasn't such a fool that she didn't notice him wink at the older children in turn and, in turn, see them wink back and prepare their own tales of impending illness. . . .

Miz Myrtle's fingers worked the worn leathery circle feverishly, as she sat with hooded eyes lowered, the blackness of her lap her entire field of vision, not listening to the now-shamefaced boy hurriedly finish his speech, mumbling "The Morgan family was real lucky because not a one of their children succumbed to any sickness. That was a really rare thing to happen in those days. Mrs. Morgan nursed them through sicknesses very successfully. She was a very good wife and mother—and doctor." The clapping sounded like fat drops of rain hitting a tin bucket—*splap, splap . . . splap.* Then sun and silence.

The next child was hurried onto the stepstool: the girl in the dotted dress (red specks of color against a creamy ground, and Miz Myrtle checked her own hands, seeing if the brown blotches had somehow turned, gone back to the way they'd been, once) wasted no time launching into her narration. "How the Pioneers Dressed, by Etta Louise Oliver," she said precisely, capitalizing each important word aurally. A safe topic, thought Miz Myrtle, no matter what sort of print the girl's dress was.

As if feeling Miz Myrtle's approval, Etta Louise singsonged pertly, "When a plains wife wanted a new dress, she couldn't go down the street to the local dress shop—first of all, there weren't any *sidewalks*, only wooden boardwalks, and second, a dress shop was of little importance on the plains. When a plainswoman, like our very *own* Mrs. Morgan, wanted a new dress, she had to make and dye it her*self*, from a simple roll of unbleached muslin. Or calico, if she had a roll of it. Denim had to suffice for the men of the family, and most people went barefoot come summer, to save their calfskin shoes. Sacks from flour became sturdy underwear, and some enterprising ladies constructed clothes from old blankets and even the very canvas of their wagons. The flowers and grasses they picked on the plains became colorful dyes that turned plain white cloth into butternut brown or Nankeen yellow—"

"Nankeen yellow," the red-dot girl said, and Miz Myrtle remembered the dress she'd been wearing the day of the Indians. The shade of goldenrods, only the dress had faded irregularily, with dark patches of fabric under her arms and along the bottom of her skirt. She'd made and dyed the dress when Carrie was born and had yet to be lucky enough to rip or ruin it enough to suit Josh's dictum of no new dresses until the old ones were too indecent to wear. Eight miserable, dirty, sweaty years, and still the dress looked unworn. The way it scratched at her armpits and rubbed at her neck was infernal. And the stiff skirt and long sleeves rubbed against her bug bites, making them itch.

Between her legs, the folded cloth had alternately tickled and rubbed, the moisture there hot and sticky. The only consolation *there* was the fact that she was not with child. The children never seemed to mind the searing July heat; mostly they aped their father's mock chills, his exaggerated shivering. But they couldn't produce hot foreheads (oh, she'd seen William and Pearl rubbing their brows, trying to raise enough heat to fool their mother), and therefore they'd had to help her with the chores. But somehow, even the oldest of them could turn a simple search for fire fuel into a chance to be lazy, to play when it was not time to do so. Even Olive, with her long colt legs and skirt that needed lengthening. Olive couldn't even can fruit right; one batch she'd done in '67 had spoiled that winter in the warmth of the soddy. The girl had learned her father's secret, all right—do something so badly, so wrong, that Myrtle wouldn't want the thing done by that person again. For foodstuffs could be scarce, and even though she knew the girls did it on purpose, Myrtle gave in and exempted them from helping with the food preparation. Wheat flour was hard to come by, and even corn was too precious to waste on rocklike bread and black pancakes. And the boys: somehow they'd manage to get the corncobs wet and break the sunflower stalks into brittle, useless bits. She didn't trust any of them to collect what buffalo chips could be found. She knew her children all too well—no, she knew *Joshua's* children.

"And in the wintertime, what animals the father had shot and killed were used to keep the family warm, for their tanned hides and pelts became snug coats and comfy bedding—"

It was lucky Miz Myrtle had become a good shot, and it was even more fortunate that she naturally took to butchering, dressing out, and tanning the remains of what she killed. Joshua was a poor marksman (oh, he could aim a fork at his mouth with stunning accuracy), and Henry showed promise of stepping gracefully in his father's footsteps. William was good at shooting the sod bricks of the chimney; once a chunk of sod clogged the chimney and everything in the house was dreadfully smoked and sooty.

Joshua had laughed like a coyote in heat over *that* one, as she cleaned what she could in the smoked house. And there was no switching the bottom of William (or any other of Joshua's brood); Joshua claimed that his own father's constant use of the rod had "done spoiled me to the core." Myrtle chose to think of Joshua as one apple that was blighted as a blossom.

Miz Myrtle sat up with a start when a different childish voice intruded on her memories. A boy with hair so short she could see each bead of sweat pop out of his scalp was droning on about what people planted in their gardens; no gold medal for him, she thought petulantly. Glancing at the row of seated children, she saw that she'd totally missed another girl, who sat between Etta Louise Oliver and an empty chair. Whatever her speech had been, Miz Myrtle supposed she wouldn't die just because she'd missed it. After reaching one hundred years, things like that didn't bother her overmuch. As the shorn boy rambled on, Miz Myrtle took a slow look around her, at the bunting- and flag-decorated street, at the brick and wood buildings (wood buildings, now *there* was an extravagance!), at the new pale-grey sidewalks, installed only two summers ago. Nothing like the town she'd crawled into, after the Indians came and went on the farm, leaving her alone, alive. . . .

The Morgan farmstead was situated midway between the Smoky Hill and Saline rivers, just below the site of all the trouble in the valley between the settlers and the Indians. Fort Hays and Fort Wallace were only miles away, but that still had not stopped the massacre of two hundred settlers in the valley between the Solomon and Saline rivers, the work of the vile Sioux and Cheyenne. The horse-mounted warriors, bearing lances and shields as well as the ubiquitous axlike tomahawk. The scalp takers and the woman stealers.

Word of what had happened to poor Sarah White and Anna Brewster Morgan (the thought that the Morgan woman could have been *Myrtle Clarke* Morgan was not lost on Miz Myrtle), how they were kidnapped and worse by Indian braves, spread even to the Joshua Morgan farm, isolated and seldom-visited as it was. It seemed that the coming of the Kansas Pacific Railroad, not to mention the many buffalo hunters who had preceded the trains, infuriated the Indians beyond endurance.

Even what Miz Myrtle and her neighbors called the "good Indians"—the Pawnee, the Kansa, or so the other women called them —were looked upon with growing unease during those years, the time of the uprisings. Years of seeing Indians had not made it all that easy to tell one from another, and a warrior bent on vengeance could hide his tomahawk and pose as a merely curious Indian just to get into a soddy and do evil there. But the women, Miz Myrtle included, still let them into their soddies and dugouts, let the braves taste their odd cooking, poke into their linens, peer inquisitively at their few Back East treasures, all in the hope that the Indians would be satisfied and leave peacefully. As all the Indian braves Miz Myrtle had previously encountered had done . . . until the July day when the Indians came.

And when they were gone and her family lay dead, scalped and bloodied, and the livestock ran loose and frantic, Miz Myrtle had half crawled away, across fields of ripening corn, the rough stalks and heavy ears slapping and jabbing her. She hadn't cared that they pulled and yanked at her hair, pulling strands from her uncut and unbloodied scalp.

Across many acres of land, both cultivated and wild, she had dragged herself, and the acres turned to miles, and still she moved forward, clutching a small bloodied thing in one fist, hair flying across her face in moist strands, blood leaking slowly down her legs (the cloth tucked in her pantaloons gone, fallen out somewhere), and still she crawled on, northward at first, until she reached a point where her whirring mind slowed down long enough to ask if she should go northeast, to Fort Hays and the town recently settled there, or northwest, to Walnut Center. A part of her mind that was still lucid whispered, *Josh said there's a thousand souls in Hays . . . too many eyes, too many people, too many,* and thus she went northwest, finally and literally crawling on her hands and knees, right hand fisted to protect what lay still warm and moist in her palm. And by the time she reached the collection of flimsy buildings, tents, and dugouts surrounding a buffalo sod street, she'd worn blood-ringed holes in the skirt of her hated Nankeen yellow dress.

The people of Walnut Center were kind and did not press her for details of what happened out at the farm. Men rode out, their horses' hooves kicking up choking clouds of brown, and then they rode back, many hours later, faces grim and rifles at the ready to shoot down the savages with the scalps on their rough clothing. The nine scalps unaccounted for . . . the men knew where *one* of the scalps was, after some of the women gently pried it out of Myrtle's hand before letting her have it again. It was the only way to quiet her, for her screams and hoarse shouts echoed in the hot still air, in the very spot where Main Street now stood in all its paved and brick-lined glory. . . .

In front of her, a girl with reddish bobbed hair and a pale blue pleated dress solemnly told her captive audience that General Custer and his troops had been encamped in Hays only three months before the "Morgan Massacre" occurred and mused that "if only those brave troops had been handy, the fearsome Indians who murdered Mrs. Morgan's husband and children would have been caught and hung. . . . From where she sat behind the strawberry-blond girl, Miz Myrtle snorted softly, thinking that the child needed to study her history better, especially the part about the Little Big Horn, until the girl said, "For anyone evil enough to do such a horrid thing deserves to lie in the fires of Hades for all eternity!"

What do *you* know about it, Missy? Miz Myrtle found herself thinking, and then, try as she might, no matter how hard she rubbed the small soft leathery bit in her purse, the memories came at her again, jabbing and poking all the tender places like ears of corn banging into her fleeing body that July day sixty years ago. . . .

It was the first week of July, the time when the sun beat down like a live, sweating thing suspended in a sky of unflawed and painful blue; the time when water had to be drawn dozens of times a day from the well, just to keep Joshua and the youngest boys from whimpering from the fevers they claimed to have "real bad" even if *she* couldn't detect any heat when she pressed dry lips to their cool foreheads; the time when the other children whooped and played at Indians, even though she kept telling them that such play was sure to bring bad luck, and the two eldest children were flinging chicken feed at each other instead of at the chickens; the time when her time of the month was the most bothersome, most uncomfortable in her lower belly; and it was the time of the year when a baby's cries carry like thunder, booming and echoing in a mother's ears.

The time of summer when most of the harvesting would fall on her shoulders (Joshua's ague could last for weeks, even if she could hear Joshua and the children giggling and playing in the soddy while she worked until her hands were red and cracked with tiny diamond-shaped furrows deep in the flesh and her face grew burnt and freckled in the sun), for as sure as bread rises in the baking dish, when it came to real work needing to be done, Joshua would call on his memory of past illnesses and come up with a whole collection of "dangerous" symptoms.

July only meant thoughts of deep winter coming, the time when Joshua and whichever child happened to want to play sick with him would sit by the fire, sucking mullein plant candies to help ward off more winter colds, the time when Myrtle would have to venture out into winds that sliced across the land like a razor against a lathered cheek, scraping her bare and raw with the chill hardness of it, to gather chips or simply whatever she could find to lay on the fire.

Fourteen years had come and gone, and none had differed greatly for Myrtle, save for the number and supposed severity of the "illnesses" her family had affected. Oh, true sicknesses did come and go, but true colds never seemed to last as long as the pretend variety. It was no fun to be really sick. Fourteen springs of nearly single-handed planting. Fourteen summers of almost solitary labor in the garden. Fourteen falls of hunting and trapping by her lonesome. Fourteen winters of listening to feigned coughs, of cleaning intentional messes in the beds.

"Fourteen *years*," she'd muttered to herself while she paused to push a sweaty hair out of her eyes as she used Joshua's ax to break up the buffalo chips—she liked them better in small pieces; they burned more efficiently come winter. The younger children were whooping and playing the scamp, as usual; their voices set her teeth to grinding. She longed to take her broom to each child's behind, tanning the skin darker than a week's worth of exposure to sunlight. Off to her left, Olive and Henry had stopped throwing feed at each other and were now standing around, jabbering like magpies.

"Some wife you'll be, Ol," Henry scoffed, to which Olive—thin-legged, wide-faced, chipped-toothed Olive—replied reproachfully, "Me, a *wife*? No man's good enough for *me*. . . . Besides," she'd added, in what was supposed to be a whisper too low for their mother to hear, "why would I want to be a wife? I don't want to work like an old *nag*! Why, I'd get ugly muscles all *over* me!" And they had giggled and whooped like ten-year-olds, and Myrtle bit shaking lips and blinked watering eyes, and then, when she'd looked up, she'd seen the Indians. . . .

The blue-dressed girl sat down, the end of her speech lost to Miz Myrtle, drowned out by the bloodroar in her large and fragile ears. The girl with the hangman braid got up and took her place in front of the big shiny microphone (the glare of the rising sun turned it into a cold white thing, like sun shining through a fat icicle), and began a speech about the various Indian tribes who "roamed the land in the time of Widow Morgan," speaking in turn of the bad and the good Indians, of their habits, their quirks, their violence, and this time Miz Myrtle could not banish the memories, couldn't rub them away with fingers that were already sweaty and slick with repeated circular movement, for the girl's words brought back the day when the Indians came. . . .

There were five or six of them far out on the horizon, but not far enough out that they couldn't see her and recognize her. Apparently, they were heading for Walnut Center and couldn't take the time to stop by the soddy, but they were polite enough to wave at her. Myrtle put down the ax long enough to give them an enthusiastic two-armed wave; not so much because she was overly fond of the Indians but just because they treated her with something more than her family's scarcely concealed dislike and open ridicule. Never had they laughed at her or refused to pay attention to her efforts to be hospitable. Their thanks had been said with their eyes, with simple gestures, but at least—at least they didn't make her want to chuck it all and run for Ohio. When they took food, they did it out of curiosity or hunger, not because they liked leeching off of her, *using* her day in and day out for fourteen years.

"Lookit, Henry, she's got herself some new *men* friends," Olive had drawled, not caring if Myrtle heard her or not. Joshua and the boys had heard Olive's remark, for from within the soddy came the singsong chant, two piping voices and one deep one: "Mama's got herself some Injins, Injins, Injins, got herself some Innnjiiins!"

And then *all* the children started in, Joshua's brood of wild animals, every last one of them, and Myrtle said nothing, did nothing to shut them up or show any emotion herself . . . for then the Indians came. And the side of the ax shone first icy white, then dribbled silver-red in the hard blue glare of the sun and sky. . . .

"The Indians who scalped people did not do so just to be cruel. The warriors believed that the souls of their killed enemies would belong to the person who collected the scalp and kept it. The Indians believed that the scalp was like extra strength in *them*, and the Indians of the Plains tribes used to count the scalps as replacements for members of their tribe who had died."

Scanning the faces of the crowd before her, Miz Myrtle's eyes lingered on the weathered faces of the oldsters, the ones still young enough to have been her children. How would Olive and Henry have looked with white hair and store-boughten teeth? Little Gertie and Walter with bifocals and big ears and noses? And the rest, Willie and Pearl, Carrie and Benjie and Bernard, with C-curved spines and wattled chins? And Mr. Morgan himself, an incredible one hundred and *six–imagine that*! Miz Myrtle tried to make light of the thought, but couldn't.

The riders from Walnut Center had buried them all on the spot and then rounded up what livestock they could, on the day the Indians came and went. And she'd lived in town, seen it gain real buildings and boardwalks and a big general store, and then she'd seen the first jerking, smoking car come rolling down the street, and she'd heard the wireless and seen a flying machine glide across the unbroken hard blue of the sky. After the massacre of her family, she'd done quite well for herself, working in the general store, then at the newspaper office. Finally she saved enough money to buy a boardinghouse, and then, when she seemed at the pinnacle of success in a state of the union that welcomed and encouraged forward-looking women, she'd had her first stroke.

In July 1909, the first week of the month. And almost every July, or thereabouts, she'd suffer more little strokes, like tiny chops of an ax lopping off working bits of her, leaving dead useless flesh and bone in their place. The last stroke, last year, had robbed her of her speech. And now, in 1929, her centennial, all Miz Myrtle could do was endlessly rub the scalp of her baby, the scalp which now looked for all the world like a scrap of chamois, worn from frequent fingering. On that day sixty years ago, the good men of Walnut Center had assumed that the Indians had taken the nine scalps with them, after dropping the tiniest, the cruelest one. Miz Myrtle had been too stunned to say different. And the kind women had washed her blood-flecked hands, the dots of red covering the tops of both hands like premature old-age spots. The ladies had burned her blood-streaked dress; the smell of the burning was a nose-curling thing, with raw scented smoke rising into the hot air. And soon she was settled into a dugout with a nice family who let her help with household chores for her keep, and Miz Myrtle had never had it so easy in fourteen years. Her only peculiarity was the little drawstring bag she kept tied to her apron. For a survivor of an Indian attack, Miz Myrtle was regarded as quite sane, quite brave. . . .

A burst of applause brought Miz Myrtle back to the here and now; little Miss Etta Louise Oliver was standing up and pretending to be very, very surprised as the Mayor came forward and awarded her the bright medal, the gold disk glinting in the sun, a mote of color against fresh sun-lit snow. Miz Myrtle nodded what looked like senile approval; the girl's speech had been innocuous, and well-delivered to boot. No one, in their approval of the winner of the speech contest, noticed Miz Myrtle rubbing the thing in her little bag with frantic intensity. The waiting brass band (sweating like plowhorses in their red and gold-braid uniforms) struck up "My Country 'Tis of Thee," and people joined in, save for Miz Myrtle.

Instead, she rubbed the tiny withered scalp, little Walter's scalp with a few downy hairs still embedded in it, in time to the music. The only scalp not thrown down the well by the Indians before they left. Miz Myrtle had kept it with her always, because it had been the hardest, most heartbreaking scalp she had taken that morning that the Indians came, that tiny scalp the size of a silver dollar.

Dust

Anke Kriske

Anke Kriske was born in Cologne, West Germany, in 1955 and learned English as a child in Australia. After brief sojourns back in Germany, in Canada, and on the East Coast, her family moved to the desert town of Banning, California, and then to Washington state, where she graduated from high school. She received a B.A. in Medieval History from the University of Connecticut in 1979, with minors in Anthropology and English. She is associate editor of the small press publication *Not One of Us,* which her husband, John Benson, edits. She has had more than forty stories published, some of them appearing in *Doppelganger, Eldritch Tales,* and the *Black Lizard* anthology. Her interests include graveyard restoration, Oriental art, and editing the newsletter of a local chapter of the American Cancer Society. She has a brown belt in judo and a yellow belt in karate. She completed her first novel, a gothic romance, titled *A Haven in Winter,* and is working on a horror novel. She lives in Storrs, Connecticut, and has two young children.

Anke's story is the only mystery that I received, and the only story set in a California mining camp of the previous century. There is a great deal of sadness about it as well.

Pan Town, if you wanted to call a wretched mining camp a town, was situated just west of the Sierras. The tents, wagons, and other makeshift dwellings—no one wanted to waste time building a proper house—stretched up the hillside and along the banks of the sluggish, shallow Stillman River. Two years earlier the town had not existed; as soon as gold was found someplace else, it was abandoned. The inhabitants, for the moment at least, numbered close to five hundred men.

There were three women.

My husband, Robert Maurer, expected me to associate with Mrs. Cairn and Mrs. Howard, especially now that my waistline was noticeably expanding, but I had no use for them. Mrs. Cairn sat about on a box all day and bemoaned the fate that had cast her into the wilderness. Evidently she and Mr. Cairn had thought wealth was easy to be had, and the three months they had spent in camp seemed a great hardship. Mrs. Howard read in her Bible much of the day and used words like God's will and Providence all the time, insisting that faith solved all problems. I often wondered what her comments had been when she saw the graves aside the trail leading to the mining camps. Did she think the victims of cholera or starvation or an occasional Indian attack had died because of a lack of faith? Perhaps those thoughts only proved that I wasn't what she called respectable.

My mother's mother had been a Dakota Indian, my grandfather a trapper who liked the Indians a lot better than the whites. My mother married a white rancher, who brought us to California years before the lure of yellow metal brought thousands of others.

I didn't much look like an Indian, although my hair is black and I have high cheekbones. Most of my looks came from my father. From him I got a narrow face, hazel eyes, my height, and the habit of calling a spade a spade. I guess I didn't have the upbringing of a lady. Although I learned to read and write—my father had studied awhile to be a teacher—I was also taught how to ride a horse, shoot, play poker, and judge a man's character real fast. It was a good thing, too, because my husband was a kindhearted soul from the Pennsylvania farm country who couldn't do any of those things very well.

I met Robert in Sacramento City, where my father and I had gone to sell our cattle; fresh meat was fetching half a dollar a pound in those early days when the supplies couldn't keep up with the hordes of people pouring into California. The population grew right before your eyes. Doctors, lawyers, teachers, farmers, as well as an assortment of riffraff—they all came for the gold. Robert, the youngest son of a farmer, didn't stand to inherit any of his father's small plot of land, so he decided he might as well try his luck in the goldfields. I found him looking lost at the crossroads in Sacramento and offered him a job helping us with the cattle, most of our regular hands having gone off to join the prospectors. Robert said he'd stay for a while to earn some money. When he left a month later, I went with him.

Walking up the muddy track that passed for a road to collect some fresh water farther upstream, I passed Mrs. Cairn sitting on her little rickety shipping box, sewing up her smaller boy's torn pants, while the two youngsters, aged four and six, chased each other around the tall gnarled oak tree that gave the Cairns' tent a bit of protection from the oftentimes cruel weather. She saw the large bucket I carried.

"Mina! Do you think you should be doing that in your condition?"

I glanced down at my stomach, protruding through the green blouse not much different from a man's shirt, and my wide, ankle-length gray skirt. "Gotta have fresh water." My logic did not appeal to her.

"Your husband should do that."

I couldn't imagine why she sounded indignant. "He's out pannin'," I answered.

"I should think a woman about to . . ." She went all pink and her words trailed away.

"I'm really fine. Don't you worry about me." Mrs. Cairn was such a fragile-looking thing, with wispy brown hair done up fancy, and eyes like a deer. The clothes she wore, real tight at the waist, and blouses with high, uncomfortable-looking necks, made her look even more delicate. Could be she thought all women were in mortal danger walking about with a baby growing in them. I had heard those kinds of stories, often from men who didn't know what they were talking about, of course. She would believe them; she believed just about anything she was told. Or maybe she had had a hard time with her own babies. I didn't know and sure wouldn't like to ask on account of her way of being embarrassed easily. Robert had said I should be nice to her because she was lonely and confused and scared. Since she was trying to be friendly to me, I decided to make the effort. I pulled up the other box that was used as a chair, most of the Cairns' furniture having had to be abandoned to get over the Utah side of the mountains on the way west, and made myself comfortable.

"I haven't seen you for a few days," I said.

"I've been sick," she replied. "I thought for a while that I might be coming down with cholera myself and almost called Mr. Maurer."

Robert had managed to bring a fat medical book with him from back east, and at times he acted as the local doctor. He knew a lot about animals, having grown up on a farm, so he also looked after the mules and horses. And when somebody died—and we'd had a few of those lately—he was the undertaker, on account of having an uncle in that trade and knowing something about laying out a corpse. I always said he brought home more gold dust with his side jobs (payment being reckoned in gold rather than coin in these parts) than by digging and panning.

"You look healthy enough," I said, as a way of making a compliment.

Her great brown eyes became sad. "As healthy as can be expected in these horrible conditions. I do so miss my house, and my garden, and the ladies of the Benevolent Society, and—"

"Jane! Jane!" The name echoed from the foothills as a big, barrel-chested man came running down the slope toward us. "Look what I found!" he panted, presenting a rough chunk of dirt and rock to his wife.

"That's not . . . ?" she began excitedly.

"It's not," I said. Never could hold my tongue, and there are times when I wished I knew how. They both looked at me, pain, anger, and disappointment etched on their faces for all the world to see. "That's fool's gold. See how green those flakes look in the light? Real gold don't do that."

Mrs. Cairn's chin quivered. "I knew it was too good to be true."

I tried to be helpful. "I heard that the best gold around here is found in the streams, not up in the hills."

"But the gold in the rivers and streams has to come from somewhere," Mr. Cairn insisted, head sinking down. "I thought for a moment I'd found it."

I looked up at the mountains that rose steeply less than a dozen miles to the east. "If it's bein' washed down, it's comin' from all the way up there, where the snow is. If a rich strike were closer, it would've been found by now."

"I suppose you're right," Mr. Cairn said, resigned.

I felt sorry for him. His clothes were dirty, there was a hole in his shirt, and his naturally pink face was deeply sunburned right up to the thinning brown hair. He had worked hard for nothing.

"I don't know how much longer I can stand living here," Mrs. Cairn began and burst into tears. She was good at crying, and I suspected it wasn't all natural. She stumbled into the tent on her high-buttoned city shoes and threw herself on the straw-filled mattress.

Mr. Cairn looked helplessly at me for a moment.

"I gotta get my water," I said, and left them alone. A tent was no place for an argument that you don't want overheard, but that never stopped them.

He stepped into their quarters, pausing briefly to pull down the flaps. "Jane, please," I heard him say as I quickly resumed my walk. Mrs. Cairn didn't even wait until I was out of earshot before letting loose a torrent of angry and reproachful words. The little boys stopped playing. I think they would have liked to run away, but they had been told never to leave.

I climbed up the slope to a large flat rock where it was easy to get fresh water. As I knelt down, I heard a chuckle. "Is that you, Charlie?" I shielded my eyes from the sun with my hand and looked up.

An old man came into view. He shuffled when he walked, his joints being stiff from crouching in cold water for too long, swirling sand and dirt and water in a pan until only the gold dust remained. He was still a hearty man, despite the long gray hair, beard, and deeply lined square face. From what I heard, Charlie was a lot like my grandfather, and on that account we had become friends. I think he had a daughter. I know he had a family someplace in Missouri that he hadn't seen for fifteen years and, although he never said so, he missed them. He'd been in California a long time when the news of gold exploded on the world, but he'd never gotten lucky, not even here in Pan Town, where a man once pulled a hundred dollars out of the river in a single day, or so most of us had heard before coming here.

He nodded toward the Cairn tent. "I heard that damn fool shouting. Tried to tell him how to look for gold when he first arrived." He shook his head. "That idiot still won't listen to me. Do you know what he was before he got here?"

"A clerk in a store."

Charlie snorted derisively. "That explains why he knows so much."

"Be nice to him," I scolded. "You tease him all the time. He's got two little boys dependin' on him."

"Should have thought of that before he left home." He reached over and pulled the bucket out of the water for me and then helped me up, although it wasn't necessary. "There can't be a bigger fool for miles around."

"There's a whole town of them down there, my husband included."

He laughed, the sound booming. "You are so right, my dear! So very right. But one of us is bound to strike it rich."

"I keep hearin' that and have yet to see it. Your pockets ain't exactly filled to burstin' with gold."

Charlie patted a little bulge under his jacket. "I got enough." Never one to abstain from smoking for long, he unbuttoned his shirt pocket and pulled out a homemade pipe. He took a pinch of tobacco from a brightly beaded buckskin pouch hanging from his belt, filled and lit the pipe, and puffed with satisfaction. "What more can a man ask for than a good pipe, a glass of whiskey, and a pretty woman for company?"

"You don't really want me to tell you." I picked up the heavy bucket.

Without a word he relieved me of my burden. "That's what I like about you, Mina. You know when sermons are useless."

He told me of his adventures upriver as we walked slowly down the slope, where tufts of fresh grass were springing up now that the heat of summer was over. The Cairns were still arguing loudly in their tent, and the boys sat quietly nearby, pretending not to hear. Charlie's eyes became thoughtful when he saw the children. He'd never admit it, but he felt sorry for them.

We arrived at the tent I called home. It really wasn't as bad as Mrs. Cairn made out. Like other folks, we had a bed and a make-do table and chairs, a shelf for books and a few odds and ends, a couple of dishes and cups, a change of clothes. I had never had much more than this in my entire life.

After taking off his old wide-brimmed hat, Charlie sat down on a log outside and started a small fire, feeding it the twigs and branches Robert had collected the day before. He took another pinch of tobacco out of the pouch and relit his pipe. Little clouds of smoke rose steadily as he watched the flickering fire, his thoughts far off. I started to put together my fifth batch of stew for the day and placed the pot on the iron cookstove we had beside our tent. Al Hart paid me seventy-five dollars a month to cook dinner, for which the prospectors paid him gladly, the salt meat and hardtack that made up most of the men's meals becoming quickly wearisome. Since the fire had gone out, I scooped the ashes from the stove and deposited them on my garden out back in the hope that it would help the plants grow. Within minutes I had a new fire blazing lustily. I added a pot of coffee to the top of the stove, because it would be dark soon and Robert would come home.

A few tired prospectors were already on their way back. Mr. Howard was the first. He nodded to me and pointedly ignored Charlie. They didn't like each other one whit. Mr. Howard thought Charlie was a useless old man and was still incensed about the bawdy songs Charlie had sung the night before, after getting drunk at Al's. I'd heard them all, but I guess Mrs. Howard hadn't.

"Good evening, Mrs. Maurer," the other prospectors called to me. "Find a rich vein?" they would ask Charlie.

Charlie always talked about the great hidden deposits of gold he had found. The other miners thought he was a trifle weak in the head. After all, no one had ever *seen* him with more gold than would meet expenses. He was a little strange, I had to admit. When he was alone he would write poetry: to the moon, the sun, the trees. Once he said he even wrote a poem to me. He was an educated man, perhaps more so than anyone else in town, and the story was that he had run away from something, but no one really knew. When he got drunk, he sang songs at the top of his lungs, some of them in French. I think he had a French last name, but I wasn't sure of that either. That was how it was in the mining camps in those days, a lot of digging and no questions asked. There were times when he wouldn't talk, just sat by the fire and stared into the flames like now, and I knew he was remembering. I once asked him what he saw, and he said, Hell.

The coffee had just gotten ready when Robert appeared, burdened by his pike, shovel, and pan. Shoved into his belt was an old Texas model .36 pistol, not as powerful or expensive as the new Colt Hartford Dragoons, but effective enough. The camps had gotten dangerous lately, and there was no law out here. His sandy hair was plastered against his skull from sweat and dirt. He sank down on the ground where the mud had dried and stretched out completely.

"Ain't you gonna kiss me?" I teased.

He opened his eyes. They were very blue, like the sky in the mountains. "Is that anything to say to a man on the point of death?"

"Look alive to me," I replied.

Charlie started chuckling. "I'll leave you two alone. And I'll take the stew for you, Mina." He walked off toward Al Hart's tent, where there was a good supply of corn liquor at a steep price and a few gamblers willing to relieve you of your gold if you wanted to play. Al had forbidden Charlie to come back, but Jonas Crown was looking after the establishment in Al's absence while he was gone on an overnight trip for supplies. "I'll be seeing you tomorrow," Charlie called out to us before the gathering darkness swallowed him.

The morning dawned cloudy, but it didn't look like rain today. Most of the men got an early start. I began my cooking chores. Henry Fields came by, limping real bad because a landslide had busted his leg a month back, to ask if I needed anything done. I told him no. He wasn't too disappointed, having already found plenty of odd jobs in the camp. Mr. Cairn was sent on his way by his wife. I could hear her complain from inside the tent as he went out. He waved halfheartedly to me, donned a heavy green jacket as if he expected the coolness of the morning to last all day, and picked up his gear. He headed up the road. Mr. Howard was late leaving, as he was every morning, because he had to read a verse in his Bible and then ponder what he read. He was a tall, grim man, going gray at a young age. Robert said Mr. Howard wasn't too happy here, missing the orderly life back east, but he didn't complain. The Howards were hard-working people and would make out one way or another. As soon as their stake was big enough, they were going to head out to San Francisco.

Robert snuck up behind me and put his arms around my waist. "Not looking for another man, are you?" he whispered in my ear.

"Seems a bit late for that," I said, patting my stomach.

"Not when there are only three women in camp, and only one of them is lovely."

"You should have talked this way last night," I told him and kissed him. "I might have cuddled up a little closer."

"A little closer and you would have been in my skin." He held me by my shoulders. "I won't be gone too long," he said in his most serious voice.

I sighed. "You don't need to worry about me."

"I know. I just don't want to be far away, in case. Besides, you need more wood. I'll be back by midafternoon."

"Just remember to save some of those pretty words for when you come home." I watched him as he walked toward the hills, exchanging a few words with the other men.

Cooking is boring work. You can't go far because you have to stir the pot often to keep the stew from burning. I sat on the log and did a little sewing while I waited. Mrs. Cairn, followed by the boys, carried an armload of clothes to the river to wash. Mrs. Howard came by to see how I was doing. She was learning, I had to admit, for she no longer wore her most impractical clothes. Knowing I was busy, she didn't stay long.

I was pouring my batch of stew into a bucket when I heard the jangle and creaking of a wagon. I straightened up and saw Al pull the reins hard to make the horse stop. "I brought you new supplies," he said, stepping down from the wagon. Al was a big man, square-jawed and broad-shouldered, with a red-hot temper that matched his hair. His shirt was unbuttoned and the sleeves rolled up to the elbows, revealing the bulging muscles. "Nice piece of salt pork, isn't it?" he inquired, unwrapping a slab from the canvas.

"That'll do just fine," I said.

"Got another one just like it. Cheap, too." Al knew how to make money. When the local supply of rabbits ran out—the deer having left the area soon after the first panners arrived—Al found ways to get supplies from a few nearby farms and once a month visited the bigger towns toward the coast. While the other men broke their backs, he worked comfortably at his saloon, the only one for miles. Someday he would go back east a rich man without ever having panned a single day. He aroused a lot of envy and dislike in town, some of the men saying he cheated them, hinting, though not too loudly, that he wasn't above stealing a little. Of course those very same men went right on back the next night and got so drunk they couldn't remember how much gold they had deposited in his huge hands. "This is the best I could do for carrots," he said, tipping the basket toward me for easier inspection.

I examined about a dozen. "Quite a few look rotten." I shrugged. "No one will notice."

He put the carrots out back with the meat; then he returned to the wagon, lifted the sacks of potatoes as if they were feather pillows, and stored them for me. He told me what gossip he had heard on the trip and left us a third-hand week-old Sacramento newspaper, before loading up the stew and urging the horse on. Al stopped one more time to talk to Henry, now looking the worse for wear and obviously hurting. Henry climbed aboard and presently they disappeared amid the tents that were scattered like mushrooms on the forest floor.

I continued to work, cutting up carrots and potatoes. The pot was soon full. Mrs. Cairn did more wash. Henry, evidently having been given a job by Al, began hauling wood. His face was pale from pain, and he stopped frequently to drink liquor out of an old canteen. The sun climbed high and the air grew hot.

Robert came home around three and went off to collect firewood. I had just made coffee when I saw a procession coming toward me. Mr. Howard was leading a mule hitched to a little cart. A half-dozen men were following it. Mr. Howard stopped a ways off. He took off his hat.

"Mrs. Maurer, is your husband about?"

"Should be back any minute." I walked toward him.

"I don't think you should look." He reached out to stop me.

But that was when I saw those dusty boots. I rushed to the cart. Charlie was lying there—dead. His eyes were open; one hand was clenched. A little trickle of blood ran out of his mouth.

"I found him at Weaver Creek by the big oak tree, just before the creek empties into the Stillman. Must have happened late this morning or early afternoon. He was lying face up. Looked like he was struck down." Mr. Howard glanced upward to the heavens, and I knew he was thinking that the good Lord had punished another wicked sinner. Ashes to ashes, dust to dust.

Poor Charlie. He looked so pathetic and small in the cart. His tools were heaped by his side. The old hat lay on his chest. The stem of his pipe poked up through the pocket. I took a closer look among his possessions. "What happened to his tobacco pouch?"

"I didn't see it," Mr. Howard replied.

"He always had it with him," I protested.

"Mina?" It was Robert. He let the wood fall where he stood and ran to join me. For long minutes he stood silently at my side.

"I'll fix up a grave for him," Robert said simply.

"Do a good job," someone in the little crowd yelled. "He might have been crazy at times, but I sure needed his advice when I got here."

There was a general assent among the men.

I left then, too upset to stay. I didn't cry. We weren't brought up to be that way. Poor, poor lonely Charlie, so far from home. I scrambled over the road determined to find the leather pouch. It seemed important to bury him with it.

I reached the spot where he had been found. Weaver Creek barely qualified as such. In the summer it became a mere trickle and sometimes not even that. There were bushes growing along the embankment, several oaks, and a path worn wide and hard by the many men who had tramped here. There really weren't many places for a pouch to lie hidden. I searched very carefully, not taking my eyes off the ground. I climbed higher into the foothills, then doubled back. I couldn't find that pouch. It disturbed me. Charlie had always tied the pouch securely to his belt on account tobacco was far too expensive to be lost. It should have been with him.

When I returned to town, Robert was busy digging a grave on the grassy knoll on top of a little ridge where the others were buried under crude wooden markers. Charlie had been laid out nice and proper on the ground. I went to kneel beside him. He looked a lot better now: his eyes had been closed, like he was sleeping, and the blood wiped off.

"Charlie, where'd you leave the pouch? I don't feel right sendin' you on your way without it." I stared at him. Maybe it was the Indian blood in me; my father always said Indians could feel things that other folks couldn't. Charlie dying like that, his pouch being gone—I didn't like it.

"Robert?" He stopped working. "Was there anythin' wrong with Charlie? He wasn't shot or nothin', was he?"

He laid the shovel aside and climbed out of the shallow grave. "I didn't check his body, but his clothes didn't show any sign." He kneeled down on the other side of Charlie.

"Look here," I said, pointing to the belt. "See this bit of leather? That belonged on the pouch. Don't that look like it was torn off?"

"Could have happened anytime since we saw him last."

"Charlie without his tobacco was a lot less likely than Charlie without his corn whiskey. He'da come straight into town if he lost it, but Weaver Creek is the long way back from his usual prospecting area."

"He might have just been wandering around," Robert said.

"Maybe," I conceded reluctantly. "Did he have any gold on him?"

"No. But he probably spent it all at Al's last night."

"That don't make sense. If he'd run out of gold, he'd a gone pannin', not roaming about."

Robert nodded. "Seems reasonable to me. I can't say that I like the alternative, though."

"We got to check the body," I insisted.

"I suppose you're right," Robert replied. He remained as still as a deer hiding in a thicket.

I knew what he was thinking: if we found evidence of murder there would be trouble. The last man caught stealing, less than an ounce of gold, had been hanged within an hour. If a man had done murder, he could expect no better.

"We can't do it here," Robert said, "completely in the open. Tether the mule over here. I'll drag a couple of boxes over. It will make it a little harder to see."

"We could haul him back into a tent."

"Too suspicious."

Seemed to me it wouldn't make a difference in the long run, but Robert was like that. Keep things looking nice as long as possible.

By the time I had the mule munching away at the grass, Robert had the boxes arranged. We didn't get much attention. Most of the men were off at their panning. Mrs. Howard was making the evening meal. Mrs. Cairn looked toward us now and then, but she was busy hanging up her boys' shirts and her husband's green jacket on her washing line. I saw Henry sitting out by his tent, but he was drunk already and it looked like his busted leg was giving him too much trouble for him to bother with us.

We set to work. Robert was carefully checking for damage when he ran a hand over the back of Charlie's head. "There's a bump here," he said.

"Could he have gotten it when he fell?"

Robert looked perplexed. "I'm not sure. It's very close to the spine, not the easiest place to hit falling backward." He lapsed into silence.

"You thinkin' about the blood in his mouth?"

"His lips aren't split." With difficulty, he pried open the jaws, stiff with death. "Doesn't look like he bit his tongue. He might have regurgitated blood." He probed the back of the mouth, his face betraying extreme distaste. He frowned. Gingerly he withdrew his fingers and wiped dark matter on the grass. "It's like the insides of his head aren't right, up toward his brain."

"Like he was shot?" I said, thinking out loud. "Like someone hit him on the head and, while he was unconscious, propped open his mouth and fired up into his brain?"

Robert winced at my description. "A gun would do more damage than that. The bullet would go through the skull."

"Not with one of those little derringers. I've seen what they can do and it ain't much, unless you aim at the right place. Lots of men carry them, hidden in a pocket. The whores in Sacramento City use them too."

"Seems like a lot of trouble to kill Charlie and try to make it look like it was natural. Why attack him for a pittance of gold, if he had any at all?"

My face must have betrayed my feelings.

Robert took my hand. "I'm not saying you're wrong, Mina, it's just that I don't know how we would prove murder when there wasn't a reason." He looked at the body. "I'm not even sure I could recover the bullet, assuming there is one."

"Does that mean you won't do a thing?"

"I didn't say that. There must be another way to figure out what happened. The men will be quitting soon. I'll start getting them together."

I scrambled to my feet. "I'm going to see if I can find that pouch."

He grabbed my arm. "Mina, I don't want you climbing about out there."

"I can take care of myself. I'm not like that Mrs. Howard, who don't know what it's like out here, or Mrs. Cairn, who's weak and scared. Remember, I was born in wild country."

"It isn't the country that worries me. It's these men."

"Ain't any one of them been anythin' but nice and proper to me. I don't think that if one of them killed and thought he'd gotten away with it, he'd be stupid and hurt me." Robert looked like he was ready to fight me on that point. "I won't be gone long," I promised, and hurried away.

The sun would be setting soon, so there wasn't much time. I thought I knew where I had to go. Chances were good that Charlie hadn't died where he was found, there being no signs of a fight. It was likely that he was killed a little way off, but not very far, because dragging a body can be tricky business when you're afraid of being found out. Now old Charlie liked to sit in places where he was out in the sun and read. It was one of the reasons he wasn't much of a prospector. I had found him a few times like that on a little out-cropping of rocks and young trees.

I kept climbing and looking among the scrub. The fourth place I tried I found the pouch. I pulled it out from among roots exposed during the last heavy rain. I stood up straight. From the outcrop-ping of rock, the murderer would have had a good view of people coming or going. When it was safe, it would have been a simple matter to drag the limp body down to the creek. Peering at the ground, I thought I could detect a trail, though the killer had apparently tried to brush the ground with branches afterward.

I scampered back to town with my prize.

Darkness was approaching, and I saw the lanterns and torches as soon as I reached the outskirts of the camp. About fifty men had gathered by our tent, and long before I got there I heard the angry voices. The loudest was Henry, protesting that Charlie wasn't worth all this trouble and it wasn't right that Al wouldn't serve liquor until after everything was settled. A few other men shouted that Henry ought to keep his damned mouth shut.

"I found the pouch," I said, pushing myself through the throng. When the men realized I was there, they made way for me. Mrs. Howard was standing beside my husband, looking grim as she always did. Mr. Howard was still tying up his mule so it could graze awhile on the bit of grass that hadn't been trampled to death by the prospectors. The Cairns stood bewildered at the edge of the crowd. I saw the boys peeking out from behind their tent, where they had evidently been told to stay. "It was on the rocks."

An angry murmur arose in the crowd when I described how I had found the pouch.

"Now see here," Mr. Howard said, pushing his way to the center. "That doesn't mean anything. Charlie could have lost it quite naturally, not missed it for a while, and then was heading into town when he fell down dead."

"Maybe you have reason to want us to believe that," Henry shouted. "You were the one that found him."

"Along with Corey Peterson. You can just go and ask him if you want."

"Still seems convenient," Henry mumbled belligerently.

"It most likely would have to be one of us, though, wouldn't it?" I said. Mr. Howard looked at me as if he thought I should keep my mouth shut like his wife. "All of the men here, with few exceptions, head out early and stay out late, some stayin' out for days at a time. Those goin' far woulda been gone early, before Charlie made up his mind where to go, right? That leaves the people that do their pannin' close to town. The married men stay closer to home. Henry, too, because he can't get around. Frank and Charlie because they were old and tired quick. Corey because he's been feeling sick lately and stayin' close by."

"What about Ted Johnson?" Mr. Howard asked.

Robert shook his head. "Ted's still too weak from his cholera to do much of anything."

"You keep bringing up other people's names," Henry said accusingly to Mr. Howard.

"I don't like the tone of voice you're using," he snapped back.

"You don't like anything about me. And you didn't like anything about Charlie. Tried to run him out of town at one point."

Mr. Howard stiffened. "He was a disgrace. Getting drunk. Shooting off that gun in the middle of the town."

"Wasn't the first and won't be the last," someone shouted.

"I'm a God-fearing man—"

"So was the last one we hung," came another shout.

He looked around, and I could detect a bit of fear in him. He hadn't expected that kind of reaction. Most of the men respected Bible-toters. They didn't steal or cheat and they pitched in quick when help was needed, but gold does strange things to a man. Any man. And Mr. Howard with his overbearing ways was not popular.

"We can try to find out where everyone was in the morning," Robert said quickly. "Who saw Charlie?"

There was a chorus of "me"s and "I"s. It didn't take long to figure out Charlie was last seen about nine walking slowly upriver.

"All right," Robert said. "I checked in on Ted very early, then I

passed Frank Fellows going up in the direction of Indian Creek."
Frank concurred.

"You were in my sight off and on," another prospector told
Robert, "all morning."

"I was way out in the hills until just about an hour ago," Mr.
Cairn announced.

His wife nodded emphatically. "I would have seen him if he had
come back earlier."

"Henry, where were you?" Mr. Howard demanded. "You were
the one closest to camp."

Henry patted his leg. "You think I can drag a body far?"

"It wasn't far if Mrs. Maurer is right," Mr. Howard replied.

Henry's pale eyes had a shifty look to them. "I'm too weak to
have attacked a man."

"He was hit on the back of his head," Robert said, "and then it
looks like he was shot in the head through his mouth."

"And gold fever gives a man strength," Mr. Howard declared.
That silenced Henry.

"You haven't exactly been able to work the fields," Mr. Howard
continued.

"I make enough gold helping out," Henry asserted, unable to
remain still. "Another two weeks I'll be back to panning. Could be
you're anxious to get to San Francisco and upped your stake with a
bit of Charlie's gold."

"I would advise you to stop casting aspersions. I am certain
enough men saw me to prove I was not near Charlie." He jabbed at
Henry with his finger. "Can you do the same?"

Henry fidgeted uncomfortably.

I spoke up. "I saw Henry a few times in the mornin'. Be awful
hard for him to have killed Charlie and gotten back in time to get
all that wood for Al."

Henry looked relieved, like he hadn't remembered that, which
was likely on account of him being drunk much of the time.

"Hey, I don't recall Al being in his tent after eleven or so,"
Henry said. "He usually is."

"What?" Al shouted from the back of the ever-increasing crowd.
Anger in his eyes, he forced a path through the men and came
straight for Henry.

"I'm just saying you did something irregular," Henry said
quickly, and slithered into the background.

Something irregular. A memory stirred in my mind. I wanted to be wrong. I wanted to think Charlie had been killed by one of the gamblers or the like. "Mrs. Cairn, how many jackets does your husband own?"

"Only one, why?" she asked.

"He was wearin' it when he went out. How come you could wash the jacket when you said he didn't come back until this evenin'?" I held my breath, waiting for her reply.

"No, he wasn't wearing it this morning. How can you say something like that?" Mrs. Cairn declared indignantly. "You're accusing him. He was out working, as he is every day."

A man who thinks fast would have said he came back for a few minutes and dropped off the jacket without seeing his family. Mr. Cairn glared at me. "You are mistaken." There was a tremble in his voice.

I felt a chill then, certain in my heart that we need look no further for Charlie's murderer. But I did not know how to go about proving this, and invoked Charlie's spirit to come to my aid and put clever words in my mouth.

"I did not wear my jacket," Mr. Cairn continued. "I never came near the town until this evening."

Corey, eyes narrowing, lifted his head. "I recall a jacket."

Mr. Cairn tried to shrug off the comment. The other men tensed, waiting expectantly, willing to give Mr. Cairn his due but suspicious of him, because after an hour of talking and speculating this was the first time a man had been caught in a lie. We don't like liars. Up here all you had was your good word to prove your worth.

"How much gold you bring home today?" Henry asked, hobbling closer and sticking his face right in front of Mr. Cairn.

Mr. Cairn's nose curled up like he smelled a skunk. He took a step back. "An ounce, I suppose. I panned for it."

"Where?" Robert demanded.

Mr. Cairn shoved Henry aside and stepped up to Robert. "At Indian Creek. The lower end. Someone must have seen me."

"Ain't been any gold found there in months," I pointed out.

He looked at me with contempt. "I was lucky."

"I tried it yesterday," Corey remarked matter-of-factly, "and I sure wasn't lucky."

Robert cleared his throat. "Did anyone see Mr. Cairn late in the morning or early afternoon?"

There were a few muttered comments, all denying he had been observed.

Robert looked at Mr. Cairn with newfound contempt.

"You're saying that I would jump an old man?"

"An old man who said he found a rich vein of gold," Mr. Howard snapped. "None of us around here believed him, but you could have thought different, and you didn't like him because he made fun of you. Those sound like tempting reasons to steal and kill."

"What kind of a fool do you think I am?" Mr. Cairn snarled. "All old Charlie ever panned was sand!"

"He always had some gold," Robert said softly.

"Search Cairn's place," Al demanded. "See how much gold he has."

"I forbid it!" Mrs. Cairn screamed. "He wouldn't kill anyone, not even an old derelict." She stamped her foot when the men moved toward her tent. "Will you listen to me?"

Mr. Howard grabbed Mr. Cairn's arm to make sure he couldn't go for his gun. "Where is the gold you found?"

"On the bottom shelf," he mumbled, perplexed at the swift change toward him. Things happen fast and impulsively with no law to hold men in check. "Hidden in a blue bottle. It . . . it really isn't much."

"Come on," Al shouted and led the way to the tent while Mrs. Cairn sobbed that we didn't have the right. Her boys saw us coming. They ran to her, their eyes brimming with tears. Mrs. Cairn gathered them into her arms.

Al strode into the tent. "I need more light," he bellowed. Three lamps were placed on the small round table. Al took the bottle—it must have held medicine at some time—and removed the cork. The contents he poured out on a nearby plate. "Not even a quarter ounce," he proclaimed, as he restored the gold to the bottle. "Search the place for more." He pulled a hunting knife from his belt. From the way Mrs. Cairn screamed you'd have thought he stuck the knife in her instead of the mattress. While Al and Corey quickly despoiled the bedding, Robert pulled a little trunk out into the open.

"You can't do that!" she wailed as he raised the lid and took out the first garment, a frilly white petticoat. She started to sob brokenheartedly from humiliation.

"I'll look through her things," I said to Robert. He gladly left the task to me and searched elsewhere. She had a lot of petticoats and chemises and stockings. I couldn't imagine why she needed so many. I picked up each item and laid it across a shipping box.

The men in the crowd pushed one another to get a better look at the proceedings. Mr. Cairn cussed as well as any cowpuncher, offending Mrs. Howard so much she had to leave. I heard a dish break. Clothes were tossed out none too carefully. Straw from the mattresses was everywhere. A child's book fell on the ground and was inadvertently crushed by Al's heavy boot, making the boys wail piteously.

"Please make them stop," she beseeched me.

I looked up from the trunk. "I don't see how. Maybe I can make them be more careful."

I had no more than turned around when Robert pulled a derringer with a two-and-a-half-inch barrel from under Mrs. Cairn's sewing. You could have heard a mouse scurry about, so silent did everyone become.

Mrs. Cairn's mouth fell open. She was afraid of guns, I knew, and would never put one there.

"Is it loaded?" Robert asked.

"No," Mr. Cairn answered fast, while Mrs. Cairn nodded in agreement.

"It would be the only gun not loaded in Pan Town." Robert checked. There was no bullet inside.

As if a signal had been given, the men renewed their passionate search. Corey even dug up the hard-packed ground in the tent but found nothing. The men looked at one another, wondering if they had indeed made a mistake.

Am I wrong, Charlie? I thought. My gaze strayed from the tent to the protective arms of the tree. "Could Charlie's gold be hidden there, in the branches?"

"Let's find out," Al said. He hadn't but walked halfway toward it when Mr. Cairn tried to run away. Mr. Howard had to hold on tight, and then it took two other men to make sure he didn't break loose after all.

Mrs. Cairn kept screaming that her husband couldn't commit a murder. I'm sure she still believed that. No one else did. "It won't do any good," I told her. "Stay calm for the sake of the boys." She clutched my hands painfully hard, and I had to struggle to free myself from her grip. The children, seeing the state their mother was in, fled for the thickets where they had played happily so many times. "There's a chance nothing more will happen," I lied, keeping a sharp eye on Robert and Henry as they dug around the tree. A lanky boy of eighteen deftly climbed into the branches, poking his fingers at every fork.

"Hey!" Everyone looked toward the youth. "This something?" He leaned down and handed a small tin box to Robert.

"That's mine!" Mr. Cairn shouted, his eyes wide with fear, the sweat pouring down his face.

I eluded Mrs. Cairn and approached my husband. "Look familiar?" he asked me.

"I'm not sure," I admitted, tilting the heavy box so it caught light enough for me to read the faded writing. "Charlie mighta had one like it at one time." I turned to Mr. Cairn. "What's written on the lid?"

He simply looked at me. "I don't remember exactly."

"Mrs. Cairn?"

She stared back blankly.

"It says Biedermeyer's, Saint Joseph, Missouri. Charlie was from Missouri. More than one person can swear to that. I never heard that you been there. You sure didn't have cause to pass through Missouri on the way west from Illinois." Carefully I pried off the lid. Heads craned forward to see. "Gold dust. Four or five ounces at least."

Al took a closer look at brown flecks amid the yellow. "Tobacco." He spat out the word. "I used to yell at Charlie for getting his damned tobacco mixed in with the gold." In three steps he was in front of Mr. Cairn. He grabbed the frightened man by his shirt. "Didn't you have enough time to pick out the tobacco?" His voice became louder. "Where did you get the gold?"

"At different places," he stammered. "I saved it up."

"Tell us where your claim is!" a hoarse man shouted.

You could smell Mr. Cairn's terror. I could imagine Charlie sitting on his rock when his murderer approached. Charlie might have teased Mr. Cairn again, showing him what even an old man could do with a little brains and experience. There was a fight. Charlie got hit in the gut and went down. Somehow the pouch came off. While Charlie was doubled over like that, Mr. Cairn hit him on the head, shot him, took the gold, and rushed to camp. He couldn't hide the tin where his wife might find it and question its presence. He slipped out of his jacket, climbed partway up the tree, and deposited the tin. Then he ran away as far and as fast as possible.

Maybe at first Mr. Cairn just wanted to shake out of Charlie the location of the strike. Maybe he went out that morning with the idea of bringing home gold even if he had to murder for it. Either way, the results were the same.

"The gold's mine, I tell you! Please. You must believe me."

I couldn't abide his lies any longer. "Then how come your wife's been complainin' all this time you're not bringin' home enough to feed the boys?"

"Does anyone here think this man is telling the truth?" Robert demanded from the crowd.

Upon hearing a chorus of *no* in reply, Cairn made a last desperate attempt to escape, pulling every which way. "I demand that you release me!" Mr. Howard held tight.

I don't know why he thought saying that would do any good. Guess he forgot where he was until Corey brought up his bay horse, all saddled and bridled.

"No!" Mr. Cairn screamed, the color leaving his face. Someone tied his hands behind his back. A dozen hands set him on the horse. Mrs. Cairn started screaming hysterically, tearing at her hair, clawing at me. Robert shoved me aside and held on to her while she pounded his chest with her fists and kicked him with her fancy high-buttoned shoes. Robert, his face showing dismay and abhorrence for what had to be done, dragged her away to our tent.

Corey took his horse up to the tree. Al was already there with a thick rope in his hand. He tossed it over the nearest limb. The boy slid the noose over Mr. Cairn's head. Mr. Cairn kept kicking that poor horse, but as long as Corey held on to the bridle the beast hardly moved. Then he let go, at the same time as Henry gave the animal a smart slap on the rump. The horse moved, but it was slow, and Mr. Cairn had a long time to feel the horse slide out from under him. He bucked and jerked and twisted, his face garish in the flickering torchlight. His tongue protruded, his eyes bulged. His legs kept on kicking the air. I caught Mr. Howard's eye.

"Whether a man betrays another for silver or for gold," he said, "this is his fitting reward."

I nodded. Hangings are cruel, but murder is evil even when only an old man dies. I watched, feeling no pity for this man who had robbed me of a valued friend.

Mr. Cairn arched his back, still holding on to life, despite the rope cutting into his flesh. The men hadn't done the hanging right. His neck should have broken or he should have choked quick. Instead he writhed in agony. It took awhile for Mr. Cairn to die of strangulation in the middle of the silent crowd.

We were the only family so to speak that Charlie had, so they brought me his things, the little he owned: a bedroll, his tools, a book of verses. There was a letter inside the book for me and Robert. It said that his real name was Horace DuChesne. He had left home on account of debts from bad speculating. Never having been close to his family, his passing would be no problem, especially after all these years. He said he found his gold with us, Robert and me, and in the hills and valleys and the blue skies.

Mrs. Cairn was weeping in our tent. The boys were still hiding, and Robert said we shouldn't go looking for them until the body had been taken down. That was what he and Mr. Howard were doing now. I put Charlie's possessions away. In a few hours, I'd go look for the boys. Robert and me, we decided to give them Charlie's gold. We had enough for ourselves.

Planting Time

Lucy Taylor

Lucy Taylor is a full-time writer based in Fort Lauderdale, Florida. Prior to free-lancing, she taught English in Japan, worked as a licensed massage therapist at a Florida spa, acted as a special correspondent and book reviewer for the *Richmond* (Virginia) *Times-Dispatch,* and was on the staff of a sports magazine based in Tampa, Florida. She holds a B.A. in art history from the University of Richmond and has an insatiable love of travel that has taken her as far as Lhasa and Katmandu. Her fiction and nonfiction have appeared in *Thin Ice, Women of Darkness, Magna, Forum, Pencil Press Quarterly, Florida Parent, Caribbean Travel and Life, Not One of Us,* and *Cavalier,* as well as over two hundred other publications. She is currently working on a horror/suspense novel.

I rejected this story at first and told Lucy why, and during our conversation the topic of what particularly scared us came up. A short time later Lucy resubmitted the story with changes—one of them being the scary thing, and I promptly bought it. Chessy is the youngest Woman of the West in this volume.

"Be a brave girl and hold out your hand," the old Indian said.

Five-year-old Chessy bit her lip and stared at the drawing she'd scratched in the sand, a crude version of the kind the Navajo made when they wanted to work magic. It was a circle about three feet in diameter that Chessy had filled with simple shapes: a quarter moon and lopsided stars and the stick figure of a man lying beneath what looked like a giant spider.

Now as she watched, a small segmented scorpion, phantom pale, skittered across the drawing toward her hand with upraised and venomous tail. So fascinated was she by the deadly creature that she didn't hear her mother approaching until Angelina screamed.

"Chessy!"

Angelina shoved Chessy out of the way and stomped the scorpion into a jellied, lifeless pulp beneath her sandal.

"This thang's evil. It can kill ya," she said, holding up the squashed insect.

Angry tears glittered in Chessy's black eyes. She looked around for the old Indian but he had gone, vanished into the pulsing bands of heat radiating up off the macadam of the distant road.

"Ya oughtn'ta killed it," she muttered, jabbing at the bed of the arroyo with her drawing stick. "Willy, he likes scorpions."

Her mother flinched. She hauled Chessy to her feet, brushing the dirt off the seat of the little girl's jeans. "We don't know nobody name of Willy," she said harshly. Then, more kindly, she added, "Get on home now. It's past suppertime, and I made your favorite, corn fritters."

Yes, we do know Willy, Chessy thought. He used to hang around the package store drinking beer and playing cards till right after Papa left town. And I liked Willy, even if he was a Navajo. He gave me a Kachina doll one time, but Papa tossed it in the dumpster out back of the Shop 'n Save.

Chessy wanted to say these things, but she didn't dare. Nothing had been right since the night her father left, that night when Mama was crying, stubbing out one cigarette after another before she'd hardly smoked it, and Papa was stuffing clothes into a knapsack in such a rush that he grabbed up one of Angelina's blouses by mistake.

"When you comin' back?" Chessy's mother kept repeating. "When you comin' back fer us, BobbyRae?"

But BobbyRae, his eyes dark and ominous as the deadly clouds from which funnels descend, didn't answer. When he came to kiss Chessy good-bye, the sweetness of the peppermint he was sucking mingled sickeningly with the smell of Jim Beam. Angelina locked herself in the bathroom, but Chessy stood at the window and watched as the lights from her father's Bronco receded down the road till they shrank to pinpoints as distant as the stars.

Nearly a month after Papa left, excitement blazed like a brushfire through the Bitter Springs Trailer Camp. Chessy heard it from the other children first. A coyote had dug up the torso and part of an arm of a man who'd been murdered and buried out by the arroyo. For a while there, Sheriff Stubbs came around almost every day, but then there was a bank robbery in Tuba City, and he had more important things on his mind.

Truth was, her mother told her, nobody cared much about the knifing of an old Navajo medicine man, especially one like Willy McDaniels, who'd got the white folks hopping mad by winning the Swansea County lottery (by magic, some said) and then proving what everybody already knew—that Indians got no common sense —by flashing the cash around.

Maybe if he'd a put the money someplace safe instead of in his bootheel, he'd be alive today, Angelina said.

Chessy wondered how her mother knew where Willy kept his money, but she was scared to ask.

"You wash up and put somethin' on that don't look like you been rollin' in the dirt," her mother said as they walked back toward the trailer where Angelina's decrepit orange Pinto sat rusting in the yard. "You never know but Papa might be walkin' in the door this very night."

Chessy wanted to believe that. Oh, desperately. Especially now that Willy'd said he'd help her bring BobbyRae home. But it was hard sometimes to believe her mother, because what her mother said kept changing. One minute she'd be lacquering her nails and putting streaks of henna in her lustrous black hair, hollering at Chessy to keep the TV low so they could hear the Bronco if it pulled up outside; the next minute she'd be in the bathroom with the water running, thinking Chessy couldn't hear her sobbing.

"Oh, BobbyRae, how could you?" Angelina cried out one time. "What'll Chessy and me do without you? How're we gonna live?"

Lately, though, her mother just sat by the window and stared out toward where the cracked, pebbly earth met the dirt road and a small sign pitted with BB shot read BITTER SPRINGS, ARIZONA, POP. 203. Beyond that, the dry, scabby landscape was dotted with half a dozen trailers, many of them, like Angelina's, with clothes flapping in the hot breeze like distress flags.

Toward twilight, when the sun dropped like a bleeding bullet hole over the rim of the horizon, her mother would take Chessy out for a walk, always with her head bent toward the ground, mindful of the tarantulas and scorpions and creepy-crawly things that, like Angelina herself, ventured forth as the desert cooled.

And if, in the distance, the dust from an approaching car became visible, Angelina's head would go up, her eyes would strain, and she would come alive for those few seconds before the vehicle came into view and proved to be some Navajo's dilapidated jeep or a busload full of tourists "seeing Indian country," not the Bronco with its CB antennas and the I DON'T GET MAD, I GET EVEN bumper sticker.

At supper, munching on corn fritters that had soaked up too much grease in the skillet, Chessy watched her mother's eyes dart to the telephone again and again, as if tugged by invisible cords.

"He'll call soon," she told her mother, trying to cheer her. Hadn't Willy promised, after all? But Angelina looked so mournful that Chessy couldn't help but add, "The drawing ain't finished is why he ain't called. He's still in Mexico."

A shudder jittered up her mother's spine. She jabbed her fork at the beans on her plate, and they skidded away like shiny black beetles.

"I told you Papa's gone down to Albuquerque to get him a pipe-fittin' job."

"Willy says—"

"There *ain't* no Willy!"

"Willy who got murdered down to the arroyo," said Chessy. And she described for her mother the crooked grin that the killer had carved out like a second smile below the Indian's Adam's apple.

"Damn busybody women," spat Angelina, eyes bright as a cornered cat's. "They'll embroider a killin' clear to Christmas, pass it around so each one can add on a few more lies like they was stringin' beads. But tellin' such things to a child. It ain't decent."

Later, after the supper dishes were cleared away, Chessy watched her mother's head loll back against the sofa and her lips quiver with rhythmic snoring. She wanted to sleep too, but she was afraid—lately her dreams were of blood soaking into the cracked earth of the arroyo, blood that little lizards tracked webby footprints in, where centipedes were trapped and mired in the sticky scarlet even as the old Indian lay dying.

"Bobby, BobbyRae," Angelina moaned, but no one heard her except the listening child.

When she was sure her mother slept deeply, Chessy scrambled into her clothes and slipped outside into the vast desert tapestried with shifting skeins of moon. She shivered a little and felt a tug back toward the security of the trailer, for the desert at night was a landscape changed, haunted with shadows and gliding shapes, a spellbound place, and Chessy knew tarantulas the size of coffee saucers scuttled among the cactuses and rattlesnakes performed their deadly, undulating dances under the stars.

She skirted the few trailers parked between her own and the road and skidded down an incline that, in wetter seasons, became a riverbank. Finding the stick she'd left behind earlier that day, she set about to finish her drawing. All the while she listened for funny old Willy with the boil on his jaw, who'd let everybody think he was dead.

She was hunkered down on her hands and knees, scrawling a new moon into the upper quadrant of her sand drawing, when she heard the old Indian coming. Someone else might have thought it was the rustling of a bat's wings or the low hiss of a tumbleweed overturning, but Chessy had heard him too many nights, nights when the old Indian crept outside the trailer window and peered in, his eyes bright and pearly as moonscape, the bloody slit in his throat gaping.

The sound that Willy McDaniels made was a low, insectile hum caused by air pushing through the hole in his throat. It was a wide gash, which gave him the appearance of having two mouths, the second one a kind of jack-o'-lantern grin where the flesh flapped down like a distended lower lip. Otherwise, he still looked pretty much like the old Navajo Chessy remembered seeing in town. A chaw of smokeless puffed out one bristled cheek, and he wore a tooled belt with a heavy silver buckle and chunky boots shaped more like the boxes they were bought in than the feet they enclosed.

Willy McDaniels grinned his double grin at Chessy and her picture of the man and the spider thing. He whispered through his open throat, a nasal wheeze, "You done real fine. Your drawin's pullin' at your papa, givin' him dreams. He's on his way home now. I see him clear."

Chessy beamed, proud of the drawing she'd produced according to the old Navajo's instructions.

"Now it's plantin' time," said Willy.

He held out his good hand, the one with all five fingers. When

Chessy saw what it contained she cringed and drew back, remembering her mother's words.

"Will it hurt me?"

"Can't," said the Navajo. "It ain't for you."

Chessy held out her hand. Willy McDaniels dropped the scorpion into her palm.

"You sound mighty cheerful this morning," said Angelina, sipping coffee so strong the aroma filled the entire trailer.

Chessy sat in front of the TV set and finished her bowl of cereal. The characters from Sesame Street were singing a song about numbers. Chessy was humming along.

"I got a surprise," she said.

She was about to tell her mother about the scorpion when the phone rang. Chessy and Angelina both grabbed for it, but Chessy, fleeter, won. She listened for a moment before passing the receiver to her mother.

"Somebody's playin' a game," she said, standing close so she could listen in.

At first there was only the swish of empty air, followed by a kind of wet gobbling for breath and labored, heat-struck sobbing. Goose bumps broke out on her mother's arms.

Angelina listened to the obscene sounds with repulsion and was about to hang up when she realized that the tortured breather was panting, "Lina, Lina."

"BobbyRae?"

"I'm sick, Lina. Feels like my guts are busting. Can't drive anymore. Ya gotta come get me."

More panting, choked and wheezy. Like the mutt BobbyRae left shut up in the Bronco one scorcher of a day, the windows rolled up, doors locked, while he dropped into Harley's Bar and Bar-B-Q for a quick one that turned into several. Guilt-stricken, he'd brought the dog home, but the animal was near death, breathing like somebody was standing on its chest. Like BobbyRae sounded now.

"Where're you at? What's happened?"

"Route Eighty-one an—"

"Can't hear you."

"—an' Claypool Junction. Come get me. But don't tell nobody."

"It's all right," said Angelina. "They don't know it was you killed the old man."

Chessy was standing as close to the phone as she could, but now she jumped back, staring at the receiver as though a rattlesnake had crawled out of it.

"What I mean is—" said Angelina. "Chessy, wait!"

But Chessy, her eyes huge as dimes, ran out of the kitchen, slamming the trailer door.

Even driving the sputtery Pinto 80 mph over flat, nearly empty roads, it took Angelina half an hour to reach Route 81, which arrowed north toward a swell of bosomy foothills close to the Utah border. Claypool Junction, twenty miles to the east, had originally been a Navajo trading post. Now it was reduced to a shabby motel, a Texaco station, and a lumpish red adobe museum with a CLOSED sign on the door and a sullen-looking Indian woman selling jewelry at a table by the road. The Bronco was parked around back of the museum, near the telephone booth where BobbyRae must have made his call.

Angelina parked the Pinto and tugged on the door of the Bronco. BobbyRae pitched out sideways, half in, half out of the truck. Pushing him back inside, Angelina climbed up into the cab. She tugged his head onto her lap.

In spite of the heat, BobbyRae's skin was dry and cool, his lips the dessicated brown of cactus pads. His mouth was clenched tight but his throat worked vigorously, and the look of wide-eyed amazement on his face suggested a man who had just unknowingly stumbled off the edge of a cliff.

"Stomach—" he began. A pinkish froth burbled up over his lips. With Angelina's help, he got his head to the window and puked.

"I'm takin' you to the hospital," said Angelina. She reached for the ignition, but BobbyRae was flailing his arms now, clutching at his own throat like a man trying to choke himself, and one hand knocked the car keys onto the floor behind her feet. She reached down for them. Something scuttled across her fingers. She jerked her hand back and let the keys lie.

BobbyRae moaned and thrust out a tongue so lacerated it looked skinned. A pale and hairy pincher about the thickness of a pipe cleaner began to probe the gap between two teeth. His mouth opened wide, so that Angelina had an unobstructed view of the scorpion gripping his tongue, its front legs positioned on the lower teeth, the stinging tail uplifted toward the roof of his mouth.

"Oh, Jesus, Bobby!"

BobbyRae coughed mightily. The scorpion dropped into Angelina's lap, then skittered down onto the brake pedal and between her feet under the seat.

"Help me!" gasped BobbyRae. His throad was working again, rippling from below the Adam's apple. A second scorpion backed out of his mouth. BobbyRae tried to swat it, but the glassine tail thrust up and stabbed directly in the hollow above the upper lip. BobbyRae screamed, beating himself wildly about the face, as the scorpion fell onto his thigh.

BobbyRae's throat began working again, this time with more powerful contractions. He struck at himself, spitting blood and bits of tooth as his throat undulated. A scorpion still larger than the last crabbed its way onto his raw tongue. He spit it out onto Angelina.

Brushing frantically at her clothes and hair, Angelina leaped out of the truck. The horror she felt at BobbyRae's appalling predicament was rapidly giving way to self-concern. An image had come into her mind, as sudden and unbidden as a scream, of Chessy hunched down in the dirt, gazing up at Angelina holding the scorpion she'd just killed. *Willy likes scorpions.*

"I'll be back, BobbyRae. I'll get help," she called, before roaring off in the Pinto.

The last she saw of BobbyRae, he was convulsing in jagged spasms on the seat of the Bronco, tearing at his throat in an effort to stem the repulsive tide that disgorged relentlessly from his belly.

Halfway back to the trailer camp, an itching started at Angelina's armpits and groin. By the time she passed the sign for Bitter Springs the sensation had spread to her scalp and felt like someone was sequestered inside her skull, setting fire to the roots of her hair. The burning spread from follicle to follicle. Then it began to descend along her face, licking inside her ears and eyelids and deep inside her at a spot where not even BobbyRae's most ardent thrustings could have reached, the fire penetrating her with agonizing intimacy.

She glanced at herself in the rear vision mirror. Beneath her swollen eyelids something ticked, a pulsing from behind her eyes. Her vision blurred. Sight doubled. The Pinto swerved into the left lane, bucked onto the shoulder of the road, and skidded to a halt near a stand of cactus.

Angelina clung to the wheel, struggling to breathe against the agony of the procession exiting her every orifice. Her mouth and ears, the passages inside her nose, and those between her thighs filled up with tiny avid mouths and wriggling legs. The pain wrung tears from her and in them shimmered flecks of matter, bits of legs and feelers. Angelina clamped her mouth over the steering wheel so hard her front teeth shattered, but still the fiery tide outpoured. Her body had become a hive, a churning nest. With every nerve ablaze and raw, she howled her daughter's name.

In the sun-baked arroyo, the centipedes tumbled over Chessy's plastic spade so thickly that they resembled tangled hair. She worked steadily, methodically, shoveling up sand and stomping it down, along with its living contents, into a circle greasy with the bodies of crushed and dying creatures.

She hummed to herself as the living centipedes scattered. Many of them fell into cracks in the arroyo; others were killed or maimed as the child's nimble feet trod them to slime. A few of the crushed bodies still twitched with life as she spaded them over with sand.

Willy McDaniels, insubstantial as the heat haze that shimmered off the arroyo, rattled off a thin song.

"Plantin' time," sang Chessy, following along.

Just As I Am

Joyce Gibson Roach

Joyce Gibson Roach, a fifth-generation Texan, was born in 1935. She has a B.F.A. and an M.A. from Texas Christian University. Her study of ranch women, *The Cowgirls,* won the Western Writers Spur as the Best Western Nonfiction Book in 1977. She added another Spur in 1987 for a humorous narrative, "A High-Toned Woman." She is past president of the Texas Folklore Society, belongs to Western Writers of America, and is a member of the Texas Institute of Letters. Currently she's working on a book about the prairie land close to the ranch outside of Keller, Texas, where she's lived for the past twenty-five years. *Eats: A Folk History of Texas Foods,* which she coauthored, was published last year. A musical folk drama, *Nancy MacIntyre: A Tale of the Prairies,* premiered October 1989. She has two children.

This humorous story set in Texas during revival time had me laughing out loud almost from the beginning; it's also a very touching story. You can see why Joyce has been twice honored by WWA.

The words came sweet and soft and oh, so familiar to my fourteen-year-old ears. They were playing my song.

> Just as I am, without one plea
> But that Thy blood was shed for me,
> And that Thou bidd'st me come to Thee,
> O Lamb of God, I come, I come!

The long call of revival had commenced. The locusts of summer buzzed. The June bugs flew with a whir of wings and landed with a tiny thud on the backs of believers who set their teeth against the onslaught of tiny legs that clung to the cotton material of shirts and dresses. Women and children who usually cried out at the attacks of such creepy-crawly things murmured not. Swarms of lesser insect creatures hovered by the hundreds around the bare light bulbs hanging on the tops of tall creosoted poles and departed from time to time to trouble the members of the congregation. Fans moved furiously. A blister bug got down the collar of Brother Martin's shirt. His wife went after it with quick fingers. Invitation hymn or not, a blister bug's got to be attended to. It was hot as hell, and not just from the enthusiasm of revival. Those who lived in Texas in August weren't nearly as impressed with the thought of fire and brimstone as others in some parts of the universe.

Tears poured down my cheeks. The sweat poured off my forehead and mingled with the flow from my eyes. I was getting pretty wet at the collar by the time I was fixing to make my move down the grass aisle toward the wooden platform at the front of the arbor. The tears were instant; I'd been working on the sweat part since early afternoon. Oh, Lord, I was perfect, blameless, contrite, and absolutely without shame as I bolted down to the altar to demonstrate to the assembled sisters and brothers that the power of the Almighty had seized my life, my all, for the sixth time that very summer. I come, I come; oh, yes, Sweet Jesus, I come.

August! There was nothing like it in the whole year. My hometown, located in west Texas, had never been known for riotous living, not either in August or any other month. The Horned Toad Café and my mother's table provided some memorable meals, but neither food nor entertainment ever came close to orgy. The rural community on the prairies was, in my youth, isolated by distance and slow cars from such sinful places as Fort Worth and, God forbid, *Dallas!* Farmers and ranchers and those who catered to their needs made up most of the population. School was about as much activity as most of us could tolerate. Many of us looked to church for entertainment and edification, and the church was not found wanting. We liked summertime revivals, and, although the grown-ups would not admit such folly, there were other folks, judging from the numbers gathered as each church took its turn, who got a certain pleasure in revivals, too. Mid-July to August was the season, the time, to gather Lukewarm Christians, Back Sliders, and New Material into the fold. Only a round of loud gospel singing, hellfire preaching from someone strange from a place at least thirty miles away, and a drenching, dripping, all-the-way-under baptism, usually performed in old man Tubb's stock tank, could set our feet on the path to righteousness once more.

I looked on the first revival of each summer just like a debutante looks forward to her coming-out party. My family approached the season with fear and trembling. You see, revivals had a strange effect on me. I do not know whether it was the music or the preaching or just a combination of things, but whatever the cause the results were the same. At the first call by the minister for rededication, I plunged down the aisle to give my heart anew to the Lord Jesus Christ, my Savior, and to whatever cause He had pending. Sometimes I gave myself to Christian nursing in the darkest jungles of Africa, sometimes as a gospel singer in the slums of some big city like Breckenridge, sometimes as missionary to the Indians in Arizona, and once to teach sewing to the poor little black children in my own community. Everybody knew I couldn't medicate, sedate, educate, sing, or sew a stitch, but I also believed in miracles. Every time the invitation was given, my mother sat down. She knew what was coming. Sometimes others were struck by the same lightning, and we raced down the aisle to see who got there first to give their lives to whatever cause was hanging fire that evening.

The summer of my fourteenth year was, in a way, the high point of a very successful revival career, which was the only kind of career there was for those too young to hold down a real job. I'll never forget that summer as long as I live, never. I was tall, had stopped wearing my hair French-braided so tight that the skin around the outsides of my eyes was in a bind, and, for the first summer of my life, felt relaxed. Gosh, what a relief! I had a whole different visual experience with my eyes finally out of traction. Headaches were gone and I quit grinding my teeth, which I had always done in trying to free my scalp from such intimate association with my hair. Boys were beginning to look at me, without contempt at least, although without any marriage interest. Too formidable, too pious, too good yet for any real interest from men, I could still feel their eyes on me, especially at church when I left my pew to make the flight to the altar.

But wait, I'm leaving out the best part—the genesis of what went on before and led up to the exodus to the altar. Oh, yeah, and my name is Nancy Ann MacIntyre and I was an only child. You ought to know that, at least. I always get ahead of myself. I mention the "only child" part because it helps explain all kinds of peculiarities. People could say, "Well, she's an only child, you know." They used it to excuse some of my transgressions—which were mighty few, by the way. Besides, I lived in a town full of only children. Mrs. Johnson, the neighborhood gossip and one of my best friends, used to say that the Depression was the best method of birth control known to mankind. She said it wasn't necessary for me to understand what she meant. I didn't even care.

Well, like I was saying, there was a certain order to things. Religious matters began for the young folks of all denominations an hour before regular revival services. Mostly we had sword drills, which commenced when the leader read out a scripture and then said "Go." The first one to find the scripture was the winner. The Baptists always won because they were long on memorizing the books of the Bible and spent many winter Sunday evenin's practicing up for the summer. The Methodists, Presbyterians, Pentecostals, and Disciples had sword drills at revival too. A person such as myself had to go to all of them, as well as two or three more in other communities close by. A person had to make choices about some of them, but even if you missed one or two you got pretty good at knowing the Bible.

There was another game we played with Sister Elizabeth, who was one of the leaders at her church. Elizabeth Morris was a maiden lady, whatever that means. She started out revival season just lovin' us little old children to death and ended the season by predicting that we were all going to hell, which had to be OK because Sister Elizabeth insisted that she wouldn't be there. The game that caused her to make such dire predictions about our future was called "Fill in the Scripture." She gave a topic and we found appropriate scriptures quick as we could. For instance, if she said find a scripture about love, there was "God is love," "God loveth a cheerful giver," "Love thy neighbor as thyself." But there were other scriptures that someone always happened across, such as "Let him kiss me with the kisses of his mouth: for thy love is better than wine" (Song of Solomon 1:2). We were off and running, then. And the more times we played the game, the more familiar we became with the unusual answers. Sister Elizabeth would move on faster and faster. "Sports," she said. "Who can tell us about Bible sports?" One kid jumped up. He was ready with Genesis 26:8, "Isaac was sporting with Rebekah his wife." "Animals," she said, her voice rising. Someone quoted her a line about ox and asses. "Women," she shrieked. Bubba Ray Thompson replied with a plum about whores, and Sister Elizabeth hit the door, running to tattle on us to our parents and shouting about the evils of our generation.

There was a little time before regular services began, and we girls would stand around in little clusters giggling and talking. The topic of the big house across the street from Mount Zion Church came up, and that was good for several minutes' speculation. Mount Zion was a funny name for a church in such a flat place. It's an Israelite word, and we didn't have any places with foreign words on them.

The church ladies referred to the place across the street as "the house of ill repute." We didn't know what ill repute was. The house across the street did need paint, and its two stories looked pretty spooky at night. So a dark house in need of paint was what a house of ill repute meant to us. The house faced the opposite direction from the church, so we couldn't see anything but the back side with mops and buckets and the clothesline showing. I particularly never connected anything very bad with the place because I had a good friend living there. Texanna was her name. Texie, as I knew her, bought baked goods from me every year, and I made a pile out of that one house. I sold cookies and cakes and pies baked by the church women for missionary causes. Because of Texie's house, I raised the most money of anybody. All the churches let me sell for them and they were really proud of my efforts, and I saw no reason to let anybody else in on my territory by telling them where I did such a booming business. Surely that wasn't a sin—just keeping my mouth shut.

Mother knew of my acquaintance with Texie. She never said anything about her, but she told me never to go inside the house. It was hard on me not to go in because Texie was such a good and mysterious person, and a child or someone such as myself always loves a good and mysterious person the best of all. Anyone would have loved my friend if only they'd known her. She was tall like me, and pretty, which I wasn't yet but planned on being.

I asked Mother once how old she thought Texie was, and Mother said she was probably in her late twenties or early thirties. I knew she was considerably older than me because she had bosoms, which I was just beginning to get. I hoped mine would be as nice as hers. I cannot bring myself to say "breasts" for bosoms. Breasts is a loathsome word contained in the Song of Solomon. The deacons and elders met once to see about having the book of Solomon removed from the Bible. Since having the book removed seemed too large an undertaking even for all the brethren in town, they just decided not to ever teach or read from it and to instruct young people not to use the vile words contained in it. But you will get my meaning when I use the word "bosoms."

Well, back to Texie. She had jet-black hair which framed her pale, white face. Her eyes were dark too. Sometimes she'd sit on the rail of her porch that went all around the front and sides of her house. Another porch went all around the front and sides upstairs: a gallery, they called it. If I found her sitting like that, I'd go up and talk to her. I think sometimes she'd sit out of an evenin' knowin' that I'd pass by about the same hour on Wednesday and Sunday. I could spend a little time with her without anyone seeing that I was on the front of the house. We just talked about pleasant things: about me, mostly, and what I was doing at school or at church. She'd ask me what I wanted to be when I grew up and was I going to go away to school or to work or had I seen the movie that month or how did I stand the heat in the summertime. She never talked about herself and I never asked anything. Anyone's common sense tells 'em not to ask questions of a good and mysterious person.

She told me about her name once and how she was named for Texas and for her mother, Anna: Texanna. She was my friend and I was hers and I counted myself lucky. I always asked her to come to church and assured her that she would not have to sit alone, that I'd sit with her. Sometimes I would do my missionary duty and quote scripture or sing her a song. The one we liked to sing together was her favorite and mine too, and it was the one that got me started down the aisle the quickest. Texie had a rich alto voice, and we could do the nicest harmony:

> Just as I am, and waiting not
> To rid my soul of one dark blot,
> To Thee, whose blood can cleanse each spot,
> O Lamb of God, I come, I come!

It was so nice sitting on Texie's porch singing the sweet songs of salvation and thinking religious thoughts about God's mercy and goodness and how He loves us all. Well, I was doing all the talking, but Texie seemed like she enjoyed listening. At least she smiled a lot.

But back to revivals. I have this problem in talking. I always lose my place and start telling things that don't need to be told. Well, anyway, when we girls had visited awhile longer, the crowd began to move on toward the arbor at the back of the church building. Choosing a fan was the next order of business. Fans served a multitude of congregational functions. Mothers fanned sleeping babies with them; men covered yawns behind them; ladies whispered behind them; some swatted flies and mosquitoes with them. And let me tell you, if you turned one of those fans sideways and hit a kid's knuckles with it, you could stop a riot, it hurt so bad.

The first ones to gather got the best choice of the pictures. The fans were constructed of heavy cardboard with a stick glued on for a handle. The only funeral home in town distributed the fans to all the churches as advertisement. It seemed sort of strange to me. Everybody knew what the funeral home's business was. Didn't seem like they needed to advertise, but we were mighty glad to have the fans, of course. There were Bible or religious scenes on the cardboard faces of the fans. You could have one with an angel on it looking protectively down on two little children crossing a bridge above a raging torrent. There was one with Jesus knocking on a door. Another showed Jesus entering Jerusalem, and one had the Last Supper on it. My favorite, which I usually had to scuffle for, was Jesus praying in the Garden of Gethsemane. You could even see the sweat as drops of blood on Jesus's brow. Bubba Thompson usually got in a snatching match over Jesus in the Garden and he'd tell everyone that I was the only person in the world he'd ever seen that sweated as much as Jesus in the Garden. I hated that boy.

The schedule of events was fairly regular regardless of denomination. Events is usually what each part turned out to be, and they generally ran in this order: the entrance, the singing, the praying, the testifying, the edifying, the exhorting, the inviting, and the rededicating.

The grand entrance of some female members of the community into revival services was an important element in the education of the young women of my age. We were exposed to members of other congregations, but, of more consequence, we came to know a type called high-toned women. These ladies, only one or two in each denomination, seemed of but one type. They were large, fleshy, buxom, and completely sure of their importance to the community and to God's kingdom universal. When they entered the aisles, independently or together, they looked like great ships turning their bows into the wind. The earth trembled and so did we. Their power was undeniable. They were not necessarily "girded about with truth" but they, in truth, were girded: corseted, staved, and shored up. August heat hot enough to make the locusts beg did not keep these ladies from appearing in full Christian battle armor ready to serve the Lord, provided they did not faint first. Fainting was, of course, not unheard of during revivals. The spells usually occurred when the service became heated with Pentecostal fire. My mother was the first to point out to me that perhaps corsets and not God had cut off their wind. I supposed the Lord was pleased with high-toned women. We certainly were.

To get everybody quieted down, the song leader would tell us to open our paperback books, which we used for revivals because they weren't so expensive to replace when folks carried them off. Everybody enjoyed revival singing. We nearly always began with a chorus of "Hallelujah thine the glory, Hallelujah, amen; Hallelujah thine the glory, revive us again." Then there would be lots of bloody songs, with words like "Are you washed in the blood of the Lamb?" "Alas and did my Savior bleed?" and "that His blood was shed for me." The bloody songs were always referred to as Methodist philosophy. We liked to sing them, but we wanted the blame placed squarely on Methodist shoulders and the Wesley boys. For the children they sang things like "I've got the joy, joy, joy, joy down in my heart." Then at the end of the meeting we sang songs like "Almost Persuaded" or my favorite.

After the singing came the praying, produced spontaneously by someone the preacher called on. Sometimes he would call on one of us older children to pray to show the parents how we were coming along in the prayer department. There was always a special musical rendition after the praying and after more group singing. Usually there was a mixed quartet or sometimes a solo.

When the special music and the "amens" that followed died away, we got ready for the testifying. The preacher planned ahead of time for one person to come to the front and start it, and then anyone the spirit moved arose to enumerate his past sins and his present cleanliness because Jesus had washed his sins away—in blood, naturally. We young people never testified, of course, because we were too young to know about hard sinning, but we could tell from the testifying that we had a lot to look forward to.

After the testifying, and while the regular preacher introduced the visiting minister, the congregation made seating adjustments and prepared to settle down for the edifying.

The preacher had but one job and always the same: to tell the gathered assembly in the most dramatic and stupefying way possible about sin—all the different kinds of sin and how we were living in it, committing it, and could be saved from it. The style depended on the preacher, but it all came out with the gaiety of a Wagnerian opera. Fist pounding, hand clapping, finger snapping, and floor stomping were guaranteed to keep the attention and to prove sincerity.

Those revival preachers spared the congregation nothing. They were far ahead of medical research in telling of the dangers of alcohol and tobacco. Dancing and swearing were dwelt on with equal intensity. The emphasis then was a negative one, on *not* doing rather than doing. Every morning I got up not drinking, swearing, smoking, or dancing and knew what a wonderful Christian I was being. I told you already that I had no small vices. I was nearly perfect.

After the preacher had covered all the bases on sinning, he proceeded to the exhorting. That did not take long. He explained how you would feel when the Holy Spirit hit you, and he begged you to let it come upon you. Members of the congregation began to look around to see if the spirit was going to descend on anyone they knew.

By the time the invitational hymn was beginning, some members, and especially the high-toned women, were already moving out to stand beside the worst sinners—teenage boys, hardened husbands, and total strangers whose spiritual conditions were unknown and thereby constituted reason enough to stand by just in case.

After three or four verses and a satisfactory amount of new material had been gathered at the altar, the preacher called for prayer, during which time he wanted "every head bowed and every eye closed" while he made an appeal for Christians to rededicate their lives to some specific or general cause he named off. When they'd sing, "Just as I am, though tossed about/With many a conflict, many a doubt/Fightings and fears within, without, O, Lamb of God, I come"—then I went. I didn't really have any fightings or fears either within or without, but that was my cue, and by the time every head was raised and every eye opened, there I stood, all tears and sweat. Afterward, there was a lot of handshaking and crying. Then we all went home to rest up for another night.

We never knew by any calendar date when the revivals were. Usually I met Peggy or Beth Ann, and when I asked them to come over, they would look as if they had just taken the veil and reply with their tongues dipped in sugar, "No, thank you. We are in a meetin'." Boy, I would race home and take a bath so I could beat 'em there. You might go to heaven unwashed because "no man knoweth the hour," but you didn't go dirty to a revival.

Well, like I was saying, the affairs of my religious life came to a head that very summer. One Wednesday evening after the mid-week service, all the church men met to plan for a special all-church revival in August. To stimulate interest and show we weren't backwoods Christians, the preachers in one accord with the elders and deacons decided to invite what was then considered a new-style evangelist, a professional revivalist, and put him on late in August after everybody had their turn.

When the evangelist pulled up to the church late that summer in his red convertible he was wearing a red plaid jacket and his wife had blond hair, which was brought about by a bottle of bleach. One fact was abundantly clear: He ought to really be able to tell us about the wages of sin because he looked as if he'd been in the middle of a bunch of it and on a regular basis. He had a real sweet face but that man's hair was plastered down with some shiny stuff and—well, he looked cheap, that's all, cheap. Folks around town were grim. There was nothing to do but go through with it.

My daddy, who was a leader and one of the planners who had voted for the pair, talked about it more than he should, but only at home. Lord, we were embarrassed, or planned to be. Daddy went about apologizing. When people wanted to know why Daddy was apologizing, he wouldn't go into detail but just sort of left them hanging. "You'll see," was all he'd say. It wasn't working out quite like the town planned. What they thought was that after the usual round of the usual events in the usual order at the usual time, our church, which was hosting the big event, would get the Best Revival Award or something like that. At least, that's the way I had it figured.

The man and his wife were staying at the old parsonage near Mount Zion church. It was vacant and used for special guests. Sometimes visiting preachers stayed in the homes of the congregation, but it was just as well that provisions had been made ahead of time to offer the extra little house. Nobody would have taken that man and his wife in. They had come two days early to "get everything ready," whatever that meant. There was a stir up and down the road. The pair found some help and brought in extra pews. More light poles were set up, and you could smell the creosote all over town. They didn't extend the size of the arbor, though. Lord, that arbor was a terrible amount of trouble. We just did it to remind folks of pioneer times; we didn't really need that arbor anyway. You'da thought we were having a circus.

On the first Sunday evening, people gathered early. Everybody knew and everybody was coming. Brother Tobias, who was in charge of the Love Offering plates, which was the way we always paid revival preachers, was heard to mutter and then go get some straw baskets. He said we'd need extra for sure, but that is only a bit of hearsay I'm repeating. I never heard it myself, but only overheard it when my daddy repeated it to another man.

I may as well get right to business in telling about that preacher. The evangelist's services were really something. Would you believe that instead of the special music being sung, the preacher blared it out on a trumpet while his wife accompanied him by knocking out a boogie beat on the piano? Boy, fans were whipping back and forth like everyone was trying to cool down Hades. Tongues were wagging. Feelings were running high. Other than the music, nothing out of the ordinary happened, but from what I could gather from listening to grown-ups, the man was just warming up.

The second night was better than the first! I had never seen such a sight in my life. That preacher was drawing them in. A good hour before the opening hymn, I went by Texie's house. She was sitting on the rail just like she was waiting for me. I nearly ran up the steps. I had walked as carefully as I could so as not to sweat more than usual, but I forgot all about it when I saw her.

"Texie, have you heard about the preacher and his wife?" I squealed. "You never saw anything like it. She's got white hair, white! And she can play that old black piano faster than anybody I ever heard. She pats one foot and keeps up the pedal with the other."

Texie laughed at my excitement. "Nancy Ann, it can't be that bad. Haven't you ever seen a bleached blonde before?"

I said, no, I hadn't, and I'd sure never seen one who jumped up and down on a piano bench and smiled and shook her head while she played. And I told her I never heard such a horn played by a preaching man before. I put in all the motions when I detailed how he wet his lips and pursed them and how he spread both feet apart and then raised the silver horn higher than his head and then let out with "When they ring those golden bells for you and me."

"But you didn't say if you liked it or not," said Texie.

Did I like it? "Oh, Texie, if it's done any better in the big city than here then I'm willing to be cheated!" I fairly shouted as I used a corny line I had read one time in a Eugene Manlove Rhodes story. "Oh, Texie, come on over. You've never been before. Please come. God might touch you. You might get saved. Then you could come regular and you could sing in the choir and help with the Lottie Moon offering and everything. And I know the WMU could use you."

Texie didn't reply right away. "I've seen them both over at the little house. I talked to her just for a minute. She came over to borrow a little sugar Friday night." Texie didn't say any more, but what little she said surprised me some. She just sighed and squeezed my hand and told me to go on or I might not get a seat up close and near an aisle. "I can hear what goes on from here," she said.

Have you ever noticed how things can change in ever so short a time? It's like rain in August. Nobody ever expects it. But suddenly, the clouds are there and—*wham*—it rains. Well, that's the way the meeting was. It didn't take me any time to get used to the change in services, and I liked it a lot. But just when things got so good, they didn't stay that way.

Things got awful, terrible. I got to really listening to what the man had to say. I had more to ponder than the music because the preacher ended up by pointing his finger at me before the week was out. He preached in a different way. He didn't shout much or pound the podium. Instead he whispered or he hissed and one time he actually cried. His sermons always mentioned hypocrisy, and when he went into detail about the hypocritical disease I knew I had been an unsuspecting sufferer from it. I was beginning to think I might not ought to go down the aisle anymore. And knowing I shouldn't go down the aisle anymore nearly killed me. God would be so disappointed. The congregation would be disappointed. It was wrong to go. It was wrong not to go. Oh, what was wrong and what was right? Nobody had a right to make me question what had always been right in my religious life. The preacher confused me worst of all when he quoted a verse from the song instead of letting us sing it. He made us quit singing! He said, real quiet, "Just as I am, poor, wretched, blind; Sight, riches, healing of the mind, Yea, all I need, in Thee to find, O Lamb of God, I come, I come!" He whispered the part about blind. Was he talking to me? Well, if I was blind, wouldn't I be the first to know?

By Wednesday I hated that preacher, and the hatred was multiplied tenfold because I knew he was right. He would see through me. He wasn't blind. In just three days' time everything went from white to black, from excitement to sick to my stomach. To make matters worse, Bubba Ray and two more boys warted me every night. They talked ugly so I could hear. It wasn't anything I hadn't heard before. I knew all those words even if I didn't use them myself except in a case of extreme provocation. But they kept looking at me in places they shouldn't have had their eyes, and I sure didn't know what to do about it or even what it meant.

It wasn't just me that was bothered. Everybody was stirred up and acting awful. I tell you, I've never been so miserable in my life. I had to make up my mind about what I was going to do on the last evening. Was I going down the aisle or wasn't I? What if the preacher named off some new cause I hadn't heard of? What if God meant for me to do a great religious work, maybe in China instead of Africa where I had already signed on? Could I refuse and maybe miss the opportunity of a lifetime to spread the word and minister to the sinners overseas? I thought of going to talk to the preacher ahead of time. Maybe he'd let me in on what he would be calling on people to do on the final night. I couldn't bring myself to do it, though. That man's services weren't anything like what we were used to. He didn't follow the order of events at all. He hadn't asked anybody to do one thing on any of the other nights except let the love of Jesus in our lives and to love our brothers and sisters. I'd already done that. Anybody who knew me could tell you that.

I took two baths a day trying to keep the sweat down, but it did no good. Sweat poured off of me worse than I ever remember. I was even dreaming at night, bad dreams, about what happens to those who don't lead good lives and those who are hypocrites; then I'd wake up sweating and wondering if that was my punishment for being a hypocrite. I was going to sweat myself to death and die of dehydration. Dehydration is bound to happen in hell. That was it! I was going to hell.

While I was pondering the wages of my sin, the men from the churches came over on Thursday night and talked into the late hours outside in our back yard. They were sure enough all stirred up. Their voices rose and fell as they pondered what to do, but they finally decided there was nothing bad they could pin on the man or his wife either. They couldn't ask him to leave in the middle of a revival. Crowds were the largest they'd ever been. The problem was they didn't know whether the crowds were secretly laughing at our church, thinking about the predicament we were in, denominationally speaking, or whether they were just curious or what. The deacons were in an awful uproar. I wished I could go talk to Texie about it all, but we weren't that good friends. She couldn't possibly understand about the trials and tribulations of Christianity. I wished I could talk to somebody, but what could I say: "I'm a hypocrite; I'm a sinner; I sweat too much; I may go to hell, how about you?" That's all I could think of. I tossed and turned in my sleep that night and dreamed of the altar where I was on my knees, moaning, Just as I am . . . just as I am.

The last night of the revival came. Earlier in the afternoon, I asked my mother to French-braid my hair.

"Nancy Ann, why would you want to do that again? I thought you liked having your hair more grown up. You're fourteen years old now. Besides, I'm tired of doing it." Mother seemed put out, but she was braiding the whole time she was talking. Her hands were cool and soft against my moist and sticky neck. I couldn't tell her why I wanted my hair braided. I just did. Something ought to be like it used to be. Braiding my hair was the only familiar thing I could remember after the week I'd been through—we'd all been through.

I arrived early but not early enough to beat the crowd. I'll bet there were a hundred and fifty people there, and the whole town population couldn't have been more than five hundred. Folks were gathering, flipping their fans like mad already, and hunting good seats. There were plenty of aisle places left in case I wanted one. You absolutely will not believe what happened then. Just as I was about to find me a spot, I saw Texie coming across the road toward the arbor! Seeing her coming at a distance was like an answer to prayer. "Thank you, Lord, for bringing my heathen friend. You will love Texie. She is so good and so pretty. Thank you, God. Thanks be to God," I murmured under my breath. If ever I needed someone with me who didn't know me, it was now. Texie could sit with me, and whatever I decided about going down the aisle or not would be OK. Boy, I fairly ran toward her.

The crowd was in the way and not inclined to get out of the way and I got tangled up. When I caught sight of her again, she wasn't alone. Bubba Ray and another boy were with her. They were still half a block away but I didn't have to be close to know by the looks on their faces that they were talking dirty. And they didn't even know her. How dare they speak to a stranger so! And Texie a visitor to a revival. I fairly flew toward her. Just as I got close, I heard Texie call Bubba Ray by name and tell him to leave her alone. He laughed, said something else I couldn't hear, and ran off, the other boy following close behind. How in the world would she have known Bubba?

"Texie, Texie," I hollered breathlessly. "I'm so sorry. You just wait till I get my hands on—" I was cut short and never finished my sentence because someone else was calling my name.

"Nancy Ann. You come here. Don't you go near that woman." It was one of the visiting high-toned women, and there was anger in her voice.

"But Sister Andrews, she's my friend, Texie. She's come to the revival and she is going to sit with me. It's all right." I looked at Texie and smiled and waved and tried with the look on my face to make it all right. The look on Texie's face scared me. But even in the midst of it all, I'll never forget how Texie looked. Her black-as-midnight hair was brushed and clipped back on one side with a silver hair clip. She had on a soft yellow dress with little print flowers in it and white gloves and white shoes. Never in all my life had I seen or known such a good and beautiful creature, and never had I seen such hurt on a face that pretty.

It was just like a dream then. Sister Andrews grabbed me by the arm and shouted—yes, shouted—for my mother. Mother was pretty close by for her to have heard, and she must have thought something had happened to me because she came running, scared nearly to death. There were twenty or so people within hearing of what was going on. Every eye was on us.

"Take your girl and tell her about her friend while I deal with this harlot," commanded Mrs. Andrews.

"Nance, are you all right? What is going on? What did you do?" my mother demanded to know.

"Mother, I didn't do anything wrong. I just asked Texie to sit with me. I told her she could come and be welcome and maybe get saved. And she came because I told her that the preacher was different and the music and all." I was hysterical and fought to get back through the crowd that had gathered around us. By the time I pushed my way through, Texie was gone, just disappeared. Mrs. Andrews was marching back to the arbor, and I mean marching.

Even though there were plenty of folks at the back where we were, a bunch of others were beginning to sing from their paperback books, and in an instant those around us turned and went to their seats, their curiosity satisfied. Whatever they were saying, I couldn't hear, and I didn't care anyway.

I just stood there sobbing with Mother's arms around me. "Mother, what did I do? What did I do?"

"Nothing, nothing, Nancy," whispered my mother. She stood right there in the road with her arms around me, rocking me just like a baby. She took her soft, sweet hands and pushed my head down on her shoulder and stroked my cheeks. In words simple and true she explained about Texie. I understood. But it was her explaining about Sister Andrews that hurt. I can't remember exactly what she said, but when she got through I knew that some people who said they were Christians weren't all the time, but only some of the time, and that I had to honor them for that, but only some of the time and not all the time.

"But can you tell me what I did wrong?" I asked again.

"Probably just about the most Christian thing you've ever done in your life. Even better than going down the aisle. Better than going to Africa, even." Mother's voice was shaking, and she cried just like her heart would break. Her tears covered me sweeter than baptism. "Let's go home, Nancy. We don't have to stay tonight."

"No, I want to stay. There's something I still have to do."
Mother and I wiped our tears and found a seat at the very back. No
one noticed our coming. I didn't hear one word of what the
preacher was saying. If there was special music it was lost on me.
No trumpet or piano penetrated my mind. I spent the whole time
thinking, thinking, studying it out.

When the call was given, I kept my seat through all the verses
and the repeats. For the first time in my life, I sang all the words,
read the meaning clear, gave up the call to Africa and parts unknown. God loved me. God loved Texie. Sister Andrews was on
her own. I didn't need to go down the aisle or anywhere, anymore.

Sunday Morning, Wednesday Night

Johnnye Montgomery

Johnnye Montgomery was born in 1936 in Iraan, Texas, and grew up on ranches in West Texas. She is a graduate of Columbia Business College in Odessa, Texas, and Midland College. She has worked as a Southwestern Bell Telephone Company service representative, Ward County Extension Service secretary, Milchem Drilling Fluids secretary, mud engineer, staff engineer, technical writer, district manager, and sales rep. Her work has appeared in *Sunshine Magazine, 1001 Home Ideas, New Holland News, Woman's World, AIMplus,* the *San Angelo Standard, Mature Living, Country Living, Women's Circle,* and *Country Woman.* She lives in Midland, Texas, with one daughter.

This story evokes many emotions—happiness, a few tears, a feeling of nostalgia. It is particularly skillful and bittersweet; again, it is set in Texas.

"Grandmother! Grandmother, can you hear me?"

There was a haze of light around the room as far as her vision extended, sometimes with dust particles dancing across it, sometimes clear and heavy, casting shadows of the chair down upon the bare oak floor. Now and then someone would set a water glass on the bedside table, and the light would fall through it and cast a rainbow upon the folded sheet over her chest.

There used to be rainbows after a rain in Texas, when she walked home from school along the dirt road beside Mr. Kingston's cotton field, and the alfalfa that grew beside the fence line would droop over with the weight of the diamond drops of rain, and the fresh-washed green of the fields would stretch out under the clean blue line of the horizon, lying beneath the distant clouds looking like just-picked cotton bolls dusted in charcoal; and extending from one side of the sky to the other would be a perfect rainbow, with each band of color so distinct you could almost reach up and peel the whole thing off the sky, the way you would peel a ribbon stick-on from the Masonite board in the art room at school.

She always walked in the hard-worn, sandy places in the road, to keep her shoes clean, and as she walked she kept an eye out for little wrinkled red rain bugs to take home to the twins. Those little bugs, bright and velvety, tinier than the eraser on the end of a pencil, came out after a shower and hurried in every which direction on tiny hairlike legs. Pick them up and they would play possom, but if you held them in your closed fist, they soon began to crawl, and you had to keep nudging them with a finger to make them play dead again, or they would escape and crawl out of your clenched fist and up your arm, then drop off to the ground while you still thought you had them.

There were often grotesque black tarantulas, propelling their hairy black bodies across the road on long stilt legs, menacing and businesslike. She shivered, thinking of them.

"Grandmother, are you cold? Henry, get a blanket, she's cold."

No, I'm not, she thought, it's just that tarantulas always make me shiver.

"They said to be sure she kept warm. Look how thin she is. Can she eat at all?"

Yes, but what would be the use of it? she thought. Besides, they never bring me anything that tastes good. I would eat a watermelon.

They used to grow watermelons in between the corn rows, down by the irrigation ditch, where there was a little wooden gate and you raised it to let the water from the ditch into the field, and there were two hills of watermelons, one on each side of the ditch. She would take the twins to play hide-and-seek in the cornfield, and she would always be *it*, and when they had run to hide, their cotton heads bouncing through the green blades of the tall corn, scrambling for a place, she would take Grandpa's hatchet off the nail in the toolshed and run lickety-split to the ditch where the watermelons grew. There, standing before the biggest ones, she would kneel and press with all her weight on each melon, listening for the heart to crack. And when she heard and felt the crack, she would split it open with the hatchet, reach in with her bare hand, and take out the succulent, seedless heart, and with juice running from wrist to elbow, would press the meat against the roof of her mouth, savoring the sweetness, until the twins tired of hiding, and came out and ran to the back yard, calling, "Allee allee in free! Sister! Sister! Allee allee in free!"

She had tried and tried to teach them to say it all, to say, "Allee allee out's in free," but they could never get it right.

"I just wish she would come to long enough to recognize us."

"Oh, I think she does, sometimes. She opens her eyes and stares at Mama every now and then, and I think she recognizes the doctor."

Mama? No, Mama died the year she was sixteen and had just finished high school. She made her graduation dress herself, out of yards and yards of white organdy, with self-covered buttons going all the way down to the hem, and the bodice scooped low, so that the amethyst pendant Charles Robbins gave her lay on her breast like a single primrose in a brown field.

She had come home immediately after graduation, not staying for the dance, and she had stood at the front door of the house that night in her new-made graduation dress while Mama lay dying, and the air was heavy and sweet with the scent of forsythia and honeysuckle, and across the field she could hear fiddles playing "Maiden's Prayer," and she held the wonder and the tragedy of the night in her heart like a jewel to be treasured all her life. And the next day, when Brother Carlson and Papa were sitting at the kitchen table with cups of coffee and big slices of pineapple upside-down cake that Mrs. Donovan had brought over, eating and drinking and discussing the funeral arrangements, Charles had come down the road in his white shirt and black graduation pants. She had met him at the gate, where the wild pink roses climbed in and out of the picket fence, and led him around to the back. He had kissed her in the milk house, pressing her back against the cool enamel of the icebox. It was her first kiss, and for years after that, whenever she remembered Mama, she remembered Charles's kiss.

Later that summer Bryan came to visit her, and came again and again, and when he kissed her one night, leaning over her on the back porch and touching her lips as gently as a feather, she closed

her eyes. And all that summer, as she lay in bed waiting for sleep to
come, she would count on her fingers all the kisses she had received, but she always started with two, because Charles had kissed
her first.

"How much longer do you think it might be, doctor? I really
can't stay past next Sunday. I have two teenagers at home, and you
know how difficult it is. . . ."

He came toward her through the haze of light, and his hands
were white with a pallor that had never been warmed by the sun,
and coarse black hairs sprouted sparsely over the soft white fingers. He gently lifted her face with one hand under her chin and
looked from behind his tiny flashlight into her eyes.

Bryan had been pale like that, unbelievably pale to a farm-raised
girl used to seeing the sun-baked shoulders of the farmhands. She
had heard the stories from Miss Henry in the post office and all the
other women who had come when her mother had died. A lifetime
of duty to a sickly mother, then hard study, then his vocation as a
minister had left his skin with a pallor that had never known the
sun, they said. Perhaps it would have been a shock, seeing the
feminine whiteness on a man, had it not been romanticized before-
hand until the sight of him, with the contrast of the black hair,
could almost make her catch her breath in wonder.

She had married him in his own church, redolent with the scent
of carnations from the flower bed outside the window, a scant six
feet from the lectern where he delivered those eternally earnest
sermons, and they had left the church through the door back of the
alcove housing the baptistry, climbing into the waiting Chevrolet
two-door coupé and driving the three blocks to the parsonage,
where they spent their wedding night—and all the nights save two
of their married life.

She could see, as if it were yesterday, that first day, the tremor of
his pale soft fingers as he unbuttoned the six ivory-colored taffeta
buttons on the sleeves of her dress, and feel the fluttering in her
breast as she turned her back to him so that he could unfasten the
back of the taffeta bodice, forty-four buttons, all the way down to
the hipline. And when she saw the white hand with the black hairs
running down the fingers and over the knuckles, as he reached
around to cup her breasts in his tremulous caress, she thought she
would surely die of joy.

"It's hard to say, actually, but if you need to go home, I wouldn't worry about it. . . . Look this way a bit, Mrs. Carson, that's a good girl. . . . She has a better rhythm today, and her vital signs look good." He snapped off the flashlight and the room went dark for just a moment before she could focus again. He spoke with a lisp, in a soft and melodic voice.

All her life, she had fallen in love with tender men with sweet, soft voices. It was Lewis's voice that she had loved first of all.

It was late August when Lewis came. That first day, she had been at the clothesline, Sharon at her feet, and the wind was whipping the sheets against her face, when the car drove in and Bryan had called out the window, "Bertie, I've brought company for dinner."

And during grace, she had lifted her eyes to find him staring at her, Irish eyes startling in a sun-reddened face, with black curly hair lying too long against his neck, shirt sleeves rolled up nearly to his elbows, looking more like a field hand than the new school superintendent, and when he answered "amen" to Bryan's grace, the sound had touched a hidden spot deep in her stomach.

And there was a Wednesday night only a few weeks after Bryan Jr. was born, when she had stayed home from prayer meeting to nurse him out of a colic attack, sending Sharon to church with Bryan. She was sitting out on the front porch in the swing, rocking Bryan Jr. and singing him to sleep, when Lewis came down the road, crossed the street, and opened the latch of the picket gate, swinging it open with a little squeak of the hinges, letting the wood slam against the rubber inner tube tied to the post to absorb the shock of the closing, and had as naturally as if he had done it every night of his life, sat down in the swing beside her, taking the sleeping baby from her arms and holding him in his own. With his free arm, he drew her into his broad embrace, and the two of them sat on the front porch watching the stars appear, and a huge pumpkin moon lifted itself over the town as they gently pushed the porch swing back and forth.

She mentioned to Bryan the next day that Lewis had come by for a while, and nothing further was said. But after that, every Wednesday night she found reasons to stay at home, and every Wednesday night Lewis came over. And then she began to stay home from Sunday school, getting to the church disheveled and out of breath, just in time for the sermon.

She couldn't remember the Wednesday night when they had left off sitting on the front porch and taken to sitting in the darkened parlor, but she remembered with still-thrilled clarity the night he had kissed her and loosened the tie on her housedress.

"If only she could speak to us, remember us."

"She had the most wonderful mind. Remember all the stories she used to tell of our less-than-proper families? I never could be sure she wasn't just making that all up, could you?"

"You know, it was almost as if she was embarrassed to be so perfect, so she made up stories to make us more at ease."

My lord, she thought, but you're right; I made a lot of it up, I guess to cover the truth about my own story. And the truth was, it never seemed to be so bad. I never felt that I was bad, even the night Bryan discovered us.

Lewis was so smooth, and his skin was so red, with the thick black hair covering his chest and growing like a tail down his back and in between his buttocks. And she had always closed her eyes, until one night he said, "Open your eyes. Look at us."

And she had looked. How different they were, he red and freckled and hairy, and she a dark gold, and he had said, "God, how lovely you are! Look at your breasts, like golden balls." And his face, looking down at her, reddened, and he compressed his lips and squeezed shut his eyes.

And she learned to squeeze him inside her, and squeeze and squeeze, to make it happen again and again, until the hour was up. And he would relax and leave her arms all businesslike, slipping into pants and shirt as if he were alone in his room at the teacherage.

But he was always there the next Wednesday, and the next Sunday.

And she found that Bryan was more exciting afterward, and if she found herself imagining that it was Lewis she was holding instead of Bryan, well, it made it better for Bryan, she reasoned, so who was hurt?

Then came the Wednesday night when Bryan came back to the house. No one at prayer meeting, it turned out. And she had heard the lilt of the children's voices, and the squeak of the picket gate, and there was no time for anything except an agonized scrambling for scattered clothing.

And while she and Lewis were attempting to dress and trying to think what to say, Bryan had taken his new necktie, the navy one with gold stripes that she had given him for his birthday, and had gone into the closet and hanged himself with it. The awful moment, the terrible moment when Lewis threw open the closet door and lifted the pallid body, and pumped the chest to force life back into the failing heart, and Bryan awoke, eyes bulging and red, and said, "My God, I am sorry."

She had never known whether he had meant it to be a prayer or was apologizing to her or to Lewis, but they had made up, incredibly, and when the night had ended, Lewis was gone and she and Bryan were locked in each other's arms.

If there had been gossip, the years took care of it, and she became the perennial Sunday school teacher and ideal minister's wife, cooking, attending meetings, forever sitting in the front pew with the widows, the newly converted, and the penitents.

And then there was Sharon's eighth-grade commencement exercise, and she had made her a white organdy dress reminiscent of her own high school commencement dress, and after the ceremony was all over she had lain awake, listening to the sounds of crickets outside in the summer night bursting with the scent of roses and althea, and finally, unable to lie sleepless another moment, had left the bed and walked barefoot, the hem of her white cotton nightgown floating phantomlike around her ankles, to sit in the porch swing.

And across the street, under the cottonwood tree, she saw the red glow of a cigarette.

The next morning she prayed for forgiveness while she swept sprigs of grass out of the sheets at the foot of the bed, and the day went by, and the following days, and the months, and the years.

And Sharon and Bryan Jr. graduated and went to college, and Sharon married a man with four small children, and promptly had two more children, and Bryan Jr. moved to Chicago and distinguished himself as a physicist.

And all the while, Bryan was dying of prostate cancer, having been repeatedly assured by their family doctor that this was the one nonmalignant form of cancer. No one, he said, died of prostate cancer. Bryan had taken three agonizing years, finally, to die of the cancer that no one dies from.

"Her eyes are changing, don't you think, doctor?"

"Yes, she's losing ground. If she has any other children, I suggest you call them."

"Yes, she has a son. We'll call Bryan."

Bryan. Oh, Bryan, forgive me. I never meant to hurt you. But it was good, wasn't it, Bryan?

Outside the window a mockingbird was singing, lifting himself off his perch on the telephone pole with the pure glory of his voice.

"Grandmother, can you hear me? Grandmother!"

She was wearing the white organdy graduation dress she had made herself, with an amethyst pendant resting on her breast, and the sweet sounds of fiddles playing "Maiden's Prayer" wafted out over a cotton field. And Charles's tender lips brushed hers in the shadow of the milk house while the smooth enamel of the icebox pressed into her bare shoulder blades.

"Mama, Bryan is on his way. Mama! Can you hear me?"

Sister! Allee allee in free, sister!

And the rainbow was getting closer and closer, and she could see the colors and the puffed clouds beyond, and she could reach up and touch it now, and beyond the rainbow, Bryan and Charles and Lewis and Mama and Papa. And now she could taste the melting sweetness of the biggest watermelon.

Allee allee in free.

Rain Shadow

Melanie Tem

Melanie Tem, a social worker, has worked with abused and neglected children in foster and adoptive homes, and with disabled adults. Previously she's published in numerous little magazines as well as *Whispers, Women of Darkness, Fantasy Tales,* Lisa Tuttle's as-yet-unnamed anthology, *Isaac Asimov's Science Fiction Magazine,* and *Women of Darkness II;* and collaborations with her husband, Steve Rasnic Tem, have appeared in *Asimov's, SF International,* and *Post Mortem.* Novels just completed are a dark fantasy and a mystery, first of a planned series featuring an elderly and disabled sleuth. She is working on a realistic/magical realistic/heroic fantasy/dark fantasy about grief and a hero's journey. And she has finished a novel written with Steve. She has also published numerous articles in professional journals. A native of rural Pennsylvania, she lives in an nineteenth-century Victorian house in old north Denver with her husband, children, two dogs, and two cats.

When Melanie submitted this story set in present-day Colorado, she said in her letter that her husband termed it "magical realism." It is also an incredibly moving tale.

The cottonwood stood in silhouette against the winter wheat field, against the wide sky blue as the eyes of a newborn baby. Blue as Becky's eyes would have been, newborn, but instead they were colorless, transparent, and always would be.

As she closed the screen door and paused on the back stoop, Annamarie could see detail in the tree: strings of bark, brown on darker brown. Stiff little bits of cotton still clinging here and there like fetal ghosts, their usefulness long since past for this season. In a fork well over her head, the empty cup of a bird's nest, intact and waiting.

One of Ma's books said there was usually as much of a tree underground as you could see above. Some of the things Ma read in books were hard for Annamarie to believe, but this wasn't. Knowing the cottonwood as well as she did, she understood that it sent its roots deep and wide, wherever they needed to go to find water, and that it could thrive here because it didn't need much. Probably the roots grew all the way under the house, made a foundation for it. Probably she was standing on a net of roots right now.

Ma said there were plants, entire species, that hadn't existed at all before there were mountains. Then animal forms had adapted to the plants, and then people, like herself and Becky, had adapted to it all. Annamarie had only a vague understanding of how it all worked, and none of her mother's passion to know, but it pleased her to think how everything fit together, how without adapting to each other she and Becky would not exist.

Now she was adapting to Parker and to Troy. She could feel it happening, feel herself changing cell by cell.

Ma hadn't grown up on the high plains. She'd come here because of Pa and stayed out of love, though certainly not love of the land. Ma hated it here. She hated the mountains, hated the prairie, hated the dry winds, the thin air, the sunshine three hundred days out of the year.

Annamarie didn't have to stare at the cottonwood to keep it in her mind; it was always there, like Becky. But it pleased her. It was so much nicer to look from a little distance at an individual tree like this, where you could see its twigs and branches and its overall shape. Whenever she'd visited southwest Virginia where Ma had grown up, she'd been saddened by the sight of all those trees blending together, blurred by kudzu. She'd come away with no real idea of what any one of them looked like.

She knew what Becky looked like, although she'd never seen her. She knew what Troy looked like; she could hold his face in her hands and he knew she was there. She knew what Parker looked like, although he was a man and she could still hardly bring herself to look at him directly.

She opened the door a crack and called, " 'Bye, Ma! Have a nice day!"

"If you won't be home for supper, call," her mother said from the dimness of the book-lined back porch where Annamarie could just see her, bent over to get meat out of the deep freeze for supper. Chicken; this was Monday. Her brother Dale had always loved Ma's barbecued chicken. Since he'd been blind he made such a mess with it that Ma always complained, but she fixed it once a week anyway.

"I'll be home for supper, Ma. The usual time."

"No plans with Parker tonight?"

"He and Troy might come over after supper."

Ma swung down the heavy lid of the deep freeze, harder than necessary. Annamarie knew she didn't like Parker and was afraid of Troy. White-wrapped package in one hand and a book in the other, Ma went back into the kitchen.

Annamarie checked her watch. She couldn't be late to work today; it was month-end. Ever since Pa had died, her salary supported the family, along with Dale's disability checks and the rent from the Miller boys who worked the farm. She hadn't missed a day of work or even been late since she'd gone back after Becky's funeral.

When she stepped off the stoop, barn cats scattered, but not very far, and only a few of them hissed or flattened their ears at her. There were more this morning than yesterday, more this year than last, and some little ones. She had never seen the litter, and now here they were, half grown.

As soon as she was out of their way, the cats would be back at their bowls, where the oatmeal she'd set out for them still steamed. Twelve servings of quick oats every winter morning, sometimes a pancake or French toast cut into cat-sized bites. She liked to think of the cats making their way through the frozen grasses to the one small white house by the one huge cottonwood where they knew there'd be oatmeal.

Over the car roof she looked again at the cottonwood. Beyond it was the faint gray irregularity that was Denver, one hundred miles due west, and then the thicker blue-purple streak of the Front Range. In Virginia everything had been so close that there had been no horizon.

Ma said there had been no high plains at all, no grasslands, no American desert until the Rocky Mountains had been uplifted. Rain had fallen wherever it chose, with nothing to stop it or give it

direction. Whenever Annamarie imagined all those swollen rain
clouds traveling unimpeded off the Pacific Ocean, imagined dino-
saurs and swamps and kudzu where the single cottonwood grew
instead, she was grateful.

She pulled out onto the road. Randy Miller was out fixing fence;
she tapped her horn and he waved without looking up.

At the Rauk place she turned toward town. Enid Rauk was standing at her gate, a very old woman, dry and brown and thin as dust.
Marcus wasn't with her; she looked different, standing on the
prairie by herself. The wrinkles of her face were so deep and
twisted that they obscured her features; the wrinkles had *become*
features, and you couldn't see mouth or nose or eyes. Ma said Enid
and Marcus both looked as if they were eating themselves because
there was nothing else to eat, drinking their own body fluids to
fight off the thirst. As long as Annamarie could remember, Ma had
been wondering aloud, almost savagely, why the couple didn't just
die and blow away and get it over with.

Annamarie waved, but Enid was gazing off over the fields, her
furrowed face lifted to the cold morning sun. She slowed down,
wondering what to do. Inside her, Becky woke up and came to
explain; Annamarie looked in her rearview mirror at the woman by
the gate and saw the beauty.

This road, too, was utterly straight, the edge and measurement
of a section of land, and she didn't have to think about driving it.
She didn't have to think about work yet, either; her ledgers were in
order, with everything she'd need the minute she sat down at her
desk.

So she thought about Becky, and the cottonwood, and the cats,
and, tentatively, Enid Rauk. These things made her happy. She
thought as much as she dared about Parker and Troy. She talked to
Becky a little and Becky answered, wordlessly, but without any
doubt as to her meaning. She sang a quiet, joyful lullaby, a love
song, not quite out loud.

Vivian Schilling heard her daughter's car pull out of the driveway, heard it all the way on the hard-dirt County Road 30 until it
turned toward town onto 31 at the Rauk place. It wasn't that she
particularly listened for it. Sounds traveled like bullets in this thin
clear air, like rocks with messages wrapped around them, whether
you wanted to receive them or not.

Her hand and wrist ached from holding the package of frozen chicken. She set it in the sink and curled the arm in close to her body. With her other hand she laid the poetry book on the counter, opened it at random, and read two quick Wallace Stevens poems that had no even lines in them and no messages like rocks. As usual, that made her feel a little better.

This chicken had scrabbled in the yard with its fellows last summer. Vivian, of course, had no way of knowing which particular chicken this one had been. There had been flocks of them in the barnyard every summer she'd lived here, and flocks of bigger, redder chickens around the house in the Appalachian hollow where she'd grown up.

She had fed this chicken, and she had killed it. She would cut it up, legs from breast from heart, and fix it for supper tonight. When they all ate it, the anonymous bird would, in a way, be alive again in each of them.

Or maybe, she thought perversely, it worked the other way. Maybe each of them would die a little because of the chicken's death, because a dead thing had nourished them. Maybe death instead of life was passed through the food chain from one species to another, or from one person to another and another through love.

She checked in the cupboards for tomato sauce, brown sugar, and vinegar and made a mental note to call Annamarie later and have her pick up a gallon of milk on the way home. By the time Dale had his breakfast and his afternoon cookies and milk, there wouldn't be enough for supper. Vivian hated running out of milk; everybody was so thirsty out here.

She also hated having to keep track of everything, being the only one who noticed. Dale couldn't, of course, and Jim had always been too drunk or too tired, up all night playing poker or laying irrigation pipe during the twenty-four hours he had the water from the ditch. Every once in a while Annamarie would say, "Never mind, Ma, I'll take care of it," but then she'd get the wrong kind of toilet paper or they'd run out of milk after all.

If Annamarie married Parker she'd have to keep track of a lot of things. That boy of his, that Troy, wasn't right. He'd take everything Annamarie had and more. She'd never get out of this place.

The big striped tomcat appeared at the window above the sink. Sometimes, when she first felt autumn in the air, Vivian would

imagine all those cats converging from the fields on her unpro-
tected house, and she'd close all the curtains, shut all the inside
and outside doors.

The tomcat settled itself into the window well, which was half
full of old dry snow, and stared implacably down at her. She tried
staring back; this was *her* house. But the animal didn't flinch, and
finally it was she who looked away.

She found herself then gazing out the front room window, between the floor-to-ceiling bookcases; individual titles were lost in
the morning glare, so that only the comforting impression of many
books remained. There were the mountains. There were always
the mountains. Clear, blue, deceptively beautiful. A hundred miles
away, and casting their rain shadow this far and farther. Rain
shadow: where rain destined for this place didn't fall because the
mountains blocked it. In Virginia, rain fell everywhere.

Even after all these years, even though she knew she stayed for
love and had no choice, a sudden glimpse of that view could make
her breath come short and her groin ache as if she were looking
straight down from the top of the tallest building in the world.
Some days she moved around the house with her head bowed and
her eyes slitted, trying not to see, wishing she'd been the one made
blind.

But the house was possessed by the rain shadow, haunted by it,
and she didn't need to see to know it was there. So some days she'd
stand at the windows for as long as she could before Dale needed
something or Annamarie came home or Becky called to her, staring at the mountains, a book in each hand for ballast.

Now she listened. The house around her was silent. Dale
wouldn't be up for a while yet and Becky for the moment was
keeping to herself. Vivian strode through the kitchen and the front
room and out the door.

The tiny rectangle of lawn between the house and the irrigation
ditch was brown now. In summer it would be startlingly green.
Vivian stood on it for a moment, hugging herself against the bright
cold wind, then cut across the road and clambered up the ditch
bank into the field, heading due west.

Enid Rauk was out walking too. Marcus wasn't with her; Vivian
didn't remember the last time she'd seen Enid without her husband, equally weak and withered, and the sight made her skin
crawl. The old woman looked like a dust devil between the flat

ground and the flat sky—insubstantial, but with energy and form. Vivian knew almost nothing about her, except that she'd been born almost a hundred years ago in the house she still lived in.

Enid didn't look up to see her, which was a relief. Vivian wondered savagely where the old woman could be heading on a blustery morning like this, stumbling and swaying. Then she realized that Enid wasn't heading anywhere; she was just moving across the land, holding her hands out to the wind and her face up to the sky. Maybe, Vivian thought, she was looking for Marcus.

Vivian turned away from the sight of the old woman and went on her way. She walked and walked, and never seemed to get any closer to the mountains. After a while she stopped, panting, and looked behind her. Her house was small and distant, the single cottonwood beside it like a stick. But when she turned back, the mountains were the same as always, a hundred miles away, and she was still trapped by their parching shadow.

The wind, out of the northwest, was colder out here. Clouds gathered over the mountains, thick and gray. It would storm by evening.

She hurried back toward home, shivering violently and stumbling over the hard furrows. Enid had disappeared. She could feel the mountains at her back. A white shadow flickered at the corner of her eye, and she heard a baby's cry. Without stopping, she shouted, "Dammit, Becky, what do you *want*?" But there was no answer.

Knowing she'd been gone too long, she hurried, fell to one knee going back across the ditch, had trouble getting up. A single bird flew by, very high in the utterly blue part of the sky; she could see sun on its gray-blue wings, hear its single-note cry.

Before she had the door open she heard Dale calling. She heard his panic, knew how she would find him: standing in the doorway of his room, holding onto the jamb with both hands, his face twisted and his eyes flat and glazed. "Ma!"

Instead, he was standing in the middle of the front room, hands out, slowly pivoting. She rushed to him, past Becky. "I'm here, honey. What are you doing?"

"I wanted a cup of tea. I thought I could get it."

"You could have gotten hurt. You could have gotten lost. You know not to try things like that without me."

"Where were you?"

Vivian didn't know how to tell him, so she took his hands one by
one and moved slowly backward, leading him toward his chair. For
a moment he resisted, stiffening his wrists, leaning rather than
taking any steps. Fury swept over her like a heavy wind. But then he
came where she led him, and she had to say only, "What would you
like for breakfast?"

"Good morning."
Annamarie jumped. She looked up from her spread sheets before answering, even though she knew who it was. Already her
hands were trembling with the nervousness she'd always felt whenever she had to speak to somebody who was not Ma or Dale or
Becky. Or, lately, Troy. "Good morning, Parker."
He came every morning to say good morning to her. It surprised
her that she liked that. He leaned against her file cabinet, coffee
cup in hand. He was going to say more. He would expect her to say
more, too. The two times they'd gone out for dinner, she'd had to
plan for days to have something to say. She dropped her gaze,
flattened her hands against the printouts to still their shaking.
"Did you have a nice weekend?" he asked.
"Yes," she said quickly. "Thank you." She swallowed. "And
you?"
He started to say something, then shook his head and came on
into her office. There was no chair in here other than her own; she
seldom had visitors. But he perched on the corner of her desk,
pushing her papers aside. "To tell you the truth, it was a lousy
weekend. I came back to work to recuperate."
She had work to do, but she couldn't be rude. "Why?" She
sounded abrupt and rude despite herself, and she blushed.
He sighed. He was wearing a soft yellow shirt and a gray tie with
yellow designs in it. Every day she looked to see what Parker was
wearing. "It's hard being a single parent," he said. "Especially to a
kid like Troy. Especially on weekends."
She didn't know what he meant, exactly, but she was afraid to
ask, so she just nodded.
He smiled sheepishly. "Sorry. I know people who don't have
kids get bored hearing about the trials and tribulations of parent-
hood."
Inside her, Becky turned. Ma was the only person she'd told
about Becky, and Ma had already known.

"There are times when I almost understand why my wife left."

"She *left*?" Annamarie was so shocked that she looked straight at Parker, saw how close he was to her, and hastily looked down again. Her mouth was dry.

"Said Troy was taking over her life." Parker took a sip of coffee and smiled again, sadly. "Most of the time I like taking care of him, but sometimes I feel there's nothing left for me."

Suddenly Annamarie spotted an error in the ENCUMBRANCES column. She reached for her red pen and heavily circled the number. Parker was sitting in her office, on her desk, among her papers. She wanted him to leave so she could trace the error, get her work done, do her job. She wanted to ask him about Troy, about what it was like to have a child who changed, a child you could hold. But she didn't dare.

Parker stood up. "Well," he said, "I'll let you get back to work." He drained his cup, then lifted it and raised his eyebrows at her. He wanted something, but she didn't know what. She looked away in acute embarrassment. "Where's your trash?" he asked.

Annamarie panicked. It was under her desk. She pushed her chair back and it banged into the wall. When she leaned over to reach the trash can, she saw that her skirt had pulled up above her knees. With one hand she tugged it down while she reached for Parker's cup with the other. "Here," she said sharply. "Just give it to me."

He leaned across the desk and handed her the cup. Drops of cold coffee dribbled across her wrist. She braced herself for his fingers to brush hers, but he didn't touch her. "Thanks," he said, smiling directly at her. "Nice talking to you," he added on his way out.

All day, although they weren't together, mother and daughter watched the storm clouds moving in. All day, although they were watching the same storm, what they saw was not the same, and what they said about it—to themselves, to each other, and to Becky —was not the same at all.

From her second-story office window, Annamarie could see the distinct straight line between gray sky and blue sky. By midmorning, the thick gray—which she understood came here from the Western Slope and, before that, from the Pacific Ocean—blurred the purple of the mountains. By lunchtime, more than half the sky was filled in.

Parker stuck his head in while she was eating her lunch. "Storm's coming," he observed.

She managed to smile and nod, although he'd made her spill tomato juice down the front of her blouse and she was embarrassed to wipe it off while he was there.

"I need a favor," Parker said.

Her heart was pounding with terror: of having to talk to him, of his leaving before they were finished talking. Inside her, Becky cooed and stretched soothingly. "OK," she said. Her voice cracked, and she cleared her throat.

"I took my car to the shop this morning and they said it would be done by noon, but now they're saying it'll be tomorrow. Could you give me a ride home?"

She took a deep breath. "Sure."

"The complication is, I have to pick up Troy. But that's pretty much on the way."

"Sure," she said again, and added, "No problem," grateful to Becky for telling her what to say.

"Troy loves snow," he told her, and his voice was so tender that she was able to keep her eyes on his face and to smile back.

Clouds massed. Something was about to happen. She wished, suddenly, that Parker could meet Becky. She didn't know whether that was possible or not.

Vivian couldn't escape the approaching storm. Like so many Coloradans, native or transplanted, whoever had built this house had prized the mountain view. From every one of the windows with a westerly or southwesterly or northwesterly view, she saw the cloudbank closing in, and she knew that if she closed the drapes it would be worse, because then she'd *feel* it coming, hear the change in the sounds moving through the thickening air, smell the cold electricity.

"Ma, there's a storm coming," Dale said half a dozen times that day. "Ma, something's going to *happen*." As if she didn't know.

She allowed herself to frown at his foolishness, since he couldn't see her anyway. She said only, "I know," and went on with whatever she was doing for him.

Much of her day was taken up doing things for Dale. Washing his face after lunch. Reading to him. Leading him from his chair to the bathroom and back again, past all those windows with the westerly view.

"Dammit, Vivian, you ain't doin' that boy no favors!"

But that was just a memory of her husband talking. He had no substance. When he'd died, he'd gone away altogether. She didn't know why some people did that and others, like Becky, stayed around. She couldn't imagine that Jim had any more reason than Becky to rest in peace, but most of the time she was glad he did.

"He's just blind, for Chrissake, he ain't a vegetable!"

She didn't have to listen to him. He was dead and gone. After all the years she'd taken care of him—dragged him home and into bed; cleaned up after him, vomit and broken bottles and hurtful words; done the field work herself or with the kids when he was too drunk to sit on a tractor; brought him chocolate cake and milk in the middle of the night when he was out changing tubes, the pickup headlights on his hands and on the streaming water—after all that, he'd died. Just like that. Left her altogether. After she'd stayed with him for love. After he and the kids and the land had kept her from getting what she needed.

"It didn't snow in Florida," Dale said.

It was twenty years since he'd been away at that college for the blind in Florida, half his life and a third of hers, yet he talked about it as if he'd just now come home. She'd missed him. She'd worried about him; the teachers had tried to convince him that he could learn to live on his own. She'd made sure to fix barbecued chicken for his homecoming meal. He'd been going to stay at home just till he could find a job in computers: here, in this tiny, dry, backward prairie town. Vivian had told him he'd never leave again.

"It rained, though," he said. "There were hurricanes. You could feel them coming in off the ocean."

"Well, that's certainly a useful skill," Vivian said testily, scanning yesterday's paper for items that might be of interest to him. Annamarie would bring today's paper when she came home tonight. That was soon enough for Dale. Day-old news bothered Vivian, but there was no point in complaining about it.

"I'll bet you could see them, too," Dale said.

Vivian read him a story about the growing drug problem at the high school, and over the edge of the newspaper she couldn't help seeing the gray and darker gray fill in. All those clouds made the sky thicker, deeper, more enormous. She was not part of this or any other aspect of the landscape. She was swallowed up by it, erased.

In the Appalachian hollows, rain or snow gave little warning; sometimes leaves would twist to show their undersides just before a storm blew in, but little else. Here on the vast high plains, you couldn't help seeing what was going to happen long before it did, and the tension was a dark gray ghost.

Becky rested on her grandmother's shoulder like a snowflake. She rustled the newspaper, passed cold feathery baby's fingers over Vivian's eyes, made it hard for her to read. Vivian didn't know what the dead child wanted from her, why she couldn't rest easy in her grave. Becky was like the pale skin of ice on the cats' water bowls on a cold dawn, like the pale skin of dust on the westerly windows the day after Vivian had washed them.

Vivian was used to hauntings. In the damp, green, crowded hollow where she'd grown up, ghosts had been as profuse and commonplace as any other growing thing. Bits and pieces of spirits had fogged the leaves, rippled the creeks, fallen with the rain. Bodiless footsteps had creaked the floorboards and tree limbs at night, often waking Vivian sometimes but never scaring her. Wordless voices had yammered and cooed, but they hadn't been demanding anything from anybody, hadn't meant to call attention to themselves. They had come easily, and there had been enough for all of them and her, too.

Out here, nothing came easily; sustenance was eked and wrested and hoarded. That, of course, was why Becky had died before she'd been born: there was only so much life this place could sustain, and Becky would have been too much life.

A long time ago, trying to understand this land where she had apparently chosen to live, Vivian had read about the rain shadow. The North American rain shadow exists because the mountains happened to uplift north–south, while the dominant direction of air circulation worldwide is west–east; in central Europe, where the major mountain ranges run east–west, there are no deserts, no high dry plains.

Luck, then. The lay of the land.

At home, Vivian hadn't been afraid of ghosts. They took nothing from her. Here, in the rain shadow, in the path of the oncoming storm, she was afraid of Becky, and Becky wouldn't leave her alone.

She turned to the back page of the paper. Marcus Rauk had died yesterday. She should have known.

By midafternoon, it was snowing hard. The sky had become solid gray-white, and the hard rutted fields were rapidly turning the same flat color. Here and there was a lone cottonwood, very black and particular, or a row of telephone poles like a seam, each stitch turning white on one side. Ground blizzards obscured roads, ditches, fencerows. Drifts mounted. Vivian couldn't see the mountains now, but she could always feel them.

Dale complained that the house was chilly. She brought him a sweatshirt and a blanket, helped him put them on, turned the heat up. She saw no sign of the cats. Their bowls were filling up with snow.

Hugging herself and swearing under her breath, Vivian rushed outside to retrieve the bowls. With the first few steps her slippers got wet and her bare ankles numb. By the time she'd brought the bowls inside, her hair and the shoulders of her blue sweater were white, and she was furious. It was Annamarie's fault the cats hung around, but of course Annamarie wasn't here to take care of them.

Vivian's wet slippers and sweater didn't make a full load so she couldn't run the dryer. She left them in a soggy bundle on the counter and made do with her robe and socks.

Irritably, she reflected that, no matter how much snow fell, most of it would blow uselessly away. Both the ground and the snow itself were too dry for it to make any difference. Gradually the mountains were wearing down, but she'd be dead long before they were gone, and so would Annamarie.

All afternoon Dale kept wanting water. No matter where she was in the house or what she was doing, she'd hear him. "Ma? Could I have another drink?" It made her thirsty too, and she stole a sip from every glass she took to him.

When it was your lot to take care of somebody, you did it, she said silently to Jim, even though she knew he couldn't hear her and wouldn't care if he could. You did your duty. Endlessly, if need be. Even if you yourself died of thirst, or adapted into something you didn't recognize, or turned the colorless color of winter wheat and dust, the powdery white of Colorado snow endlessly blowing away.

She'd lived in the shadow of the people she loved, and there had been little left for her. She'd had no choice. It was the lay of this land she'd stumbled onto. But Annamarie had a choice. She didn't have to give up her life for Becky. Becky had died before she'd ever been born.

When she said these things silently to Jim, it was Becky who answered, but Vivian didn't understand what she said.

The office closed an hour early. There was an air of excitement and camaraderie; people seemed almost reluctant to leave, although everyone spoke anxiously of getting home before the storm got worse.

The shy affection Annamarie felt for her co-workers made her fingers clumsy when she pulled on her boots, kept her in her office while the rest of them gathered in the lobby. She tried to frame in her mind things she could say if she were out there with them, but everything she thought of sounded silly, until Becky woke up and told her it was OK. Then, shyly, she shut her office door and went out to join the others.

She had worked with most of these people for years. Only Parker was new, and already she knew more about him than about any of the others. He was divorced. He had Troy, who was ten and couldn't see or hear or speak much but who smiled when you touched his cheek. He wore shirts the color of spring flowers, pale yellow and pale pink and lavender.

"They're saying we could get thirteen, fourteen inches out of this one."

"We can sure use it. Crops are real dry."

"Not much moisture in a winter snow, though. Won't help much. Not like a good wet spring storm."

"Remember the spring snowstorm in '83? Or was it '82?"

"It was '83," Annamarie said, and everybody nodded.

None of them knew anything about Becky, that she'd ever lived, that she'd ever died. Mel, who might have guessed, had moved to Sterling with his wife and family before Annamarie had even known for sure that she was pregnant. She blushed to think about Mel. He'd written her one letter—chatty, apologetic—which she hadn't answered because she hadn't known what to say, what he might be interested in. Now he was less real to her than Becky, much less real than Parker and Troy.

The abrupt, recurrent realization that no one here knew about Becky made Annamarie acutely lonely. She could hardly wait to get home. She'd bundle up and go play outside; everything would be blue and white and cold, the sky barely distinguishable from the ground because, really, there was little difference. The mountains would be hidden, but the mountains were the cause of all this. You could make wonderful angels in this light dry snow. They filled in while you were still lying there, and then you made more.

Annamarie found herself thinking, Maybe Troy likes playing in the snow. Guiltily, she tried to dismiss the thought. *I don't want any kids but you, Becky,* she said in her mind. *I'm glad you're my daughter.* But thoughts of Troy didn't go away, and, from the secret place inside her where she lived, Becky didn't seem to mind.

Annamarie could hardly wait to get home, but she had to stop for milk first and she'd promised Parker a ride. Here he was, in fact, coat and hat and gloves on before she was even ready to leave, looking worried.

"I feel awful about this, Annamarie. I'd never have taken the car in today if I'd known we were going to have a blizzard."

Fumbling, she looked down at the buttons instead of at him. But she managed to say, with Becky's help, "Colorado weather. You never know."

Saying all that to him took her breath away. She thought suddenly about the plants on her windowsill and hurried to check them, pulling off one glove and sticking her index finger up to the first knuckle into the soil of each one. The dirt that built up under her nail was a small pleasure, evidence that in taking care of living things she became part of them, that in letting her take care of them they became part of her.

She watered each plant thoroughly from the yellow plastic watering can she always kept full under her desk, not caring if they dripped. Now they'd be okay if the office had to stay closed for a day or two.

"It's getting *cold*," Parker said. "That's a nasty wind."

"Nothing to stop it from the Rockies to the Appalachians," she said.

"I heard on the radio that parts of the interstate between here and Denver are already closed."

With hard water, you were supposed to let it sit for several days before you used it. She didn't understand exactly what was supposed to escape into the air, but she liked the notion of something existing in different forms but still being the same thing—ice, water, snow, rain, water vapor, chemicals in the water and then into the air.

Parker was waiting, Troy was waiting, Ma was waiting for the milk, Becky was moving eagerly. Annamarie set the empty can on her desk without refilling it, checked in her purse for keys and hat, and walked out through the lobby with Parker into the storm.

After all, there had been a funeral.

Vivian hadn't seen the need. This had been a miscarriage, so early that Annamarie had hardly been showing, and the doctor had kept calling it a fetus, not a baby. He'd said there was something wrong with it, probably a lot of things, and there hadn't even been a body for burying. But Annamarie had insisted, and she'd insisted on so few things in her life that Vivian had gone along.

It had been a hot, dusty August morning, with the constant late-summer threat of hail making the cornstalks rustle from across the ditch. The Miller boys had kept driving past, looking curiously over their shoulders. Enid Rauk had drifted by, but she hadn't looked. Vivian and Dale and Annamarie had gathered around the cottonwood, where they'd all—even Dale—stared at a spot on the hard ground where there was no grave. Nobody'd said any words. Annamarie had cried.

Restlessly, surreptitiously, Vivian had taken a step backward into full sunlight, then a step forward into shade again. Still testing, still unbelieving, still a stranger though she'd lived here forty years. In this thin, dry air there was a sharp line between sunlight and shadow, a temperature difference so explicit that she could have told with her eyes shut which she was in. Back east, the moisture in the air blurred such hard, sharp lines, and things changed gradually. Out here, a thing was either, abruptly, in one form or in another.

Annamarie had cried and cried. Vivian had cried too, in sorrow for her daughter and in relief. Dale had fidgeted, had sung a hymn in his low dry voice. Then they'd all gone back inside the cool house.

Annamarie had grieved for a long time, and Vivian had lost patience. The miscarriage had been for the best. Raising a child alone, especially a child who would have been *not right,* would have ruined Annamarie's life. She'd have been trapped in the rain shadow the way Vivian had been trapped. The child would have taken everything from her, would have dried her out. Now, she had a chance again to escape.

But she refused to take it. Instead, she'd named the fetus for her grandmother, Rebecca, nourished it with things she'd needed for herself, and made it grow into a baby. The spirit of a baby, a form without a body and a voice without words. And as Becky flourished, so did Annamarie. Vivian saw it happening and didn't understand. Any more than she understood why things grew out here at all: buffalo grass and Indian paintbrush, brown-eyed Susan and yucca and apache plume, the lone cottonwood with its brittle cool shade.

Any more than she understood what Becky wanted from her, why the child couldn't rest easy. After all, there had been a funeral, and Annamarie spoiled her, gave her everything she wanted.

And now Annamarie was getting herself involved with that man Parker, and with that child of his Vivian had never met, the little boy who couldn't see or hear, who needed so much, who would take so much. It was slow; Annamarie had always been shy. But the more time she spent with Parker and Troy, the less shy she was, the more full of life, the happier. Vivian saw it happening, and couldn't deny it, and didn't understand.

"Ma!"

Dale was calling from his room. Vivian turned away from the snow-filled window and realized that his tape must have ended. She hurried to turn it over. His room was dark, of course, and she stumbled over his shoes.

He was fumbling with the tape recorder. She pushed his hands away. "Where were you?" he demanded. Coming out of the dark like that, his voice sounded just like his father's. "I needed you."

"I was just watching the snow."

"I called and called."

"I have more important things to do than wait on you all day," Vivian told him testily, but she knew it wasn't true.

There was no sky. There was no ground. There were no roads marking the edges of anything, no fields or fences or buildings or trees. There was only snow.

Snow twisted like white yarn around and around the car. The car swayed. Snow sucked at the wheels, half swallowed them, stopped them from turning. Snow sheeted all the windows so that nobody could see out or in, drifted up past the headlights and taillights to cup their red and yellow glow and throw it back.

"We can't go any farther." The engine noise had been so muffled by the snow that when Annamarie switched off the ignition there wasn't much change in the sound. She reversed the key half a turn so the radio and heater would stay on. "I can't see the road."

"Do you want me to drive?"

She laughed a little. "You can't see the road either. Anyway, they've probably got it closed all the way from Denver to Limon by now."

Both of them reached to turn up the radio. Their hands collided, caressed. Parker took his hand away, but not with any particular haste or determination. It pleased and surprised her to notice such a thing; it also made her terribly nervous. With Mel, she hadn't noticed a thing until it was too late.

She fiddled with the tuner, turned the volume up and down. Ghostly bits of voices mewled and murmured under the blanket of static, but she couldn't make out any words. She turned the radio off. There was a rush of quiet.

There was only snow, up and down and to all sides, a deep shadow of snow that absorbed everything. Snow blurred the sturdy white farmhouse into the rest of the vast white landscape.

Vivian was being blended, too. She felt it, fought it. She and Dale and Becky would be absorbed by the blizzard, and only Annamarie, somehow, would keep her own form.

She sat in the hushed, lamplit living room and read to Dale from the new *Sports Illustrated*. Boredom buzzed in her mind like static. He could get the magazine on tape, but she didn't feel right making him listen to it alone. Snow fell and rose outside, making long layers. Becky floated around the house like snow herself, cold and white and bone dry. She wanted something. Vivian didn't know what she wanted.

Vivian glanced at the clock again. Annamarie would be home soon. The storm would slow her down some, and she had to stop for milk, but she'd be home for supper.

"We can't just sit here and wait, can we?" Parker demanded. "I mean, you hear about people freezing to death like this."

"Usually those are people who got out of their cars and tried to walk. The State Patrol will be out, and we're on a main road. They'll get to us."

What she said was true, but he was also right, of course. People did die like this, froze to death on the prairie or died of its dry heat. That had been happening for centuries, millennia; death as long as there had been life.

It wasn't that distinctions blurred. It was that, in this bright clear air, things showed themselves to be exactly what they were, and that was many things.

Annamarie had no particular wish to die, now or ever. She had no particular determination to live. There was, after all, only snow, and the four of them wrapped up together in this stuck car:

Annamarie herself. Not the same person she'd been five years ago. Not the same person she'd been this morning. Not the same person she would be tomorrow, when the blizzard was over and she was alive or dead. It was warm in here; she took off her hat and scarf. The cool gallon of milk for supper leaned heavily against her ankle.

Becky, warm and safe inside her mother where she belonged. Waiting for something important to happen. Pushing with her tiny hands and feet against the very insides of Annamarie's body: opening her up, keeping her open.

Parker. Again and again he leaned forward to clear a patch of steam from the window with the heel of his hand and the cuff of his pale yellow shirt.

Troy, asleep under a plaid blanket on the back seat. Only his dark hair and the red soles of his rubber boots showed. He's a beautiful little boy, Annamarie thought. I could love him. She braced herself for Becky's protest, but none came.

There was only snow, and the four of them, and the mountains. Annamarie could clearly feel the mountains: a western edge. She was steadied and stirred by her knowledge, virtually instinctual by now, of where the mountains were, of how they were different from the plains.

Parker cleared another spot on the window and hastily peered through it before it fogged up again. "This is unbelievable."

"We get a couple of big ones like this every winter," she told him. "Eight-, ten-foot drifts, whiteouts, temperatures way below zero. But by next week you'll hardly know it snowed."

It amazed her to be chatting so easily with him. Becky showed her how, gave her courage, gave her voice. Knowing that Becky lived inside her steadied and oriented her like knowing where the mountains were without having to think about it.

"You know what they say," she added cheerfully. "If you don't like the weather in Colorado, wait five minutes."

Parker chuckled. She had made him laugh. Pleasure suffused her. She slid her hands inside her heavy coat and laid them flat on her stomach in gratitude.

It was still snowing, but more lightly now. Vivian couldn't help but see individual flakes and clusters of flakes against the deep blue sky. The fallen snow—sheets of it, drifts, dry waves—had a luster; though she herself could see no moon or stars, there must be some infinitesimal light that the snow could catch and use.

Annamarie was over an hour late. If she didn't get home soon, Vivian would have to go ahead and fix supper for Dale, milk or no milk.

Worry for her daughter buzzed in the back of her mind. It was not unlike the worry she always felt for her, and always would feel as long as Annamarie lived in this place. The fear that she would be suffocated by head-high snow with no moisture in it, that she would freeze to death on a windswept plain, that in the dry air of the rain shadow she wouldn't ever become part of anything greater but would stay herself, dry and brittle and lonely, forever.

Wind shook the house, rattled the window. Vivian clutched the sill.

She could hardly tell where County Road 30 was in front of her house. It had all filled in, and the ditch banks, and the furrows in the fields. More features erased, when there hadn't been many in the first place. Probably Annamarie was just waiting out the storm someplace, although you'd think she would have called. Probably the phone lines were down.

The thought crossed her mind that Annamarie might have escaped. Maybe she'd driven off just ahead of the blizzard and was at this moment pacing it eastward. Vivian had looked at an ecology map; you didn't really get out of the rain shadow much before Iowa. Maybe Annamarie was on her way to Iowa. Maybe she'd never come home again. Vivian would miss her. But she'd know that her own life had been worthwhile if one of her children managed to break free.

"Ma," Dale said behind her.

"In a minute," she told him.

"Go to college," she'd urged her daughter, again and again. "You'll never get anywhere without a degree. A woman, especially."

Usually Annamarie had just smiled or frowned or shrugged, hadn't said anything. Recently, though, she'd retorted, "Dale went away to college and what good did it do him? He just came back here anyway."

"Dale's *blind*."

"I don't want to go to college. There's nothing I need to learn that I can't learn right here."

"But there's nothing to learn here! This place is arid!"

"*Semi*arid," Annamarie had corrected with a smile. "Things grow here."

"I don't know why they bother."

"Becky grows here."

"Annamarie, stop it. Becky is dead. She was never born."

"Well, she grows. And so do I, because of her."

"If you don't stop this, she'll take everything from you. She'll take all the nourishment you need and leave you with nothing. Just like the mountains. If the mountains had never been formed, this place would be a lot different."

"Different, maybe, but not better."

"There'd be rain."

"Why don't *you* go to college, Ma? Or move back east, where it rains?"

Her daughter's simplistic way of seeing the world infuriated Vivian. "Don't you think I'd do that if I could? I've got Dale to take care of."

"You've got your own life, too."

"No, I don't!"

"Dale could take care of himself if you'd let him. They taught him how at that college. Lots of blind people—"

"Dale is my son."

"Well," Annamarie had said reasonably, "I could stay with him. I'm not going anywhere."

"That's ridiculous. Your life is still ahead of you. Mine is gone. Given away."

"Well, take it back, Ma. I have."

Vivian had supposed she meant Parker, but he was just more of the same. He and his son with the empty eyes, the sucking mouth, the clawing hands.

"Ma," Dale said. "I thought I'd go shovel the walk."

Panic seized her. "Don't be silly. It's still snowing."

"The snow's letting up."

"It's dark out there."

He chuckled. "It doesn't matter to me if it's dark."

"Well, it matters to me. You stay inside with me."

She felt the presence of Becky on the back of her neck and reached up to brush her away. The coldness and dryness of her, all the unnamed things she needed.

"What do you want?" she whispered. Her breath appeared for a split second on the windowpane, but Becky wouldn't tell her the answer.

Annamarie's watch had stopped, and Parker didn't wear one. They dared turn the radio on only once in a great while, for fear of running out of gas. The diffuse light reflecting between the sun and the snow didn't seem to change at all from one hour to the next, and there were long periods of time when Annamarie wasn't sure where she was, except that she was with people she loved in the shadow of the Rocky Mountains.

She shifted her weight against Parker and stretched her legs. Lying across both their laps, Troy stirred and whimpered. She didn't know the exact moment when they'd started huddling together, when Troy had let her hold him as easily as his dad, when she and Parker had first kissed. By now it seemed as though they'd been together a long time already and would be together a long time more.

Every few minutes, she'd check on Becky, and the baby was there at the center of her, lively and demanding as always but different somehow, changing. Annamarie wondered if Becky could feel cold, or fear, or loss, and realized she knew almost nothing about her. She wondered if Parker knew Becky was there. As her mind cleared again, she doubted it.

But Troy did, she was sure. He looked up at her with his brown eyes that didn't focus, and he said, "I love you," which was one of the few things he could say, and she knew it was Becky he was looking at and talking to, Becky who made him smile.

"He's a beautiful little boy," she said again to Parker.

"Yes, he is," he agreed again.

"My mother thinks having a child like Troy traps you."

"A lot of people think that. Troy's mother thought that."

"She says there isn't enough of anything to go around, and other people can take what belongs to you."

"Troy gives more than he takes," Parker said. "Because of him, there's more to go around."

Becky was still there, but so small and deep inside her that Annamarie could hardly find her. Something was happening.

"It seems to be letting up," Parker said, clearing another spot on the side window. "I can see individual flakes instead of just sheets."

Annamarie leaned forward and Troy squirmed. She laid her hand on his cheek and he calmed. High headlights were materializing out of the scattered white. "It's the State Patrol," she said.

Though she was looking the other way, she felt Parker turn to her the way she felt the presence of the mountains. She met his gaze—and scattered bits of white like ghosts, which all her life had threatened to fill her field of vision, suddenly came into focus, showed themselves to have always been in a pattern and a form. "Marry me," he said. "Will you marry me?"

She had taken her hands away from Troy to peer through the windows at the rescuers, who were pulling up beside them now in their hulking yellow four-wheel-drive. Troy said, "Mama," took her hand in both of his, and brought it back to his face.

Doors closed dully, and men in padded suits slogged through the snow toward them, shouting muffled words. "Yes," she said quickly to Parker, and he kissed her quickly, and then there was a wrenching pain and a soaring sense of freedom as Becky worked herself free and scattered toward the mountains.

Vivian had fallen asleep in her chair. When she woke up— groggy, her head fuzzy and her tongue coated as if with dust or snow—Becky was sitting on her lap.

The child had no weight, of course, and when Vivian put her hands up they passed right through her. Yet she was insistent, tugging at Vivian's hands and hair, making a seamless sound like the sighing of the wind or the rustling of the wheat or the drone of a tractor so far toward the horizon that it became bodiless and unattached and took on a meaning of its own.

She didn't know where Dale was. She didn't know where Annamarie was. She sat up straight, heart pounding, and—fearfully, because she couldn't help it—looked out one of the windows facing west. She could see the mountains, dark on the far white horizon, and she could see that the snow had stopped.

Becky keened and chortled, plucked at her cheeks. The book she'd been reading about rain forests slid to the floor. She heard a dull, rhythmic scraping from outside, and headlights swept across the windows as a car pulled into the driveway.

Vivian got up and walked to the kitchen, with Becky pulling at her robe. The dark narrow room smelled of barbecued chicken and of sacrifice. The striped tom sat in the window well again, its back to her.

Dale had shoveled almost the entire driveway. She watched him working, strong and capable, flinging snow into the blue night air, packing it so that it wouldn't fill in the path he'd made. She watched Annamarie get out of the car, carrying the sleeping Troy in a green plaid blanket, Parker beside her with his arm around her shoulders.

She saw Enid Rauk stop and talk with them, a tiny figure so bundled up you could hardly see her face. She shouldn't be out in this weather, Vivian thought, but as the old woman went on her way it was clear she was where she belonged.

She saw Becky leave the house, a dry white cloud. Then the child dissolved into the prairie, absorbed into the rain shadow, used for all she was worth, and Vivian knew she herself could leave, too, when the time was right; she could find her own place; she didn't have to stay here anymore.

She turned on the light and went to make hot chocolate.

History
of the Branded Heart

Jo-Ann Mapson

Jo-Ann Mapson is a fourth-generation native Californian. Her short fiction and poetry have appeared in numerous small journals, including *Suisun Valley Review, California State Poetry Quarterly, Lunar Retorno, Gambit, Nob Hill Gazette,* and *The Elephant-ear.* In 1986, "The Red Nighties Network" placed first in the California Short Story Competition sponsored by the Squaw Valley Community of Writers and the *Nob Hill Gazette.* Her first collection of short stories was published this past November by Pacific Writers Press. A third-generation horsewoman, she teaches horsemanship as therapy to juvenile offenders. This story was a Christmas gift to her husband, artist/illustrator Stewart Allison. They have one son and live in Costa Mesa, California.

This was one of the first contemporary stories for the anthology, and I knew from the first paragraph that I wanted to buy it. Other stories of these two characters recur in Jo-Ann's collection, and she's currently compiling a novel about how these two characters met.

All my life I've been told my sins are countless and will send me to hell. So I'm going for broke. I wait until Hank's asleep before I go through his wallet. Standing here in the bedroom naked, using the moon as a flashlight, I'm no better than a prostitute hunting for a little something extra. But I do it anyway. I have to know.

Two tens, four ones. A parking permit from the college where he teaches. Every day he sets it on the dashboard of his Austin-Healey so it won't mar the chrome of his bumper. He is an untenured

professor of folklore and mythology, a Ph.D. The closest I've come
to finishing college is lying here in the crook of his arm. But I'm
not stupid. Even before my fingers close on the tissue-thin doctor's
receipt, I have suspected.

Hank's heartbeat, until tonight, has always been like a medium
trot on a well-seasoned horse—those measured beats as important
as the spaces. But tonight when I listened, offhandedly at first, then
closer, as if I were hearing gossip about myself, there were lapses.
It skidded into a rushing gait, all wrong, before it settled.

"What's this?" I asked, my finger on his nipple like I was taking
his pulse.

"Just PVCs," he told me. "What I get for drinking American
beer."

"Did you see a doctor?"

"It's nothing. My heart just hammers every once in a while."

"Just hammers."

"Tap, tap. Like a rubber mallet. Reflexes."

Is it because he keeps getting turned down for tenure? Or because I make him dance the two-step when he really doesn't want
to? Could be either. All those weekend cowboys at C.C.'s Yellow
Rose and my Hank. The crowd's breathy hum-along to "Hearts on
the Borderline" while he missteps, whispering in my ear that I
should go back to college. Finish something. Different path down
the same old trail. To tempt me, as if it's his classes I would be
taking, he tells me the story of Bellerophon, the Corinthian prince
who tamed Pegasus. Folklore I, opening lecture; I've seen the
course syllabus.

"Oh, neat," I said, though putting wings on horses in my opin-
ion is overkill.

"Not entirely," he answered. "It wasn't enough that he killed the
Chimera and danced with Amazons. He got ideas about moving to
Mount Olympus."

"You make it sound like a singles complex."

He laughs. "It kind of was."

"So? Don't leave me hanging. Did he get in or not?"

"Nah. Zeus got rankled that he didn't think of it first. So he sent
a mega-horsefly to bite Pegasus and he bucked our ambitious
prince to earth. Boom. Blind and crippled. Don't you hate it when
that happens?"

Translated means: You scare me going over those fences, Chloe.

Sit right here with a book where we can be mortal together, grounded in a safer love. Oh, yes. I probably should go back to school. This inside scoop of professors' minds is going to waste. The receipt says echocardiogram. So Hank's got his own fears. But he hasn't shared them with me. He dances along, his feet not quite in rhythm with mine, grinning, as if I have no right to ask. And I guess I don't. I'm not his wife. Not even his next of kin. I'm just here stealing the blankets in his bed. Like I have been for the last eight years, waiting to go to hell.

In preparation for the Calcutta on Sunday, when the weekend cowboys will race the clock to pen three bewildered cows, the Southern Sierra Land and Cattle Company is unloading a fresh herd. I watch, sitting on an upturned Carnation bucket near the pipe corrals, smoking a Kent 100, and biting a perpetual hangnail.

Chester, manager of the stables where I board, a so-so team penner himself, oversees the animals' passage down the ramp of the truck and urges them through the chute. His black skin is covered with a film of dust, making him look a bit like a ginger-bread cookie. He barks in rapid Spanish to a lazy groom, then snaps a whip at a confused steer. He tips his hat to me, and a brief smile flashes across his face. This is as close as we come to communicating—unless I count the smudgy fingerprints on my board checks for Absalom, my horse. I stub the cigarette out on the heel of my boot.

A pain nags down my left arm that ends in the tip of my ring finger, where I wear the diamond ring Hank gave me a year ago. Suffer through an attack of the guilts. I deserve it. I look at the marquise cut, the antique platinum setting. It slips to the left, just a little too big for my finger, like Hank thought I might grow into it. Or possibly that I expected on one of my gloveless dips into the grain bucket it might fall off.

Absalom, my twenty-one-year-old Thoroughbred gelding, is tied to the hitching rail, waiting. He is lame. Tennis-ball-sized swellings mar the inside of his hocks like somebody's been feeding the mosquitoes vitamins. The vet says things like, "You could try Numatizine," and before that it was Bigel oil, Absorbine wraps, and one useless attempt at corrective shoeing. What he hasn't said is that it's time to think about retiring Absalom, that twenty-one years is a pretty fair workout, purebred or not. In England, the

Queen's horses are put down at retirement; I saw this on television, finally something on PBS both Hank and I could appreciate, though for different reasons. An old groom with pasty, well-fed cheeks stood in front of this empty pasture, explaining that once the horses have served the gentry, it would be cruel to turn them over to peasants. "Now that makes sense," I said out loud, as if the guy could hear me across an ocean, through each snippet of videotape. "So be good enough to hand over your scones and blackberry jam and suck on this gun barrel."

Hank laughed; I always make him laugh. He pulled me closer and said, "Chloe, you kill me," and proposed. I declined to answer, even though it encourages him. Hank likes it that I say no. He asks me to lunch and tells me that six pomegranate seeds alone convicted Persephone, just as I'm on my last mouthful. There'll be an earthquake, just a little rattle, and he'll remind me that the gods send them when they're displeased with mortal behavior. Or I'll step from the shower and he'll clutch me, imprinting my body on his good clothes, as if reclaiming the territory only works when I'm naked, damp, and vulnerable—and a little pissed off. It's the same old story, like watching the six o'clock news. In five thousand years nothing's changed; all that violence and despair only reinforces the old myths.

Absalom has a small outline of a heart freeze-branded on his left shoulder. He is a Stout Valentine horse, broken and trained, branded like an expensive sports car's trademark. His brand leans to left, evidence of a small resistance. The frozen hair has turned white permanently, like premature gray. Otherwise, he is a dark bay with three ermine spots on the pastern of his back left leg. He knows three tricks. He will lift his upper lip, asking for carrots, but I call it smiling. When I tickle his elbow, he "counts," scraping his right hoof in the dirt.

I'm fooling myself, thinking he'll miss our daily workout. Warm-up walk, fifteen minutes at the trot, six laps transition canter, reverse, cool-down walk. It's not expecting the off days to get better. Or even imagining winning in the ribbons again. There are a million horses in California, and for the money any one of them can be mine. What is troubling is the rubber-band rhythm of my life, stretched and deteriorating, echoed by that wet knocking in my ear at Hank's chest. It drives at me to make a decision, any decision, when I've successfully managed thirty years avoiding them.

At first I thought it was a joke, because I believed those things my foster parents told me. "No one will want to marry a girl who talks like that, Chloe. Look at you. For Christ's sake, what kind of man wants a girl whose legs are permanently bowed from strad-dling a horse? I'll tell you what kind. Only one kind. Now sit with your knees together!" Like there was a little Velcro closure in between them, or saying "Go to hell" would backfire on me.

Yet, years past that shuffling, I'm like Hank's arteries—calcified with butter, eggs, those cheese omelets I make him instead of a real dinner. Working toward the WE'RE CLOSED sign in the window forever.

Absalom turns. His eyes look like buttons, a stuffed animal's blank stare. But I know how the pupil dilates, that he can see 340 degrees without turning. That in his turning is also his trust. Be-cause the person I've loved and trusted most in my life is not a person at all but this horse, who doesn't love me back beyond the last armful of hay I've dropped in his stall because he isn't capable. My arm stops hurting; everything stops and is replaced by a numb-ness, like a groom just took the apple picker and mucked out my soul, leaving a clean, empty stall.

Chester whistles, and the dirt is turned up by the hooves of fifty or sixty head of cattle, crowding into the arena. The longhorns shuffle by, a shoulder-bouncing strut of pride. Calves bleat for their mothers, and I'll be damned if Chester hasn't gone and found a buffalo. He blends with the herd but remains separate, as if his history demands it. I recognize the blunt muzzles of Mustangs, three dun-colored mares Chester will probably turn into cutting horses. They keep to the center of the ring, herded together, as if the fence's shiny perimeter is too frightening, spooking a breed of gray cows I can't place.

"Chester! Those gray cows. What kind?"

"Them's Brahman."

"Where'd you get them?"

"Corte Madera. Way up north where they still got real land for pasture. We're trading them ours 'cause these damn cows's getting too smart. You go to herd them and they just run in the pen. That ain't no fun."

"What about the buffalo? You plan on herding him too?"

He smiles. His gold-capped front tooth shimmers like a wedding band. *"Her.* I'm gonna break records penning that mama."

"Right."

"Hey. I'm fifty-six years old and tired of losing. Want a goddam silver belt buckle to hold up my pants. Unless you want to hold them up for me, sweet thing."

"Rain check, Chester."

At third-level dressage, his mouth securely on the bit, Absalom held his own, from shoulders-in at the *travers* where I asked him to move sideways and forward at the same time. We cut this ring to pieces, zigzagging. It was my favorite gait, even above the demipirouette, where the strutting muscles of his breast danced, outlined with baby oil. We no longer compete, but in the ring he remembers, style and grace. Sometimes I just go along for the ride.

Fridays, Hank teaches a seminar to graduate students, then plays racquetball with guys he refers to as his colleagues; I've always called them the circle jerks. They're two Fellows in Art who bilked the department into paying for a semester in London so they could study the western frieze of the Parthenon in order to enrich eighteen-year-olds' minds.

But what is carved into the thing? I wondered. Is there a message in those rearing horsemen, or did they just want to be immortal, some B.C. version of the three pictures you get for a quarter in the booth down at the beach? Cartoonaroony. One big answer made up of continually evolving questions to discuss as they crack the ball into a corner where it dies.

I could tell Hank, and it'd net me a laugh, but I know what he'd say next. "You slay me, Chloe. Let's get married."

The new cattle are skittery and strange. Paired off and parted from the center of the arena, they give one of the horses room. She's down, and at first I think she's been kicked, but then her knees do that vulnerable splay and she's up, breaking the umbilical cord of the new foal beside her. Against her dun, he's a riotous paint, sorrel and white, a mysterious map of it on his face, almost like he's part cow. He wobbles. She nudges, encouraging his independence. It's spring, so there's lots of babies, but it gets to me, cracking through my layers of tough-chick. I am sent careening back to eight years of age, cantering around the fenced yard of a school where I never quite fit in, wanting to be part of the herd, so desperate for acceptance that I whinny when the teacher asks me my name, and inevitably I'm labeled hopeless. Hoping all those years and even now to find that connection—that synapse—to learn just how necessary and unnecessary parentage is, so I could break free of it just as instinct tells the mare when to stand and create tension on the cord.

She noses and laps the foal. One of Chester's Australian shepherds squeezes under the fence and makes off with the afterbirth. The cows wander back, the mare and baby accepted into the herd for the time being. It's his eyes, I think. He is looking at all this for the first time, getting a whole universe in his first blink. His lungs take breath and give back carbon monoxide to the grasses. His heart pumps blue blood that turns a common red when he's cut. His beaver tail automatically switches at flies. And here I stand on two legs, twiddling opposing thumbs, useless to own such simple gifts.

Chester looks at me from across the fence, shaking his head at my tears. He taps his watch and holds up five fingers, three times: I've got fifteen minutes. I nod and go to my horse.

Here's Absalom's third trick: untie any rope. He's got his head in the grain sack, one last feast before I tell Chester yes, put him on the truck with the cows. Corte Madera; it even sounds like a retirement community. I imagine Palominos catching the sun on chaise lounges, Ray Bans in place, reading the equine equivalent of the *Star* where it is suspected after all these years that Mr. Ed was involved in drugs the entire time he had that hit television series. I let him eat. I butt my head up against his flanks, run my fingers along the ribs, just so; I want to memorize this flesh. I want a map I can take with me, in case I might be tempted to forget all he endured for me, the depth of terror in mud puddles he vaulted but never really forgot because my heels were pressing, Go on, you can do it, for me, for a ribbon.

When Chester touches my shoulder, I have my face pressed against Absalom's breast, trying to hear the constant thump of his massive heart. The muscle is too thick, but I know it beats, not understanding any human complications, just running on auto pilot.

"Now listen," Chester says. "He'll be fine. I'm sending a couple along too. He'll have some buddies." He spits in the dirt, and looking at that little gray swirl getting sucked into the dry earth, I'm mortal, crippled. Blind.

He cuts the clinches and I pull Absalom's shoes. I hand him the
lead rope, the scope of my vision narrowing down to the diameter
of a gun barrel. And even as terrible as my heart aches, knowing it
will hurt more before it hurts less, I've made the right choice. Later
I can sweet-talk Chester into selling me the paint foal and—if we
time it right—retire together, just a girl and a horse.

Hell is the promise of ascension when you take each fence and
poise yourselves for the next one, never expecting the sting of age
that grounds you to be delivered by such ordinary gods. Lares and
Penates, Folklore 2, a peek in Hank's briefcase. It hurts, sure, but
Hank's here dancing beside me no matter how his heart rebels or
his feet trip, because he knows I can let him love me: straddle-
legged, on horseback, in between the sheets, while my diamond
winks, a stubborn eye of the history between us, as I tell him no for
the last time.

The White Woman

Ashley McConnell

Ashley McConnell was born in Germany and has lived, with her Air
Force family, in Europe, North Africa, and the United States. She has a
B.A. in Anthropology from New Mexico State University and an M.A.
in Speech Communication from the University of New Mexico, which
have been put to excellent use in jobs such as insurance secretary,
technical writer, security coordinator, and purchasing agent. She now
lives in Albuquerque, New Mexico, with the obligatory writers' cats, in
her case a pair of Burmese. This is her first sale, and she has recently
completed a mystery novel as well as a horror novel which has sold to
Charter Books, and is now working on a historical fantasy. She has also
sold a dark fantasy story to *Final Shadows*. She is a member of Horror
Writers of America and Sisters in Crime, as well as a charter member of
the Mary Shelley Society. She also likes English history and is particularly interested in Richard III. And she cannot read newspapers without scissors in hand.

At the start of the anthology, Ashley and I talked at some length
about what was wrong with most of the stories I had been receiving
and what I thought writers should be doing instead. A few weeks later
this story set on an Arizona reservation arrived; obviously she'd listened well.

*I returned to my room tonight, after a long day with the Apaches, and
paused in the dining room to consider whether to eat. I became conscious,
however, of the eyes of all present staring at me, and decided that I
would remain in my room.*

*Indeed, sometimes I wonder whether they would stare at me any more
if I were one of the Indians, come in to town for a good dinner—it does
not seem to be so very different. Whether I were an Indian or a white*

*woman alone, they would stare equally. In any case, I am acutely aware
of how very out of place I am. I suppose it is the function of an observer
to be out of place.*

Dr. Frances Williamson slapped her notebook shut and flung it
across the room to hit the edge of a picture with a crash. The
picture swung dangerously, and she leaped to catch it before it
crashed to the floor. She missed.

She was hardly behaving like a scientist and a scholar, she
thought wryly. Mama wouldn't be at all surprised.

She had gained her degree at the University of Chicago exposed
to the works and personalities of Boas, Benedict, and Sapir, but
her dissertation was on linguistic problems presented in certain
Assyrian tablets from the Middle East. Her mother had been proud
of her; every day she went to the university and sat in a cubicle in
the library, and as a result she was the first person on either side of
her family to have a doctorate. Mama liked to show her daughter
off at tea in the gracious Lake Shore house and pinched her lips
tight against the worry that her too-intelligent daughter had educated herself right out of a chance to ever get married.

But her colleagues at the university wrote and talked about
fieldwork, about "real" anthropology, a science of human culture
reclaimed from the unsystematic records of missionaries and traders. "Real" anthropology meant going out in the field, talking to
real informants, observing with one's own eyes, recording, report-
ing. Frances felt like a second-class scientist. Tea at Mama's became an agony, as she chatted brightly, superficially, with the
clubwomen about how wonderful it was to use one's mind and
contribute something to the sum of human knowledge and then
went back to a safe, clean, sterile cubicle to be left out of the
camaraderie of the people whose work she admired most.

Then Swayzet came to give a seminar on the Apache. He gave a
brief history of the Apache wars, told how the several bands—
White Mountain, Chiricahua, Jicarilla, Coyotero, Pinal, Mescalero,
Arivaipa—had been uprooted from their desert Southwest homes
and forcibly deported to Florida, then to Oklahoma, before being
allowed to return to reservations in Arizona and New Mexico. He
spoke of the surviving Apache chiefs, beaten now, returning hum-
bled to the lands they had fought for so bravely. It presented an
interesting problem: Did the Apache culture survive at all? How

much of their own ways did this defeated people retain? Swayzet urged his listeners to consider a new field of inquiry, to help preserve a culture fast sinking under the relentless assimilation policy of the white man.

Frances was thrilled. She saw herself venturing intrepidly into the wilds of the Southwest, making the Apaches "her people," becoming an acknowledged expert on one more primitive people, finally able to hold her head up beside Benedict with her Appolonian Pueblos and that upstart Mead and her Samoans. Papa Franz Boas would be proud of her. She too could dazzle young anthropology students with stories about the rewards and hardships of fieldwork. And just *think* what Mama's clubwomen would say.

Frances neglected to consider what Mama herself would say. Not to mention Father. Only one grant was available, and it wasn't much, though Swayzet was kind enough to offer her an introduction to an Apache community near Lost Springs, Arizona. Father couldn't find Lost Springs on a map and nearly forbade her to go at all. A ridiculous situation for a woman almost thirty to be in, but Father held the purse strings. She finally agreed to live in the town, and he agreed to buy her train ticket. Her father was so relieved to know she wasn't actually going to *live* out there with the Indians.

Still, she had set out that June with high hopes and visions of becoming famous—in a small anthropological way. She was sure that these silly restrictions wouldn't really make any difference. The white community at Lost Springs would welcome her with open arms, awed and respectful of the intrepid lady anthropologist doing her bit to help the Indians. She'd quickly gain the confidence of her Apache informants. It would be a wonderful, constructive, successful summer.

Then she had arrived in Lost Springs.

It wasn't so great a loss, she thought as she stepped out of the broken picture glass; Mr. Carson, manager of the Lost Springs Hotel, would add it to the bill, of course, and the cost would come out of her rapidly diminishing grant money. Once again, she regretted knuckling under. If only she'd stood firm about living out in the field with her subjects! Out there, she'd learn to do without the amenities in no time at all.

Like dining rooms, she reminded herself as she swept the glass onto a sheet of paper. What a luxury it would be if she could only ignore the stares and whispers and actually order an evening meal. It was a convenience in the morning, certainly, and the kitchen was willing to pack a lunch for her.

Well, the lesson lived is best learned, she reminded herself. Next time she would ignore them all and do things properly. This trip was almost wasted anyhow. Victoria might have learned to trust her if she'd only lived out on the reservation.

The next morning Frances duly reported the broken picture frame to Mr. Meredith, the day manager, as she waited for the kitchen to prepare her lunch. Meredith, a pimply youth of nineteen or so, took careful note and assured her that the picture would be replaced at once. That wasn't the point, but at least the hotel had been officially notified, and she refused to worry any more about it. They brought around the Model A for her, and cranked the starter, and then stood out of her way as she chugged down the dusty street and out on the county road toward the reservation.

At least Victoria Lovato didn't stare at her. It wasn't the "done thing" among her people. For all the old Indian knew, all white women drove automobiles and wore men's clothes. White-eyes were crazy, and the white doctor who was not a doctor was as crazy as the rest of them, asking personal questions and never explaining why she wanted to know. But it was a good thing to stay friendly. The crazy doctor brought canned fruit and cloth from the town store.

The old woman welcomed her inside the crumbling adobe house, gray braids flopping with her nods, and Frances settled with relief against a worn saddle and opened her notebook, taking the regulation three deep breaths.

Victoria grinned toothlessly at her, as she always did. "Good smell, eh? Smell of home!"

Frances smiled. At the university, Swayzet had warned her. "You'll think the smell will kill you," he'd said. "It's the hardest thing to get used to. They haven't got plumbing out there, you know. But take three deep breaths right away, and it won't be so bad."

Somehow hearing about it in the ivied halls of the University of Chicago wasn't the same as sitting in a tiny adobe house on a roasting-hot Arizona summer day, with a fire smoldering in the fireplace to enrich it all. The first time she'd been introduced to Victoria, she thought she'd be sick. The old woman's blank, uninformative stare hadn't helped. It had taken all summer for Victoria to smile when she greeted Frances.

Now she took three deep breaths, inhaling the scent of badly cured leather, unwashed bodies, burning piñon, and reminded herself that she was a scientist, after all, and not here to judge. Dr. Swayzet was right. Once you got used to it, you didn't even notice anymore.

Though it would be something to see what Mama would make of the "smell of home." It wasn't what she would expect to find in the spotless Chicago Lake Shore mansion, polished daily to an inch of its life by a small army of colored servants. And Mama wouldn't have a fire in August. She wouldn't need it. Mama had hot water on tap.

"Good smell," she agreed. "How are you today, Victoria?"

"Good," Victoria said. The old woman was sewing, using one of the new steel needles from the trading post. Her hands moved over the bright cotton material with quick, sure stitches. Her fingers were misshapen, one fingernail missing, another split to the lunule and growing in two sections. The joints were gnarled with arthritis. "Everything's good."

Frances nodded and opened the notebook. Victoria grinned again. "Estibitzie's boy got a new horse yesterday. They say he's going to bring it to the dance, maybe for Sam Little Fox's daughter."

The notebook closed again, reluctantly. Frances's topic, bravely outlined in her grant proposal, was Apache language related to food gathering. It would provide a solid basis for future research on cultural change, now that the Apaches lived almost exclusively on "white" foods, canned goods from the agency and beef from the scrawny herds. All summer, she'd been trying to establish a comfortable relationship with her informant just as all her colleagues had talked about. Old Victoria knew what it was that she was after; she'd told her often enough.

But every time she took out her notebook, ready to record the fricatives and glottal stops and dentals and nasals, her informant proceeded to tell her about the health of all her relatives, the prices the trading post charged, how many calves had been born two years before, who had been at her Sunrise Dance, or who got into a fight at the last branding. Anything except the old words for food. If the crazy white woman wanted that information that badly, it must be very important. It made the words too dangerous, too valuable to give away. The white woman might be pleasant to talk to, but she was white and not to be trusted.

They talked for a while about Sam Little Fox's daughter, and whether Estibitzie's boy was wasting a good horse. All the while Victoria kept sewing, a blouse taking shape under her hands. Her eyes darted back and forth between the material and the white woman as she talked about courtships and feasts and good horses long past.

Frances began to have hopes that the subject was wearing itself out when a small figure came barreling through the door, yelling at the top of its lungs. With one quick movement, Victoria put her project aside and gripped a small girl by the shoulders. The child looked up to see Frances, and her mouth fell open in astonishment.

"This is my daughter's daughter," Victoria said. The little girl, suddenly blank-faced, ducked her head. "They came in to visit yesterday after the sun went down. These young ones, they even travel in the dark time."

The little girl murmured something. She had huge liquid black eyes, and her hair was pulled back in a braid that ended somewhere around her waist. She was dressed in a cheap cut-down blue cotton smock like a dozen others Frances had seen in the trading post. School clothes, probably; the girl children normally wore the long multicolored skirts and blouses of reservation dress unless they were attending the reservation school.

"She wants to know where are your children." Victoria's eyes danced. They had had this conversation before. Back in July, Frances thought.

Frances took a deep breath and smiled at the little girl, knowing Victoria would not entrust her with the child's name. "I have no children."

The child looked confused and whispered something too quick to catch. Victoria chuckled. "She wonders if white women do not have children."

The little wretch could have been taking lessons from Grandmama. A strained smile flickered on Frances's lips. "As you know, Victoria, I have no husband."

Victoria whispered into the little girl's ear. The child looked up at Frances, her eyes big with sympathy, and one small grimy hand patted her knee. Victoria laughed again, a high thin cackle, and shooed the girl over to the hearth to play.

Frances took a deep breath and turned firmly back to her note-book. It had taken weeks to convince Victoria that she really hadn't any children, and almost as long to convince the hotel manager in Lost Springs that a young eastern woman driving the hotel's Model A out every day for three months in the heat of summer to talk to some damn Injuns wasn't jist plumb crazy.

At first he thought she might be a schoolteacher, schoolteachers being, she gathered, the only white women voluntarily unmarried in the entire Southwest. Mr. Carson refused to call her "doctor" because "You don' look like no sawbones, ma'am." She had re-frained with effort from waving her diploma in his face. He proba-bly wouldn't be able to read it anyway.

The ladies of the Lost Springs Historical Society had welcomed her into their midst with many a fluttering of teacups until they discovered that she really planned to visit the tiny Apache settle-ments on the reservation a few miles out of town. And more than once! The ladies could see not the slightest use in learning Apache gathering customs. "They're not like *us*, dear," Mrs. Hawkins had said. "So *dirty*. More like animals, really."

Frances toyed with the idea of doing a study on the number of houses in Lost Springs that had achieved indoor plumbing in the first quarter of the twentieth century but decided against it. The ladies of the Lost Springs Historical Society were rather too much like Mama's clubwomen. So she rattled out every day to visit Victo-ria, made careful field notes, took out her frustrations in her jour-nal, and wrote desperately cheery letters home to Mama in Lake Shore.

"About the yucca fruit, Victoria," she hinted. Reports made by military personnel fighting the Apache in the 1880s had suggested that the Apache harvested the fruit of the yucca plant. It could be picked green and allowed to ripen like a banana; it was edible either raw or roasted. The military was more interested in the logistics of supply for a guerrilla war, listing the foods that the Apache found in the desert, than in the words people used to identify them. Frances wanted the words; the words might give a glimmer of understanding of how the Apache viewed the world. And if science could have that understanding of one people, some-day it could have that understanding of all people.

Besides, she could get a publication out of it, and even Papa Franz would respect her.

Unfortunately, the Apache as a whole, and Victoria Lovato in particular, were not particularly interested in giving the white man any more than he had already taken. Frances could appreciate the sentiment, but by late September she could have cared less. As far as she was concerned, the old woman was being willfully obstinate, much like Frances's own mother refusing to offer a guess about the contents of a birthday present. Frances gritted her teeth and sat patiently.

Victoria nodded, peering at the cloth in her hands. Frances stared at them, torn once again between the lesson learned at her mother's knee that it is rude, my dear, to comment on another's misfortune, and the scientifically cultivated curiosity to know what happened. "Pretty, eh?" the Indian woman asked, holding the blouse up for inspection. It was bright blue velvet, with full sleeves and red fringes on the bottom.

For a moment, she reminded Frances of Mrs. Hawkins, preening herself over her new tocque. "Very pretty," she agreed. "For a festival?"

Victoria laughed, a dry scratchy laugh filtered through missing and blackened teeth. "Not good enough for festival. This is to wear to the trading post."

"Ah." Frances nodded wisely. "Of course."

Across the room, the little girl had discovered a yellow ball and was bouncing it on the dirt floor.

"About the yucca," Frances began again. Victoria glanced up quickly, and she realized she had been too sharp. Not now, she thought, don't let me spoil it all now. The summer's almost over, and I've got nowhere, and what will they all say if I come back without anything on my topic? What will *Mama* say? "About the yucca fruit," she repeated, consciously softening her voice. "What's the Apache word for it?" The tip of her pencil trembled over the notebook.

Victoria laid the blouse aside and said indifferently, "We don't eat yucca anymore. We buy food at the trading post. Do you have nice clothes like this?"

The pencil tip snapped. It took considerable effort to say, "Yes, I have many nice clothes, in my home in Chicago." And what would

a younger Victoria have looked like in a debut dress? Frances
thought waspishly. "*Very* nice clothes."

"Why do you dress in man's clothes, then?" Victoria asked logi-
cally. Across the room, the yellow ball bounced against the ceiling.

"Because they're comfortable."

"You are comfortable being like a man?"

Wait, she thought. I'm supposed to be interviewing *you*. And
we've had this conversation too many times before. "I'm not like a
man." Though I'll bet those biddies back in town think so. And
probably Mama, too. None of them ever thought past the wedding.
What more could a woman possibly want? When she'd told Mama
that she was going to Arizona to do her first real field study, that
elegant doyenne of Chicago society had fallen into a faint. Better
her daughter should become a flapper or one of those "free-love"
tramps than subject herself to those savages, that privation, that—

"Do you not do man things?"

"No," she said wearily. "Don't the Apache have wise women?"
That wasn't the right term, Frances knew. Well, if Victoria would
only tell her what the right terms *were*—

Victoria nodded again, her face going curiously blank as it did
when Frances asked a too-penetrating question. The gray braids
flopped against her ample bosom. "They do not dress like men."

"They don't dress in stupid tight skirts and silk stockings and
high heels to walk in the desert, either!"

Victoria laughed, and Frances fished in her pocket for a penknife
to sharpen her pencil, feeling vaguely as if she had won a round.

"About this yucca fruit," she repeated doggedly. "I know you
don't use it—"

A scream wiped out the rest of her sentence. The two women
spun around to see the little girl sitting on the hearth, clutching
her hand, eyes squeezed tight shut and tears pouring down her
face.

"Ah, *pobrecita!*" Victoria gasped, lumbering to her feet. Frances
was at her side as she took the child's hand and pulled it into the
light. *Pobrecita*, Frances thought. No, that's a Spanish loan word,
not Apache at all.

The little girl was still weeping silently. Frances felt like weeping
with her; the palm of one small exquisite hand was blistering and
peeling away before their eyes in a wicked burn. The smell of

burned flesh mingled with the smell of burned rubber from the yellow ball wedged back among the coals.

Victoria said something glottal and took the little girl by her other arm, pushing her out of the house and back to the well. Her notebook dropped forgotten on the dirt floor as Frances followed, stunned. The sight of the old woman soaking a corner of her skirt, oily, matted, grimy with dirt, in the well bucket called her back to her senses. "Victoria, no! You can't clean it with that!"

Victoria's eyes were cold and remote. "This is what we have. It must be cleaned."

"For heaven's sake, she needs a doctor!"

"There is no medicine man here." Victoria pulled the little girl close. All the ease between the two women had vanished. "The reservation doctor is away."

Other Indians began to gather, watching from the doors of the wickiups and crumbling adobe houses. They came closer, muttering. Frances ignored them.

"It doesn't have to be the reservation doctor. There's a doctor in town. Let me take her—let me take you both to town. I have the automobile. Let me take her!"

Victoria paused, looking down at her granddaughter, glancing at her neighbors. One or two called out guttural suggestions. The child's mouth was open in a silent scream, but the only sound was a stifled gasping. Dr. Swayzet had told Frances how the Southwest Indians taught their children not to cry; they would place a hand over their mouths, pinch their nostrils shut until the child nearly suffocated. This was the result.

"The town doctor will not see my little one." There was a fatalistic recognition of the way things were in the old woman's voice. The watchers stood silent, observing. The little girl's gasping was the only sound. Frances recognized the look—the same look she had seen all summer, the shuttered eyes and blank countenance of a human being acknowledging there were terrible things in life that would never change.

It was the same look she had glimpsed on Mama's face, Frances realized suddenly, when she had asked her mother why she hadn't studied for a degree herself. The two images blurred together for a moment, and then she was looking at Victoria, her friend, the woman she had spent all summer with, and an injured child.

"I say he will."

Victoria blinked at the phrasing. Frances was too desperate to notice. She picked up the child and ran with her to the Model A. "Victoria, get in!" she shrieked, cranking frantically at the starter. The little girl's control broke as the engine roared to life, and she buried her face in Victoria's bosom as Frances flung herself in and they jolted around back to town.

Frances pushed the old car to its limits, not daring to take her eyes off the rutted, washed-out road to check on her passengers. Neither one had ever traveled in a motor vehicle, she was sure; few enough Anglos owned one in the early 1920s, and the Indians saw no use for them while they had good horses to ride. But it was twelve miles through barren desert to Lost Springs.

They were in the outskirts of town before Frances realized she had no idea where the doctor's office was. Muttering some words that would have amused Dr. Swayzet and shocked Mama, she pulled up to the hotel.

Mr. Meredith came out to see who was in the automobile.

"Where's the doctor?" Frances snapped.

"What? Hey! Hey, what're those redskins doin' in our Model A? You get out of there, squaw woman! Get on out of our—"

"Where is the doctor?" Frances repeated at the top of her lungs, wild with fury that the idiot boy couldn't hear the muffled sobs coming from the little girl. She had to be in agony to make a noise like that.

"I'll tell Mr. Carson—"

"You shall tell Mr. Carson *after* you tell me where the doctor's office is! *Now*, Mr. Meredith!"

Victoria was looking back and forth between the two of them, holding the little girl against herself. She was silent and grim and not in the least surprised at the look in Meredith's eye.

"You get that Injun out—"

Frances grabbed his shirt and yanked him across the wooden sidewalk. "I'll get her out of there as soon as you tell me where the doctor's office is."

"Next door!" he spluttered, stumbling back.

"Victoria, come on!"

The doctor was at least as startled as Meredith had been to see Frances come in, hauling behind her an elderly Apache woman with a small child clinging to her skirts.

"Here, here, what's this?"

"Doctor? This little girl burned her hand—" Frances recognized the moue of distaste crossing the other's face, and drew herself up tall. "I'm Dr. Frances Williamson, here on a grant from the University of Chicago to do research. This child has been hurt, and we need you to help her."

"My dear Mrs. Williamson, this is an Indian child. . . . And this is a white clinic."

"And you are a doctor, sir." She bit the words off carefully.

The doctor looked from her to Victoria and the child and back again. "Why, so I am, Mrs. Williamson. But the Indians—"

Something in Frances snapped. "This is not an 'Indian,' damn you, sir! This is a *child*! Look!" She pulled the little girl's hand away from her side and showed the man.

He whistled softly.

"Did you take an oath only to heal white children, doctor?"

The man glanced at her, angrily, guiltily, and began to busy himself with sulfa and dressings.

"That's it," he said at last. "Tell the squaw to change the dressing every day, and don't let her get it wet. And put more of this on it. Do you think you can make her understand, Mrs. Williamson?"

"It's *Dr.* Williamson, doctor. And Mrs. Lovato speaks excellent English."

"Ah, yes. Quite so." He looked skeptical. The little girl had buried her face back in Victoria's skirt. "If it gets infected, tell her—" the words obviously pained him—"tell her to send me word, and I'll go look at it. Or I'll tell the reservation man. Now, if you'll go—"

He showed them out the back way. Frances led them out to the car again, only to see Mr. Carson from the hotel waiting for them.

It was a brief conversation. Carson told them that under no circumstances could the two Indians ride in his automobile back to the reservation. Frances informed him that he could send someone out for the car, and helped Victoria and her granddaughter in. As she was turning the crank, Mr. Carson said, "You will have to find lodging elsewhere, Miss Williamson. We cannot tolerate—"

"Oh, I know very well how *tolerant* you are, Mr. Carson." The engine caught, and she climbed in beside her passengers. "You can send out my things with the person who comes to get the auto."

"Miss Williamson, this is simply *not* ladylike behavior!"

"Then I guess I'm not a lady, am I?" she asked.

Her heart was amazingly light as they rumbled and jounced back down the road toward the reservation. Once she risked a glance at Victoria and the little girl, now free of pain at least temporarily, staring wide-eyed at the sage grass at the side of the road speeding blindingly by. "Am I a lady, Victoria? In my trousers and all?"

Victoria muttered something.

Frances slowed down to navigate the turn into the reservation. "I'm sorry, what did you say?"

"*Goshk'an*," Victoria repeated, more loudly. "Fruit of the yucca."

Taking Miss Charlotte Back

J. L. Comeau

J. L. Comeau was born in 1952 and is a lifelong resident of northern Virginia. She attended George Mason University, where she is currently enrolled in a course of Women's Literature studies. Primarily a writer of dark fantasy, she has published stories and poems in *Grue, Dark Regions, Haunts, Twisted, The Belladonna,* and *Good Housekeeping,* as well as numerous small-press magazines. This story marks her first professional sale. A full-time writer, she shares her Falls Church, Virginia, home with her husband and with a variety of exotic birds. She is currently working on her first novel.

When J.C. (as she prefers to be called) and I talked over the phone the first time, I mentioned the various "categories" of stories I hadn't received yet and how surprised I was at the lack in some areas. J.C. said she would do a story about fur traders and promptly sent this one —with nary a fur trader in sight. Instead, it is a deeply poignant story of two old friends.

Kate parted the ecru lace curtains above the freshly polished spinet piano she had never learned to play and peered up the road through her new trifocal glasses to see if Miss Charlotte was coming yet. Tilting her chin this way and that, she squinted through all three variegations in the lenses but still could see nothing more than an indistinct blur where the Grand Teton Mountains ought to have been.

"Dern things," she said irritably, removing the grey plastic frames from her roundish face and discarding them between the framed photographs smiling out across the top of the spinet. She could see better without them, she decided, and again looked out across the fertile valley of prime grazing land separating her household from Miss Charlotte's. Yes, now she could make out the carriage-style house way up there on the hill, imposing and splendid, fit for a royal cotillion. Beyond the big house, the Teton mountains rose up in haughty blue splendor as if deliberately arranged to enhance the view.

Miss Charlotte's English Bentley car still stood in the circular drive in front of the big house, so Kate knew it would be at least ten minutes before the old woman arrived. *Bentley car*, of all things, Kate thought sourly. It was just like Miss Charlotte to keep something so frivolous and silly. Why, Miss Charlotte seldom went any place at all except to Kate's house and back once a week; servants and other hired hands did all the fetching.

"Poop and nonsense!" Kate muttered, flinging the curtain closed.

With the loose, rolling stride of a woman half her age, she went to the kitchen and put a pot of water on the stove to boil. A Blue Willow plate stacked with sandwiches she'd made earlier rested beneath a crisp linen towel on the sideboard. Cucumber sandwiches, no skin on the cucumbers, no crust on the Arnold's Brick Oven Thin Slice White Bread. Just a tiny smear of mayonnaise— not Miracle Whip, mind you—beneath the top slice of bread. No salt, no pepper. This was the way Miss Charlotte expected her cucumber sandwiches, though for the life of her, Kate could not understand what Miss Charlotte found so delicious about them. Kate required solid nourishment like roast beef or pork chops. Something to fill the belly. But Miss Charlotte seemed to subsist upon puny vegetable sandwiches and tiny flowered cups of steeped English tea.

"Lord, what a silly woman," Kate grumbled to herself as she checked the sandwiches to make extra sure she'd cut off every last bit of crust.

Carrying the sandwiches into the parlor, she placed them on a low glass-topped curio cabinet between two weary, seat-sprung easy chairs, then returned to the front room to see if the Bentley was coming up the road yet. Seeing the black dot of the massive car still parked in front of the big house, Kate went back into the parlor and rechecked the position of the quilting frame where she and Miss Charlotte would spend most of the afternoon.

She ran her tough, weathered fingers across the unfinished quilt stretched taut across the antique maple frame, thinking that of all the quilts she and Miss Charlotte had made while sitting here in the parlor, this was certainly the most beautiful. But then, she thought that each time they'd begun work on a new one, and she figured they must have made well over a hundred quilts during the sixty years they'd lived in the valley.

Sixty years, Kate thought wistfully, touching the hundreds of diamond-shaped pieces of fabric that formed one huge multicolored star pattern that fanned out from the center in concentric ripples of blazing color: yellows and oranges and bright carmine reds. Lone Star, the design was called, and indeed the quilt reminded her of Texas, of home.

Kate sighed and wondered if Miss Charlotte was aware that it was exactly sixty years ago today that they had left Texas and traveled here to Wyoming. Sixty years! Such young women they'd been then—Kate eighteen and Miss Charlotte twenty-one. Girls, really, leaving berth and brethren behind to travel to a place they'd only heard tales of: a wild, harsh place unfit for careful-raised womenfolk, it was said.

Careful-raised, indeed, Kate thought. She and Miss Charlotte had been raised together in the dirt just like their families' cabbages and potatoes, until they'd found oil on Miss Charlotte's family farm. After that, everything changed, and she supposed Miss Charlotte could have been considered careful-raised once she got back from that prissy eastern women's college she'd attended. It was upon her return from school that the formal "Miss" had become attached to their references to each other, which had kept a certain cool, polite distance between them.

They had come to Wyoming together, Kate and Miss Charlotte, leaving Texas and childhood behind, both for the love of the same man: Miss Charlotte's husband, Lacey.

Lacey had been dead now going on ten years, and though she thought of him often, Kate was careful not to picture him as she'd last seen him, laid out in a mahogany coffin like some grotesque, bloated waxwork; no, in her mind she always saw the daredevil shirttail boy from up north who spent summers on her daddy's farm. Oh, she could see Lacey Gorham now, a freckled blond man child with the devil in his eye, dancing barefoot across high post fences surrounding scrubby pastureland, singing silly songs, taunting the bulls.

Yes, she supposed she must have fallen in love with Lacey way back then. He was her fourth cousin twice removed or some such nonsense—anyway, they weren't hardly related at all as far as Kate was concerned. Lacey had been her heart's desire, that wild boy with all his big talk about moving to Wyoming to raise Black Angus cattle—as if he had a nickel to his name. Why, Lacey's pa had been even poorer than Kate's. But Lacey wasn't ever one to let loose of his dreams. She supposed that was what she'd found most captivating about him.

It was when Miss Charlotte had come home from school back east that Lacey's dream had begun to take form. There was Miss Charlotte, suddenly a dowried maiden of marriageable age, and Lacey had gone after her in a fever, courting her ardently, finally winning her hand against the wishes of Miss Charlotte's family.

It still squeezed Kate's heart to remember the day she stood as Maiden of Honor at Miss Charlotte's grand white wedding. But then, when she heard that Lacey's best friend, Arlen, was going off to Wyoming to help the young couple start their ranch, Kate had seen her chance to remain close to Lacey. Dear, sweet Arlen Newell had been smitten with Kate for years, as she and anyone else with eyes couldn't help but see. So Kate had married Arlen Newell two months later, and together the two young couples had set off for Wyoming.

So many years ago. . . .

Arlen was gone now, too, and it wasn't because he'd been a bad husband or an unkind man that she'd felt no passion for him. No, Arlen's only offense had been a lack of whatever mysterious male sorcery Lacey instinctively exercised that made Kate's blood run hot. Until the day he'd died, just the sound of Lacey's voice in the next room could set a flaming blush to her cheeks. Sometimes Kate had loathed herself, wondering what on earth was wrong with her for feeling the way she did about Lacey—someone else's husband, for heaven's sake!

Oh, she tried to stop loving him, really *tried*. She prayed to God every night to stop her loving Lacey and asked that she *please* be allowed to love Arlen instead, but her prayers had gone unanswered. Lord save her soul, she *still* loved Lacey Gorham.

Feeling her eyes fill up, she sniffed and pulled a wadded tissue from the sleeve of her bright blue cardigan. Mopping at her face, she turned away from the quilting frame and went back to the front room window, tucking the tissue back into her sweater sleeve.

Surely Miss Charlotte would be on her way by now. Kate leaned
over the spinet and peered out of the window just in time to see the
Bentley crunch across her gravel drive and roll to a halt.

Kate was out the door and down the front steps before Mr.
Peaflower, the driver, had opened Miss Charlotte's door.

"I'll get it, Peaflower," Kate told him brusquely, shoving him
aside to grasp the door handle. She thought Mr. Peaflower was
among the most useless creatures on God's green earth, right up
there with houseflies and cattle ticks. Any man who collected a
week's salary for less than a full day's worth of work wasn't fit to
shovel cow dung, to her way of thinking.

Mr. Peaflower deferred to Kate's wishes and allowed her to
wrestle the Bentley's heavy, black-windowed rear door open, ex-
posing Miss Charlotte, who blinked and shrank away from the
sudden intrusion of sunlight. Frail with her advancing years, Miss
Charlotte resembled a pale, withered bloom wrapped in violet silk
against the dusky leather of the seat cushions. Clutching blindly at
Kate's extended arm with spidery fingers, Miss Charlotte caught
hold and slid forward on the seat.

Kate helped the old woman out of the car. "Careful now," she
said as she led Miss Charlotte toward the house.

"Thank you, Mr. Peaflower," Miss Charlotte called over her
narrow shoulder. Her voice, surprisingly, was musical and vibrant.
"That will be all for now."

As the Bentley pulled away behind them, Miss Charlotte allowed
Kate to lead her slowly up the steps and inside.

"Do you know what today is, Miss Kate? Have you any idea?"
Miss Charlotte asked as Kate settled her into a parlor easy chair.
When Kate did not reply, she continued, "It was this very day
exactly sixty years ago that we saw Texas for the very last time."

"That's supposing neither of us ever gets a notion to go back,"
Kate pointed out as she went to the kitchen for tea.

"Oh, I think that would be highly unlikely," Miss Charlotte said,
selecting a sandwich wedge from the Blue Willow plate. After a
careful scrutiny of the bread, she located and picked away a mote
of offending crust that Kate had failed to notice. Apparently satisfied, she clipped off a dainty bite and closed her eyes contentedly
as she chewed.

Kate returned carrying a woven cane tray ceremoniously stacked with all the ritual objects and ingredients constituting Thursday morning tea.

"There is no fragrance in the world nearly so wonderful as the aroma of steeped Earl Grey," Miss Charlotte announced as Kate lifted a brown teapot from the tray and placed it on the curio table between the chairs. Accepting a steaming cupful balanced on a wafer-thin saucer, Miss Charlotte selected two papery slices of lemon and one cube of sugar.

Kate sipped her tea from a sturdy mug, listening to the chatter of Miss Charlotte's china cup rattling against the saucer.

Noting an increased tempo in Miss Charlotte's teacup symphony this week, Kate opened conversation with her usual question. "How are you feeling today, Miss Charlotte?"

Instead of proffering a permissible variation of reply from a carefully scripted dialogue that she and Kate had honed to a cordial knife blade over the years, Miss Charlotte said, "I will be dead soon, Miss Kate."

Kate sat rooted, stunned. Death was not something she had ever considered in connection with Miss Charlotte, although she'd observed the old woman's steadily declining vigor for a decade or more. Miss Charlotte, dying? No, she could not embrace the idea with any sense of reality. Impossible. A sudden anger blossomed within Kate, surprising her with its ferocity. Miss Charlotte will be with Lacey again, and I'll be left here alone, she thought. Even in death, Miss Charlotte would have her way.

"What exactly did the doctor tell you?" she inquired with an edge to her voice she hadn't intended.

Miss Charlotte sniffed and raised her chin. "I haven't spoken to any doctors. Didn't see the necessity."

Oh, Miss Charlotte was an exasperating woman, Kate thought as she tried to collect her temper. "Well then," she said evenly, "what the red hell are you talking about dying for?"

"I'm not well, Miss Kate."

She detected a slight tremor in Miss Charlotte's voice. Perhaps she *is* dying, Kate thought.

Miss Charlotte continued haltingly, "I—I've been thinking about Texas lately, Miss Kate. Remembering the old days before Daddy's oil field was discovered. Staring directly into the face of death does tend to set a body to thinking."

Oh, boy, here we go, Kate thought. A long-winded account of

countless aches and pains. But what was this about Texas? Miss
Charlotte hadn't mentioned Texas since they'd left. Kate had always assumed Miss Charlotte was ashamed of her undignified be-
ginnings.

"Oh?" she replied noncommittally.

"Oh, yes," Miss Charlotte said in a dreamy tone. "Remember
Nellie?"

Nellie. Daddy's swaybacked old plow horse. A vision of herself
and Miss Charlotte rose in Kate's mind: giggling summer girls of
eight or nine, bare-legged and fancy free, squashed joyously together in the dip of poor Nellie's sagging spine.

"I remember," Kate said. "We never even got a decent trot out
of that dern nag, did we?"

Miss Charlotte laughed softly. "No, I don't believe we did."

"That was a long time ago."

"Yes," Miss Charlotte agreed.

A long silence followed during which Kate and Miss Charlotte
finished their tea and sandwiches.

"You were always the horsewoman of the two of us," Miss Charlotte stated abruptly as she rose with difficulty and shuffled toward
the quilt frame. Easing herself into one of the ladderback chairs on
either side of the quilt, she said, "I was always afraid of horses."

Kate stopped clearing luncheon dishes, remembering distinctly
how envious she'd been the day Lacey had presented Miss Charlotte with an exquisite golden Palomino mare for her birthday.
"What about Goldie?"

"Oh, Lacey just wanted for me to be more like you, I guess. He
knew I didn't care for horses."

She watched Miss Charlotte thread a needle and take a few
stitches in the quilt. "Lacey wanted what?"

Miss Charlotte sighed. "He used to stand at the upstairs window
and watch you and Major practice barrel-dodging out in the field."

She decided to let the dishes sit and took the chair opposite Miss
Charlotte, who was busily working tiny stitches into the quilt.
"Lacey used to watch me practice?"

The other woman put down her needle and looked up. "Good
Lord, Miss Kate," she said. "You cut quite a visible figure around
here. Always made me feel like a smudge on the wall to stand next
to you."

This news was beyond Kate's reach. Miss Charlotte was the one with the educated manners and the tiny waist and the honey-blond hair. Kate had always thought of herself as big-boned and gawky, what with her muddy brown hair and eyes the color of tobacco spit. "That's foolish talk, Miss Charlotte," she said, wondering what her friend's game was.

"Remember when you won the barrel-racing championship in 1944?" Miss Charlotte asked, returning to her stitchwork. "Lord, what a day."

"Yes," Kate said, remembering for the first time in decades.

She had been the first woman in the county to win the barrel-racing event at the local rodeo, and she had been thirty-three years old at the time. Her sorrel quarterhorse, Major, had been an ugly little cuss, but by God that horse could cut between rows of close-set oil barrels like a greased snake. Kate's heart fluttered just recalling the thrill of thundering across the pasture astride Major's narrow back, the sweet grass a green blur hurtling beneath his nimble hooves. Sure-footed and tough as a mountain goat, Major had stolen the '44 ribbon away from the full-time working horses with ease.

She shook her head. "That old Major, he was something, wasn't he?"

Miss Charlotte laughed. "Major? He was just a horse being a horse. It was *you* who were something, Miss Kate—wild as a Comanche out there on that sorrel, leaning out across Major's neck with the wind whipping your hair back." She paused, putting down her needle to look at Kate. "And there I was on that silly beast, Goldie, scared to death she'd pitch me right out of that ridiculous sidesaddle and break my fool neck."

Kate stared down at her fingers as she worked on her section of the quilt. How she despised her big, uneven stitches, which seemed even coarser in contrast to Miss Charlotte's flawless needlework. "Lacey gave you that sidesaddle," she reminded Miss Charlotte.

"Yes, I know." Miss Charlotte's voice acquired a slight edge. "Lacey picked my horse, Lacey picked my saddle. Everything was Lacey's choice."

Kate knew they were approaching dangerous territory, but pressed on because the subject was Lacey. "What do you mean?" she asked, embarrassed by her own curiosity. Miss Charlotte's marriage was nobody's business.

Miss Charlotte shifted uneasily in her chair. "He—" she began, then shook her head is if trying to shake away an ugly image. "You knew Lacey as well as anyone else. You know how he was, always putting on a show for everyone, trying to pretend he didn't start out poor as a churchmouse like the rest of us. He was such a *proud* man."

She thought about that for a moment. It was true that Lacey never mentioned his childhood in Texas, but Kate always guessed it was because of Miss Charlotte's embarrassment.

"Sometimes I was fit to burst wanting to talk about the times the four of us had as children, you and me and Arlen and Lacey, bellywhopping in the reservoir and sneaking Camel cigarettes out behind your daddy's barn." Miss Charlotte paused and dragged in a long, ragged breath. "But I guess I was the only one who remembered those days so fondly. Things didn't change that much for you and Arlen."

"I remember those things," Kate said defensively, telling Miss Charlotte a half-lie.

Kate remembered, yes, but in her memories she saw only herself and Lacey—always Lacey—in everything she was able to recall. The rest of the people who passed through her life had become as insubstantial and wispy as ghosts. Even Miss Charlotte sitting right across from her now was not nearly so real to her as the memory of Lacey Gorham. But somehow she could not form an image of Lacey as an adult. Even when he had been alive, she had seen him only as he'd been when they lived in Texas as children. It was the rakish, towheaded boy who would not be banished from her life. If only it could have been Arlen, Kate thought miserably.

"You see?" Miss Charlotte said, shaking her head sadly. "I've made you unhappy by bringing it up."

"No, no," Kate assured her. "It's not that, Miss Charlotte. It's just that . . ."

"What, Miss Kate? Do finish."

"It's . . . it's just that things didn't turn out the way I imagined they would when I was a girl."

"Oh, I do understand, Miss Kate. Indeed I do."

Kate's temper flared. "How can you say that? You had everything anyone could ever want. If there'd been oil on *my* daddy's property, I—" She stopped abruptly, humiliated by her outburst.

"I wish it *had* been your daddy's property," Miss Charlotte said with a grim smile. "Then it would have been *you* wearing the corsets and long dresses, riding sidesaddle and giving boring parties for boring people Lacey wanted to impress. It would have been *you* taking a thrashing every time he came home crazy drunk. And it would have been *me* out there on Major, tearing up the pasture with my hair flying out behind me. *I'd* have been out there branding and roping and running with the cowboys. I'd consider it more than a fair trade, your life for mine."

A terrible silence filled the space between them for several moments as the two women sat facing each other. A fiery hatred flared briefly between them, but soon became feeble and fell away with the sound of Miss Charlotte's sudden weeping.

Kate fought to keep her anger alive as she watched the pitifully thin shoulders tremble with sobs. What lies! Kate told herself. How dare Miss Charlotte malign Lacey so, tearing the memory of a dead man to pieces! It was insufferable! She would not stand for it! She would not. . . .

But, slowly, despite her best efforts, Kate's ire ebbed. "Was life so bad?" she asked in a whisper.

Miss Charlotte swabbed at her cheeks with a sleeve of her violet dress. "Oh, I suppose not," she said, gasping back a sob. "It's just that after Daddy sent me away to school, everything changed. Nothing was ever right after that. The girls at school hated me because I was the daughter of a dirt farmer, and when I came home you hated me because I'd gone to school."

"I never hated you."

"You didn't like me much."

"Well, Lacey liked you enough."

"Lacey never liked anything but money. My dowry is all he wanted so he could buy this ranch. Lord, Momma and Daddy warned me, but I wouldn't listen."

Kate refused to accept this slander. "That's not true. Lacey loved you, Miss Charlotte."

"Do you remember those Friday night poker games that Arlen and Lacey used to have before Arlen took sick?"

"Of course." Kate had to think. Exactly when *was* it that Arlen got the cancer? 'Sixty-eight? 'Sixty-nine?

"One night I came downstairs to get a glass of milk after I thought the boys had all gone home, but Lacey and Arlen were still in Lacey's game room, and they were talking about *us*. I knew then I shouldn't eavesdrop, but I just couldn't help myself."

Kate wondered if she really wanted to know what Miss Charlotte had overheard their husbands say in private.

"Well, I heard Lacey say to Arlen"—Miss Charlotte continued awkwardly, pausing to swallow hard—"I heard him say . . ." Tears filled Miss Charlotte's eyes anew, but she lifted her chin and went on in a higher pitch. "Lacey said, 'Arlen, you don't know what hell is till you've lived with a woman who means less than nothing to you.' " A bright tear cascaded into the powdery seams of Miss Charlotte's face.

Kate could not speak.

"And do you want to know what your husband said in reply to Lacey?"

For the first time in her life, Kate cared more than anything in the world what words had come out of Arlen Newell's mouth. Suddenly, she found she could not move or find her breath.

Miss Charlotte twisted the tissue in her hands. "Arlen said, 'No, Lacey, I sure guess I don't.' "

Miss Charlotte's words crashed over Kate's head, threatening to knock her out of her chair and wash her away. She wanted to stand up and scream at Miss Charlotte about the unfairness of it all, about ruined years and time wasted. She wanted to shriek at the sky and throw thunderbolts at God Almighty for allowing such wretchedness.

Instead, she looked at Miss Charlotte with a steady eye and said, "Arlen's dead. And so's Lacey."

"Yes," Miss Charlotte agreed with a sigh. "They're gone and we remain." She picked up her needle and resumed stitching. After a pause, she said, "You're so lucky to have your two daughters. Such sweet, funny girls they were, remember? And your grandson. Oh, he's a darling boy."

Yes. Bonnie and Sarah had been wonderful children, Kate reflected, recalling how the two of them could light the darkest hours with their antics and laughter. And now there was Bonnie's son, Jason, who brought Arlen to mind with his quiet ways.

"After we lost that first baby," Miss Charlotte said in a tone barely above a whisper. "Well . . ."

Kate remembered that night as clearly as if it had happened weeks, not decades, ago. She had gone up to the big house to assist the midwife with Miss Charlotte's delivery. A sudden rainstorm raged and howled outside, and Arlen and Lacey had gone out to help corral the cattle. Miss Charlotte's delivery had been long and difficult, her screams of pain mingling with the screams of the wind tearing past the eaves. Toward dawn, as the storm had begun to die down, Miss Charlotte delivered her first and only child.

The child had been hideously deformed, a fleshy lump devoid of human resemblance but for one horribly perfect arm and hand that extended, dangling, from its top or side or bottom—there was no telling which. Mercifully, Miss Charlotte had never seen her baby; the midwife had immediately spirited it from the room and, although it pulsed feebly with life, Miss Charlotte was led to believe the baby had been born dead.

When Lacey and Arlen finally returned from tending the drenched stock, Lacey had demanded to see his child against the midwife's advice. Tugging back the blanket covering the poor creature, Lacey's face had gone pure grey. Then a look of wild fury had come into his eyes, and he had wrenched the child from the midwife's arms and taken it out to the pasture, grabbing a spade as he'd stormed past the toolshed.

Kate watched Miss Charlotte taking tiny stitches in the quilt, apparently engrossed in her work, her face betraying nothing. "You and Lacey could have had another baby," she said, instantly regretting the righteous sound of her statement.

Miss Charlotte looked up with a mild expression of surprise, then went back to her stitching. "Lacey moved into the extra room the same night our baby died, Miss Kate." A rosy blush tinctured her pale cheeks. "And he never slept with me again."

"Why, that sorry son of a *bitch!*" Kate cried indignantly, astonished by her own outrage.

In the shocked silence that followed, she and Miss Charlotte stared at each other across the vivid mosaic of fabrics they had constructed. The serenely ticking mantel clock in the front room punctuated the quiet, somehow adding strength to Kate's angry pronouncement.

Miss Charlotte recovered first, the thin line of her pale lips drawing into a gentle curve of gratitude. "Well, what's past is past."

"I know!" Kate said, aghast. "But really!"

"Lord knows I don't like to speak ill of the dead," Miss Charlotte told Kate in a confidential tone. "But Lacey Gorham was never what you'd want to call a regular Romeo, anyway." Then, to Kate's utter and everlasting amazement, Miss Charlotte giggled.

Giggled. Just like she had when she was a girl, Kate thought, hearing the sweet, ghostly echoes of young girls' laughter as she and Miss Charlotte bucked and kicked poor Nellie, trying to get that lame old plug to move. Now the young girls were the old plugs, swaybacked relics distantly removed from breathless afternoons spent together scrabbling in the hot Texas dust: happy, carefree, bellywhopping, tag-playing, tree-climbing afternoons.

Was it really Lacey she'd been longing for these sixty years, Kate wondered, or was it what Lacey represented in her mind? Lacey, Lacey . . . defiant ruffian, sun-bronzed and strong, laughing at the world in his tattered short pants, wild and free as the mustangs that came to drink at the reservoir. Was it the boy Kate had been in love with, or a certain place in time? All at once it did not seem to matter.

Enveloped by a delicious sense of emancipation, Kate began to laugh. Not a nervous titter or a polite snicker, but a cackling howl that rocked her back and forth. *Lacey Gorham was never what you'd want to call a regular Romeo*: suddenly it was too funny for words. Tears welled up in her eyes and poured down her round, ruddy cheeks. She could not stop laughing. She laughed and laughed until her sides ached and she could hardly breathe.

Gasping and exhausted, Kate pulled the damp tissue from the sleeve of her sweater and swabbed mightily at her face. "Oh," she said, trying to catch her breath. "Oh!"

Miss Charlotte's shoulders hitched with giggles and she, too, pressed a tissue to her face. "My, my!" she squeaked. "I can't remember the last time anything struck me so funny."

Kate's laughter had wound down to a wheeze and, although her temples pounded painfully, she felt replete and satisfied, as if she'd just finished the best meal of her life. Amid much snuffling and sighing, she and Miss Charlotte at last settled back into silence, but it was a silence of a different texture than before, more natural and comfortable. No rush to fill the void, no dread discomfiture over what to say next. It was merely a spell of quiet, guileless and innocent as two rascally farm girls on an old Texas plowhorse.

"We had a good old time back there in Texas," Kate said at last, "you and me and the boys."

"Oh, Lord, yes," Miss Charlotte agreed. "You know, I can see your momma now, standing there in her big, warm kitchen listening in on the telephone party line. Remember that, how she could hold the earpiece in one hand and whip up a bowl of biscuit dough in the other?"

The image gripped Kate's heart, warming her. "Mercy, yes. Momma couldn't get over such a newfangled thing as a telephone. I remember when they put it in, do you?"

"I remember more than that," Miss Charlotte said with an impish glow in her eye. "I remember the bell ring they gave you before they had numbers."

"No!" Kate exclaimed with a laugh, shaking her head. "You couldn't."

Miss Charlotte popped up and down on her chair like a child. "Yes, I do. It was two shorts and a long, like this: *ring-ring-ri-i-ng!*"

Kate slapped her knee and smiled. "I declare! You have the memory of a butt-shot bear, Miss Charlotte. Two shorts and a long. When the phone did that, the call was for us. I remember now."

"And the operator's name was Miss Tippett," Miss Charlotte added proudly.

"Oh, that's right! Ol' Miss Tippett from Arkansas! Meaner than a striped snake, wasn't she?"

From that point, Kate and Miss Charlotte flitted from subject to subject like butterflies on blossoms, their voices rising and falling with animation and easy laughter as they swooped and soared on iridescent wings of shared memories. Their hands fairly flew over the quilt as they chattered, stitches capturing the three essential layers of their Lone Star quilt: intricately pieced top, warm cotton batting beneath, strong muslin backing below. In and out and through their tiny silver needles flashed, stitching their quilt and their pasts together, until Mr. Peaflower arrived to collect Miss Charlotte at precisely four o'clock.

When the doorbell chimed, both Kate and Miss Charlotte looked up from their sewing with genuine expressions of regret.

"Oh, dear," Miss Charlotte said, embedding her needle firmly into the quilt to mark her stopping point.

"I could drive you back," Kate offered. "If you'd like."

Miss Charlotte's pale blue eyes brightened with her smile as she rose unsteadily from her chair. "I'll dispatch Mr. Peaflower at

once," she said as she hobbled into the front room. "I'm absolutely sick to death of riding in Lacey's silly old Bentley. Always
reminded me of a hearse."

Kate took a few more stitches while she strained to hear what
Miss Charlotte was telling her driver.

"Miss Kate will be taking me back," Miss Charlotte said haugh-
tily. "I'll not be needing you again today, Mr. Peaflower, so you can
go home to your beer and television earlier than usual."

Kate could not suppress a snicker. It seemed that Miss Charlotte
had Peaflower's slothful behavior tagged and recorded all along.
Kate struggled to tidy her expression when Miss Charlotte tottered
forthrightly back into the room.

"More tea, Miss Charlotte?"

"No, thank you, dear. I really must get back to the house and lie
down." She glanced sadly at Kate. "I never did have your stamina.
And now . . ."

"Well, then," Kate said as she rose from her chair and moved to
join Miss Charlotte, "let's be off."

She gently gripped Miss Charlotte's skeletal wrist and assisted
her down the front stairs to the car shed where, with some difficulty, she managed to get them both into the cab of Arlen's beloved Ford pickup. The engine, twenty years old if it was a day,
whined and protested at first but finally clattered to life as white
smoke spewed in bursts from the swaying tailpipe.

"Lord, I ought to have gotten rid of this rust bucket years ago,"
Kate muttered as she steered the truck across the drive and turned
onto the road connecting her house to Miss Charlotte's.

"New things aren't ever as good as the old ones," Miss Charlotte
observed soberly. "These new cars are made out of tinfoil, I believe."

"I reckon," Kate allowed, noting the sudden shakiness in Miss
Charlotte's voice. A peripheral glance revealed a glistening tear
slipping down her friend's face.

They rode along in silence, Kate driving slowly so as to keep
from jarring Miss Charlotte as much as possible. On either side of
the road lay the gentle slopes of fresh summer grass, once dotted
as far as the eye could see with Lacey's Black Angus herd, now
bereft of cattle.

"I can almost hear it," Miss Charlotte said, breaking the dream-
like silence.

"Hear what?"

"The cows moaning, the cowboys whistling and shouting."

The dented truck bumped up the hill past the bunkhouse, once alive and bustling with cowhands, now tumbledown and abandoned. Soon they passed the toolshed where Lacey had gone to fetch his spade the night his only child was born. And somewhere beyond lay a small, unmarked grave.

"When our Lone Star quilt is finished, I'll be finished, too," Miss Charlotte whispered as the truck rumbled to a stop in front of the big house.

Kate looked over at Miss Charlotte. So pale, so fragile, so . . . so *old*. "Nonsense," she stated without real conviction.

Miss Charlotte turned away. "It sounds foolish, I know. But it's true, Miss Kate. I'll die when the quilt is done. I feel in my heart."

Knowing it would be useless to argue the point, Kate watched the housekeeper, Mrs. Steptoe, rush from the big house to help Miss Charlotte out of the truck.

Before the passenger door slammed shut again, Kate leaned over and shouted, "I'll see you next Thursday, Charlotte!"

Leaning on Mrs. Steptoe's chubby arm, Charlotte smiled and waved. "Thursday, Kate!"

All the way home, Kate pondered what Charlotte had said about finishing the quilt, wondering if such a thing could possibly come true. No, she thought as she climbed the stairs and entered her snug little house. She did not believe in premonitions or second sight.

She went directly to the parlor with the intent of clearing away the luncheon dishes, but instead found herself seated in Charlotte's chair in front of their quilt. She looked down at the beautiful stitchwork, admiring Charlotte's fine handwork.

The quilt would be finished soon.

With a determined step, Kate marched into the front room and retrieved her new trifocal glasses from where she'd discarded them among the smiling photographs atop her piano. She was going to have to get used to wearing glasses, she decided.

Returning to Charlotte's quilting chair, Kate adjusted her glasses and picked up a needle, once again marveling at Charlotte's impeccable stitches now that she could see them clearly. Hundreds and hundreds of tiny, perfect stitches.

Carefully, one by one, Kate began to pull them out.

Buried Alive, or: Lunar Mischief

Nancy Holder

Nancy Holder lived in Japan for three years and at sixteen dropped out of high school to study ballet in Europe. Later, she graduated from the University of California at San Diego with a degree in communications. She sold her first book, a young adult romance, in 1981, and wrote romances for five years under various names. Seven novels placed on the Waldenbooks Romance Bestseller List, and she received several awards from *Romantic Times.* Her mainstream novel, *Rough Cut,* was published in May of this year by Warner Books. Her short stories have appeared in numerous anthologies: *Shadows 8, 9, 10; The Best of Shadows; Doom City; The Seaharp Hotel; Noctulpa; Obsessions; Borderlands;* and *Women of Darkness.* A member of Horror Writers of America, she lives in San Diego with her husband, president of FTL Games, a software company, and her two border collies, Ron and Nan (not named, she insists, after a former first couple).

This is an unforgettable story of a California woman of the West from Nancy's very strange and highly riveting pen.

Heya, Kim! You listening? Lunar mischief!

That's our password, to let her know I'm OK. She's really worried about me down here, but I'm already four days down and it's a piece of cake. I can do anything for a month. Kim says I could hold my breath that long if the price was right.

I'm Terry Hammond, I'm twenty-one, and as you can see I've got long blond hair I wear in a braided ponytail, brown eyes, and a stripe of freckles across my nose. Kim calls me Flicka. I work as a teller at California First Bank and go to school part-time. By school, I mean Grossmont Junior College, where I'm taking the general ed. requirements for my Associate of Arts degree. I don't have a major, but if I did, I'd probably change it sixteen times the way Kim has, because neither of us cares about school anyway. Even though we're smart. And the bank—well, it pays the rent.

Excuse me while I scratch my nose. I have to snake my hand up my chest, turn my wrist, and scratch, scratch, scratch. Once in a while I wonder if anybody's watching me when I do that, especially if I feel the need to—ah, dig, dig, dig. We have two-way video monitors: I can see you and you can see me. Hear me, too, and me you. I can't believe they used to do this without technology—and the real pros got buried with rattlesnakes crawling all over them. I saw a guy in a glass case, once, crammed full of rattlesnakes. The case, I mean. It was in front of a market near my house in Santee, where I lived with my parents.

Boy, that was real country then. That's about twenty miles east of San Diego, and when I was little it was just us and a few other people and the coyotes. You never saw tumbleweeds so big. Then the mobile home parks rolled in, and now there're condos everywhere; and now they're calling San Diego part of the Far West, which isn't the West at all, which is true.

Am I rambling? Jeez, who am I talking to, anyhow? I thought there was a cockroach down here for a while, and he's the one I *started* talking to, but he burrowed off or whatever it is cockroaches do. On second thought, maybe he was an earwig. I had a humongous fight with my grandma when she came to stay with us after Mom died, I mean a horrible blowup over what the critter in the bathtub was, an earwig or a cockroach. Pop told me later how disappointed he was that I'd hassle my own grandmother over a trivial thing like that, but he didn't get it. What she was trying to say was that we were living like pigs, not that she had any interest in the flora and fauna of our neighborhood. We had done OK, sharing chores and all, my two sisters and Pop, but she was like that, finding all kinds of things to criticize while we were staggering around trying to take in that Mom was really gone. Of course Pop defended Gramma. She was his own mother so he couldn't see it;

besides, he had other things on his mind. So to him, an argument was an argument, period, and I had to apologize.

So maybe I'm still talking to you, Señor Cucaracha. Or maybe I'm starting to flip out. As Kim says, it would be hard to tell. I've always been a little wacko. It was sort of my stock-in-trade at school, being the goof-off, until I met Kim, who showed me how to dress and wear my hair and stuff, which allowed me to make the transition from being a ha-ha buddy-buddy to everybody to a genuinely popular *girl* (but I was never stuck-up about it). And it was Kim who introduced me to the joys of Magnolia Mulvaney's, which led me to meet Ian, who looks like Mel Gibson and—

What? What? Oh, Kim, lunar mischief, jeez, I am *not* mumbling to myself. No, I'm fine. Criminy. Go get a Coke or something. It makes me nervous when you watch me all the time.

My friends are taking shifts, you see. They made a chart with all their names on it, who comes to sit with me when, even when I fall asleep. It doesn't matter when it's night or day to me because I've got this light bulb dangling above me, which is for show, and stronger lights hidden in the corners, so the camera can pick me up. But it doesn't matter to me; in regular life, I sleep through all the earthquakes that freak out everybody else. But they worry about me, so they come and babysit me on the surface, play cards and pass the time. Phil brings his guitar and they serenade me. They've all been on the news or in the paper, being interviewed about this deal. Sweet Baby James says business has almost doubled in the eight days since I got buried, so it's paid off for him the way I said it would.

We're a tight bunch of friends, have been since before elementary school. We're kind of weird because we don't fit into the Southern California lifestyle. I mean, we aren't punks and we aren't surfers and we sure aren't yuppies. We're the last generation of real cowboys around here. I don't mean just 4-H kids raising sheep. Our parents came from ranches in Texas and Colorado and Nevada and taught us everything they knew. Trouble is, there's no place around here to do anything with that knowledge. A girl I know said the difference between the West and the Far West is that in the West they work the land, and here we pave it. And I guess that's true, because she has to drive twenty-two miles to visit her horse, Tucker. Now, back in the real West—which is everything east of us, until you get to the Midwest—kids still live on ranches and ride their horses to school.

Oh, you've got a few around here who do that, but they don't live on real ranches. You've got to understand about Santee. There are a few other places like it in San Diego County: Lakeside, Ramona, and Jamul, for instance. Bonita and Julian, too. These little towns are more out-of-the-way, so they're more Western, but they're not as Western as they used to be. I mean, most of the ranches in San Diego County are avocado ranches, or tangerine, and on the way to Julian there are beautiful horse farms, but those horses are for show, not for herding cattle.

The kids like me who grew up in these little towns are kind of like Western kids—you know, like Arizona or west Texas kids. We were all wearing cowboy boots and jeans before, during, and after it was popular, bored out of our minds, watching TV at each other's houses, and making out in dens paneled by our dads from the good stuff at Handyman's (now extinct), and waiting to get our driver's licenses so we could go commit lunar mischief.

Lunar mischief, ah, lunar mischief. You get off work, or finish your day at Grossmont Junior College, and you cram into pickups and off you go—

to the desert,
in the night,
and the moon sifts down like gold dust, like powder, like magic
on cacti and manzanita,
on deerweed and white sage,
on tumbleweeds.

Whitebone, spotlight night, and we walk carefully because this land is prehistoric. This land is Western Land. We get out harmonicas, make a campfire, and the boys hold the girls and we drink Jack Daniels like the solemn cowboys who live deep inside us. Just a sip at a time, not messy.

On our Western Land.

And when we're all settled down, and the 7-eleven shift and the Art History 101 and the fight with Gramma slide off our shoulders, we tip back our heads and we howl like wolves.

Ooouuu. Ooouuu.

And what we're saying is, It is we. Come and join us.

We feel lonely, outcast, like we're in the wrong place. Some of us
—and I'm one of us—believe the souls of dead cowboys fill us
during lunar mischief. That's why the out-of-placeness looms so
wide and clear: because we're feeling the wrongness of the Far
West, the mistake of it. How they've razed it, and paved it, and
corraled all the old stuff—the buildings and brands and spurs and
lariats—into historic buildings in Old Town and Heritage Park,
where tourists wander through and buy piñatas and burros carved
out of soapstone.

I don't for the life of me know why we call it lunar mischief. I
think we used to pull pranks out there, when we were younger and
had to lie about where we were going, and someone would drive a
best friend's brother's truck, using a fake license. When we were
silly.

But shoot, I'm still silly. I'm losing track of myself here. I mean,
I'm buried ten feet under, with a latrine at one end of my coffin
(and don't ask me how I use it, because I won't tell you), and a light
bulb dangling at the other end. I've got K rations (hokey, I say),
and all the pop and water I can drink. I'm lying flat on my back in a
tiny little box, I stink, and I'm talking to myself (I guess); and if
that's not silly, I don't know what is.

Ooouuu! Sorry, I had to let loose. Yeah, Kim, I'm fine. Sixteen
days! Far out!

I think they ask me how I am so often because they're bored, too.
At least they have each other up there. Well, I'll be up soon, won't
I, Señor Cucaracha, and then watch our dust! Because we're going
to commit the ultimate lunar mischief then. And Ian's going to join
us.

Ian. He's also a real cowboy, but he's from Australia. You see,
down there they have real cattle ranches and real cowboys, who
drive the mobs of cows down the middle of the continent, through
the bush, so they can forage before they go to market. The cowboys are on the trail for months at a time; they sleep with their
heads on their saddles and they eat jerky and damper, which is a
kind of bread with fruit in it. They've got bow legs—Ian's got bow
legs—and they wear jeans and chaps and western shirts.

You know how people talk about "cowboy lawyers" and "cowboy doctors" in *People* magazine and all? They're talking about
guys who live in states like Montana or Arizona or Texas, who wear

western clothes and maybe live on a ranch or own a horse. So they're considered cowboys with a profession on the side. Well, Ian's a cowboy sailor. He's in the Australian navy but inside he's a cowboy. Like we are.

And he must have seen that in us, when we met him at Magnolia Mulvaney's, which is a cowboy bar in Santee. It got popular during the *Urban Cowboy* craze and has stuck around. We go there and drink long-necks and dance the Cotton-eyed Joe, like our parents did back in their home states; we strengthen the bonds of our pack. It's like howling; it cements us with our dead cowboy souls, with our feeling for the true West.

Ian, who was homesick, must have felt those feelings too, because he watched us quietly, a wolf on the outskirts, looking for the one he had to go to for permission to join us. And I guess he figured I was the one, because he came over and asked me to dance. Now, usually boys ask Kim first (and lots of times, she says no, and then they ask me), so I was impressed with him right off the bat. I mean, he was so cute, with his white-blond hair and his tan and his baby-blue eyes, and a humongous dimple in the middle of his chin, and his jeans and his shirt. Yum. Yum yum. He danced better than anyone there. He asked me all about San Diego, and he complained about the freeways and the condos and the smog—

in the whitebone desert, our bodies
it is we. Come and join us
sang.

And there was a soul in him, an old cowboy soul, that talked with my old cowboy soul, and together we bayed for the West. There was a yearning between us, so bittersweet I pressed my face against his chest and cried. He stroked my hair and said, "Ah, Terry," in his funny, twangy Australian. "Let me take you," he said, and I knew he meant, take me *there*, so I gave myself to him. And we went to Laredo, and Tucson, and Nacogdoches; spurs jingled, horses nickered. The tinkle of an old piano, the creak of leather, the crackle of a campfire: I thought my heart was going to break.

We went to Indian bingo afterward, to ease our transition back into the 7-eleven world. We sat there in the long hall with a batch of cards in front of us, our nachos untouched, covering those squares

as fast as we could. Some Indian lady called out the numbers and
we hustled along, grinning at each other. Love.

I won a leather cover for a car steering wheel. That wasn't too
thrilling, because I don't have a car. Next I won a mat for the floor
and a set of sheepskin covers for the seats. When I went up to
collect my prizes, I said, in a loud, joking voice, "Gee, I hope I get
the car. Otherwise I'm going to have to eat this stuff or something."

I don't know why I said that; it just came out. But Sweet Baby
James Donaldson was there, talking to the Indians in charge, and
he cracked up. He walked up—I recognized him from his ads—and
told me he hoped I won the Bronco he'd donated from his dealer-
ship in El Cajon, which was the grand prize of the evening. But that
if I didn't, he'd love to sell me one. I told him I couldn't afford one.
He said he could make the payments low enough so I could, and
we started teasing and joshing and the next thing you know, I
suggested that he bury me alive for thirty days to attract publicity
and pay me off with a Bronco. So here I am.

Where was I?
Where am I?
Oh, there you are, Mr. Cockroach. Ooh, isn't that hot? I can feel
the heat from that light bulb on my face. It must be burning you.
You silly earwig thing. What're you doing, crawling all over it?

You know, it was lonely after Mom died. Dad was gone so much.
I was glad I had a horse. And my friends, too, with their old cowboy
souls. I wanted Dad to take us back to Texas. I wanted—

Wow, the light's glowing like a bonewhite moon. It's like the
desert, cool and serene, with the air so still the spirit moves inside
you. Oh, Ian, when I get that Bronco, we're heading east, to the
West. To Tucson and Laredo and Nacogdoches. We're going to
commit the ultimate lunar mischief, my cowboy sailor love. The
ultimate.

I know I shouldn't say things like this, but my gramma was a
real—

What? Who's calling me? Lunar mischief? Oh, lunar mischief!
Day Twenty-five? Six more days! Yes, I'm fine.

Lunar. Lunar.
For a while I thought it was the sun, but of course you're the

moon. I remember now that I couldn't figure out who you were. But now I see you, with your little black eye dot; I see you, brother moon.

Ooouuu. It is I, Flicka, your cowboy brother. It is I, and I'm basking in your glow, and I'm in the Western Land with all my family and my friends. Ian's back from the cowboy sea, and we're playing our harmonicas and putting our boots up near the fire. And the boys are holding the girls, so we'll never be lonely again.

Ooouuu. Come and join me, old gold-dust moon. My bucking bronco moon. Because we're going to get on that bronco, that bucking bronco, and we're going—

There's a noise. What is all that noise? What's all that racket?

The crackle of a fire, the tinkle of an old piano, the creaking of leather. I'm in the West. I'm the West. I'm buried six feet underneath the highway because in the Far West they pave it. I'm—

What's all that noise? Who's shouting? The moon's so bright my eyes are burning. Or am I crying?

That eye in the moon. Is that right? The eye in the moon? Or is it the man on the moon?

Ooouuu! Why doesn't anybody answer me? What's happening?

I'm staring at you, moon, and you're not talking. I see your black eye dot and you never blink; you're watching me, like God. You see the heart of my cowboy soul.

And it wasn't a cockroach in the tub, goddamn it; it was an earwig. We were not pigs. Mom didn't raise pigs, she didn't.

In the West, there are no cockroaches. In the West—

What is this? What is happening?

Sunlight! Oh, my god, I forgot! I forgot! Whose eyes am I staring at? Ian, Ian!

Oh, baby! It's time? It's over?

What? You dug me up? You dug me up?

I was not. I was not losing it. But now I've lost the bet! Damn it, you made me lose the bet!

No, wait, wait! Lunar mischief. Do you hear me up there? Lunar mischief! I'm all right. K rations. Latrine. And one fried earwig on the light bulb.

Yeah, I got a little weird there, Kimmy, but I'm OK. Ian, you there, baby? You did start to dig me up? Well, yeah, it *is* harder than I thought it would be. Day Twenty-eight?

Heck, I can do anything for a month.

And when I get that Bronco, we're heading east in a cloud of gold-dust moonshine. East.

To the West.

Kathryn Ptacek, raised in Albuquerque, New Mexico, received her B.A. in Journalism from the University of New Mexico. She has worked as an advertising layout artist and computing technical writer/editor. She has written a historical fantasy series, numerous historical romances, and five dark fantasy novels, the latest being *In Silence Sealed* and *Ghost Dance*. She's edited three anthologies and is currently working on another dark fantasy as well as a mystery series. Her short fiction has appeared in *Fantasy Tales, Post Mortem, October Dreams, The Horror Show, Pulphouse,* and two of the *Greystone Bay* anthologies. She is married to novelist Charles L. Grant and not only shares a one-hundred-year-old-plus Victorian house with him, as well as three cats, in the small town of Newton, New Jersey, but the same birthday as well. She collects unusual teapots, ethnic masks, and gila monster memorabilia.